The Oversight

'This debut by Will Eaves feels like a patch of smooth baby skin among an increasingly irritating rash of twentysomething first novels. Mature, well-paced and complicated but never showy, it is a family saga with more twists than the ribbons on a maypole . . . Eaves is a fine writer'
The Times

'In well-weighted and meticulous prose, Eaves finds the right voice for each scene, whether frivolous or full of trepidation, with each mini-denouement delivering healthy doses of wisdom and wit. A fine novel'
New Statesman

'An insightful exploration of memory, death and parenthood . . . a consistently fine use of language and an acute sensitivity to how the emotional contours of a family flex and are disrupted by events . . . [Eaves] has written that most honest of books: a coming-of-age novel the central perception of which is that one never really does'
Economist

'. . . outstanding by any standards'
Bath Chronicle

Will Eaves was born in Bath in 1967.
He now lives and works in London.
This is his first novel.

Will Eaves

The Oversight

PICADOR

First published 2001 by Picador

This edition published 2002 by Picador
an imprint of Pan Macmillan Ltd
Pan Macmillan, 20 New Wharf Road, London N1 9RR
Basingstoke and Oxford
Associated companies throughout the world
www.panmacmillan.com

ISBN 0 330 48140 1

1 3 5 7 9 8 6 4 2

A CIP catalogue record for this book is available from
the British Library.

Typeset by Intype London Ltd
Printed and bound in Great Britain by
Mackays of Chatham plc, Chatham, Kent

for Joanna

We learn to restrain ourselves as we get older. We keep apart when we have quarrelled, express ourselves in well-bred phrases, and in this way preserve a dignified alienation, showing much firmness on one side, and swallowing much grief on the other.

George Eliot, *The Mill on the Floss*

'Good evening, ladies and gentlemen. This is your conductor Martin speaking. I'm sorry about the go-slow we're experiencing. The driver has received reports of children placing things on the line in the Box area and he is currently clearing the way ahead. We'll be picking up speed as soon as he gets the OK. Once again, we do apologize for the delay to your journey today and for any inconvenience it may have caused you.'

Part One

Part One

Railway Children

Advances in railway engineering and carriage pressurization mean that your ears no longer pop when you emerge from Box Tunnel. When I was five, this was the significant announcement of one's homecoming – the elastic release of a strained tympanum, as the train slithered free of the Wiltshire hillside and, tumbling first through steep cuttings and then alongside the Avon water meadows, began its approach to Bath Spa Station. Like some landlocked monster in its lair, Brunel's tunnel screamed at you to go round, not through . . .

Box Tunnel is not the only burrow exit from the city. There is another way out (or in), underneath Fox Hill and Rainbow Woods, on the defunct Somerset and Dorset Railway – the Slow and Dirty, as it was perhaps better known. Combe Down tunnel, built for a single track, was always a less epic construction than Brunel's, though it has since become more evocative in its desuetude. Things of night and leftovers of the day – bats, foxes, vagrants from the Bear Flat – colonized its tenebrous mile and a half for nearly twenty years after the official closure in 1966, before the council walled up the entrances in 1985. Its southern section was collapsing, they said; of course, it had been collapsing for years. That was what made its soot-clogged claustrophobia so appealing. That was the whole point of being thirteen and daring oneself to confront it, without a torch: Box Tunnel hit you suddenly, and with piercing earache; Combe Down lay in wait, like an open secret. The fact that it was out of bounds to all of us at Lyncombe School was inducement enough to stagger blindly through it. But we were also, in our way, the clumsy curators of its past, kicking at the gut of the muddy hill like revenant navvies.

One Friday afternoon in the early autumn of 1983, Nigel Dooley, the games master at Lyncombe, decided to take the whole of 3TD through Combe Down tunnel on an official field trip. Dooley was young – around twenty-six or so – and attractive in a yobbish way, with dirty blue tracksuit trousers, mousy stubble and a shaggy perm, inconceivably fashionable at the time. Like all games masters, he also taught geography and took a dim view of doctors' notes. In Dooley's book, only the diaphanous and drip-fed were ill enough to miss rugby – which Peter Lillingston, who had bone-marrow disease, patently was (though even he wasn't normally excused). The decision to broach Combe Down nevertheless showed that Dooley, too, had his off-days, when the childlike intrigue of playing Pied Piper seemed preferable to the rote aggression of scrums and rucks.

Combe Down suited me fine. Like the weaker boys, I hated rugby, along with most other contact sports – though not for fear of assault. Rather, as a long-legged, agile adolescent, with big hands and pincer fingers – the sort that preyed suddenly, cripplingly, on other boys' shoulders in the corridor – I was shamed by my lack of coordination. Who could not envy the bona fide weeds, like Lillingston? No one expected a wraith to be any good at rugby; but to be tall for one's age (five feet and eight inches) and cloddish, with tentacular limbs that only ever worried the ball, or inexplicably sailed away from it on some lunatic trajectory of their own, was a special kind of curse. *Christ, Rathbone, stop leaping about and get stuck in, you berk.* Dooley's rebukes were not empty of sympathy and even earned me an eccentric popularity (I was known as the 'leaping professor').

'Ri-ight,' Dooley shouted above the changing-room babble, 'find a partner and get your rough books out. And do it qui-i-etly. This isn't a ski-ive, it's a field trip. What is it, Professor Rathbone?'

'A ski-ive, sir.'

'A field trip, that's ri-ight.'

Every teacher has tics that become the intellectual property of his cheekier pupils. Long vowels, particularly long 'i's, were Dooley's. Long vowels, partial deafness, and a tendency to use the wrong word when trying to suggest the hidden extent of his intellect. He was tolerant, too, of my feeble mimicry, recognizing in it the bright kid's refuge from creepdom. It made me popular, and him something of a hero in my eyes.

Encouraged and supported by a ripple of laughter, I nudged Gregory Bray, the solemn, unhandsome boy next to me on the bench, and said, 'Do you want to be with me?'

Bray declined to answer but curled his lip and elbowed me back harder. In the gestural vocabulary of the male pubescent, this means 'Maybe, but you've probably blown it by asking.'

'Mr Dooley, sir, please sir, can I ask a question now?'

A squeaky American accent grated on my back two fillings. It came from an oddball on the opposite bench with finger-in-the-socket ginger hair and peppery freckles. We all groaned.

'Ye-es, Schumacher. As long as it's pertinent.'

Relevant would have been a big word for Dooley, but 'pertinent' – that was a self-conscious giveaway, and we knew it. Particularly Carey Schumacher, who, instead of joining in the chorus of mockery ('Very pertinent, Nige'), chirped a ludicrous 'Yessir!' Carey was one of those nerdy boys whose unpopularity with his peers led him to solicit every authority figure with a show of attentiveness. Dooley, a fair-minded man with a high regard for effort and none at all for sucking up, had disappeared, embarrassed, into the kit room adjoining the changing area. Someone else wanted to know why we always had to do things in twos or in groups, but Carey would not be deterred. 'Can I ask a question now?' was his favourite opening: the question which made another question, and so a conversation of sorts, however superficial, inevitable.

'I was wondering, sir,' Carey called after him, defying more groans, 'why you wanted us to take our books. Because it'll be dark in the tunnel, sir, and we won't be able to write, or see what we're doing. At least I don't think we will, sir. And that's all I wanted to – hey, that's all. Ow.'

Weakly, Carey fended off a missile from the class maniac, Bruce Hartt ('Oi! Smacker!'), whose aim, through two rows of coat-pegs, was too true. Hartt specialized in making flob-bombs – boluses of masticated paper and crisp-scented saliva – to which activity he devoted the first ten minutes of every lesson, waiting usually until the final bell before splattering his chosen victim. Carey's keenness made him a candidate for more immediate correction, however; even his so-called friends, of whom I was one, could see that. Sometimes, Hartt didn't even wait for him to open his mouth, or, worse, snared him with a gesture of forbearance – 'No 'ard feelin's, Schuma-cher, a' right?'; 'Sure, Bruce. Cool' – before hailing him again – 'Oi! Smacker!' – with an exploding dollop of grey filth.

The teachers all reviled the practice; it was 'obscene', 'spread disease', 'would result in immediate suspension'. It never did.

Dooley now re-emerged from the kit room, carrying a box full of torches and Gaz lanterns, to find Carey wiping the remains of Hartt's f-bomb off his blazer and tie. (The wrong tie, too; Carey's liberal mother, who taught tapestry at the local college of art and wanted her son to be unusual, made him wear button-down yellow shirts and pressed slacks, instead of the black and grey school uniform.) Hartt sniggered.

'You. Hartt,' Dooley yelled.

'Wasn't me, sir.'

'Mouth. Shut it.'

'You're always pickin' on me, sir.'

'That's because you're an easy target,' Dooley replied, 'and if I see any more of that stuff flying around, you'll be following it. With the same results on impact, sunshine.'

Hartt's razor-haired cohorts cackled – when he laughed, you could see Craig Spillings's tonsils through the gap in his front teeth – and playful punches were thrown.

'Ri-ight then,' Dooley continued, ignoring both Hartt's fisticuffs and Carey's pleas for redress, 'in answer to Mr Schumacher's useful query, you'll be glad to hear that we're taking these torches with us – courtesy of the Caving Club – which means you'll be able to look for signs of erosion in the cuttings and continue taking notes while in the tunnel. Understood? Erosion is what we're after. Clear indications of. We did a lot on it last term, so don't give me that blank stare, Hartt. Spillings, don't think with your mouth open. River courses, land wastage, general disrepair, acid rain. Can anyone give me an example of what we might be looking for in a disused railway tunnel? Hartt?'

'Disused train, sir.'

'Disused train. Thank you. Anyone else?'

There was an uneasy hush. I thought a bit about decay. About some of the possible answers – weathering, plant invasion, simple neglect – and whether the climate was right for a little sober cleverness, just enough to impress the mirthless Greg Bray without boring or offending him, if such a thing were possible. But none seemed plausible, really, because none of us gave a stuff about erosion, least of all Nigel Dooley. Instead, I caught Hartt's eye, and saw his hand stray to a rough book on the bench with several pages already torn out. He smiled and opened his mouth quickly to reveal a ferment of white paste inside it. The smile closed and broadened into a tight grin. Carey's face began to pucker.

*

What *does* one look for in a disused railway tunnel? Something scandalous, perhaps: a wino the worse for wear after his lunchtime bottle swearing at you to 'bugger off, all yous cunts', a sixth-former and Sandra Kale, the fifth-form tart from the local girls' school, scrambling up the side of the cutting as you approach (to cheers from Spillings and his cronies). An opportunity to disappear, briefly.

I know I did wrong that afternoon. I don't want to turn the whole episode into an extended bleat; all children are cruel to each other at some point, if only because they sense that they can afford to be. Responsibility lies ahead. A small minority, however – and I was one of them – work out early on that real cruelty hides even from itself; that it is a contract of insecurities dressed up as friendship; that it is genuine diligence in the service of monsters; that, like all the misdescribed casual sex I've ever had, unintentional cruelty isn't what it says it is, because we are an intending species. So when someone says,

'I didn't mean it,' they mean something much more sorrowful for which, in a way, it's easier to forgive them. They mean that they're taken aback by the extent of the damage their cruelty has caused. At least, that's how it – what I did – seems to me.

After the launch of the second flob-bomb, Dooley ordered Hartt to clean out the kit room and mop the changing-room floor. ('Make sure it's sparkling when I get back, Cinders, or your ball's off.') And I was teamed up with a traumatized, pebble-dashed Carey Schumacher – the kind of useless compliment to one's dependability that teachers like to pay, knowing of course that it spells social death.

The main school building was accent-shaped, like two sides of a hexagon, bracketing a raised playing field that dropped suddenly on the far side into Greenway Lane and Lyncombe Vale, where a stream ran parallel to the heavily creepered railway embankments for a quarter of a mile. We put on our rugby boots to deal with the expected mud, and clattered along an antiseptic green corridor past the suspiciously aromatic art room towards the West exit. As we streamed out of the right leg of the accent and across the pitch, several of the boys in front of our dislocated teenage crocodile broke into a run, barging through the long-jump pit to one side of the rugby field and flying on to the gate at the bottom of the school grounds. If you held your arms out as you ran, the sweat in your armpits evaporated more quickly, which felt nice.

Bray was ahead of the pack, as usual, his arms wide open, teeth bared. He was about five foot three – if anything a little short for his age – and wiry, with close-cropped black hair that scrambled into fuzz on his neck, and a shadowy upper lip. He had bright, sharp, but not very straight teeth, ferrety eyes and ears that went red when he mined them for wax, which he did absent-mindedly and often. His trousers looked almost fitted and he never wore a vest. Beneath his white shirt, I could see hormonally bruised nipples and a few sprigs of curly hair around the navel.

Withdrawn in the classroom, Bray came into his own on a run. A hidden arrangement of tendons and breathing apparatus unfurled inside him; his shoulders relaxed, and the top-heavy scuffling gait that shushed grit into your shoes from behind dissolved into an easy gallop. At the age of thirteen, he had already distinguished himself in the under-sixteen national cross-country trials; but by county standards, he was a freak of nature – the rabbit on the greyhound track – showered and dressed by the time his nearest rival crossed the finishing line.

I didn't want to be Gregory Bray exactly, but ever since he'd won that Jubilee mug (the blue one) for gymnastics at primary school, I'd wanted to tell him things. Principally, that I admired him as a runner, and that – well, that this admiration was natural, unfeigned, spur of the moment. Nothing for him to worry about. Even if it kept me awake.

There was little balance of power either in our fantasy trysts (I always imagined him making the first move), or in reality. I was his friend on tolerance, though my pride never allowed me to be too grateful. My tall frame and mildly intellectual bearing, reinforced by mimicry and second-rate musicianship, made me appear self-sufficient: a boy who could have been very popular, but didn't need to be. Though this was far from the case, it served me well as a secret admirer; for my posed self-possession brought me closer to Bray, who raised indifference to public opinion to the level of high art. My air of bemusement was an affectation indulged by Dooley and others ('Houston to Professor Rathbone. Come in, Professor, do you read me?') because it provided a benign model of learning, or at least of a willingness to learn, that might just, possibly, inspire others. Bray, though, was the genuine article. Immune to praise or insult, he greeted athletic triumph and academic disappointment with the same glacial calm. His father, still unemployed four years after losing his job at Bath's crane and engineering works, Stothert and Pitt, shouted a lot at the monthly PTA.

Bray stood, now, leaning on the gate, bored, waiting for a signal from Dooley to cross the road and carry on along the public footpath to the lower reaches of Lyncombe Vale. As soon as it came – a dismissive wave – he was off, skimming the pavement and hop-scotching down the muddy passage towards the end of the embankment and the entrenched V of the railway cutting. At the back of the procession, I carried the box of lanterns and listened to Schumacher complain. Every so often he gave his beloved Rubik's Cube a rueful twist and said things like 'I got three sides yesterday. It was so neat.'

The Rubik's Cube, lest blissfully we forget, was everywhere in the early 1980s. The attractions of rotating this gridlike puzzle so as to achieve a cube with six differently coloured faces of nine squares each were sensibly lost on the trainee architects for whom it was designed – but not on adolescent misfits, who saw in it a model of order and propriety. Where life disappointed, Rubik provided cheerful resolution. Lunchtimes, breaktimes and curricular holidays (RE, Technical Drawing) were all filled with the clickety-clack of the cubists. I had one, as did the translucent Peter Lillingston; Craig Spillings, too, though his was soon forgotten when he joined the Air Training Corps and discovered group masturbation. It was the perfect displacement activity: Carey began our walk to the tunnel entrance by asking me if he could ask me a question ('Say, Daniel, can I ask you a question? Do you like Bruce Hartt? Well, *I* think he's gross'); then, after telling me what his dad would do to Bruce if Dad wasn't separated from Mom and living in Albuquerque, he fished out his cube and started to fiddle. Dooley bore down on us at this point with his Gaz freight and loaded me up; Carey was excused from carrying anything because he looked busy. And that was the last straw.

Silently, I itemized my resentments. To begin with, the whole friendship was a set-up. My father administered the art college at which Frankie, Carey's mother, taught. Carey had been introduced to me at an end-of-term drinks party in 1981, as soon as Frankie discovered that we were to be schoolmates at Lyncombe. Green-eyed, sibylline Frankie, who believed in 'openness' and gave readings of her terrible poetry every Monday evening in the Hat and Feather, told me, in Carey's hearing, how she hoped I would be 'real supportive'. Carey, it turned out, had already been through three other local schools in twelve months, but none of these had come up to scratch.

'It's the darnedest thing,' Frankie sighed. 'Carey just loved school back home, but he hasn't gotten comfortable here yet, have you, honey?'

Carey shook his head doomily. I blinked and clutched my fruit fizz. Something in Frankie's nurturing tone made my roots shrivel: her smile was ray-gun bright. She beamed it at me a while longer, then kissed her carrot-haired son heavily on the lips, and invited me over to play on his computer. 'That would be so great,' he piped.

Carey perked up a week later, when I called round. I was in a sulk after my Saturday morning piano lesson, and in no mood to talk computers. Back then, they were all overpriced bits of tat requiring vast amounts of daft instruction before they yielded so much as a blip. A fool could see that they would have to be much more sophisticated in order to serve any simple purpose, but Carey was in thrall.

'This is cool, Daniel. Watch this,' he crooned, and thumbed a bit of code into his ZX81: 10PRINT'CareySchumacher'/20GOTO10. Suddenly, his name filled the screen; Carey squealed with delight. Equally suddenly, I wanted to hit him. 'And?' I snapped, finally.

'What do you mean, "And?",' Carey stammered.

I took a breath. 'And what else can it do?' I said.

There was a silence.

'Oh, a whole bunch of things,' came the distant reply. 'Let's have a shake. Mom'll make us one. C'mon.'

In the kitchen were fresh sources of irritation: white cat hairs on every surface, and the overfed animals to whom they had once belonged pooled upon a rickety wooden table like a couple of collapsed meringues. 'Oh, shoo!' gushed Frankie and scooped them up, one under each arm. 'They know they're not supposed to do that.'

The cats escaped her embrace and retreated to a large tray of kitty-litter in-laid with filigree turds and dumped in front of the American-style, drive-in fridge. The whole room smelt of pee. An avocado tree grappled at the window and dangled its parched leaves over the gas stove on which a pot of something yellow and sour was bubbling away. Frankie drifted off to stir the mixture and nearly tripped over the tresses of her full-length Aran cardigan. There was no further mention of a milkshake.

'I guess I know what you guys'd like,' she began hopefully instead, speaking out of a cloud of steam.

'I guess I do, too,' said Carey evenly, as the cloud dispersed and Frankie emerged from it bearing a tureen of risotto. He looked at me once, long-sufferingly, as she doled out the luminous gruel. And for a moment, I felt that – with no one else to impress – I could almost like him.

The risotto lined my stomach like lead. I felt trapped. Frankie's friendship with my parents required me to be civil, since they owed their marriage to one of her aphrodisiac dope-cakes, baked at an art student party in the early 1960s. At the same party, Frankie seduced Corsham College's young caretaker and disappeared back to Connecticut with him, where she taught, wove and wrote poetry while he smoked, drank and pill-popped. Two decades later, after their divorce and Frankie's return to Bath, my father took pity, gave her a job and spoke to us in you-don't-want-to-know tones about a 'traumatic personal history'. Now Carey, her only son, had joined us, and I was told to make an effort. Which I had, I decided, before swallowing a last mouthful and making my excuses.

'That was delicious,' I lied. 'But I'm afraid I really must be going, Mrs Schumacher, because my father's taking me on a long walk.'

Frankie boggled slightly at this news, with its undertones of mystery and abduction. Carey was ecstatic, though, because he liked long walks, too. Much more, in fact, than my father, who was not at home.

'Oh gee, that's a shame. I guess he forgot. We'll just have to go on our own,' said Carey philosophically, and so we did – on a five-mile trek across Lansdown, through the beechy outskirts of Charlcombe and Woolley, and back home along the Gloucester Road. Wood sorrel and white violets, recognizable from my April issue of *Look and Learn*, were springing up everywhere. Carey trod on them and laughed. So I led him in his open-toed sandals through a large bank of stinging nettles.

It was of no use. The unwanted have low expectations; learn not to register every instance of rejection. I could do no wrong. The more I tried to shake Carey off, the more he clung to me. Now thirteen, he had two other friends, with whom he twisted his cube and played Dungeons and Dragons, but I was courted in other, more substantive ways. I sang in the choir; so Carey joined the choir. I played the piano; so Carey took up the clarinet. I ran long-distance – not like Gregory Bray, but adequately; so Carey bought himself a bright green tracksuit and started 'training'. Whenever I had the chance to walk home with Bray, my heart beating a little if I lingered a step behind to look at his neck, Carey would intercept us at the gates and offer us both warm mints. In the canteen queue at lunchtime, he would seek me out; at weekends, he would call round, uninvited, on his Chopper bike.

*

At the tunnel entrance, there was much hilarity. By the time Carey and I staggered onto the overgrown track, Spillings had already chased the wino up the side of the cutting and surprised our deputy head boy, mid-clinch, in a clump of elder. Dooley was unflappable. 'Take it easy,' he advised the drunk, and turned a blind eye to the fast disappearing, dishevelled gropers.

The lanterns were handed out, one between two, and we listened idly to a lecture about subsidence and safety precautions – 'Stick together, walk slowly, don't shout, don't kick stones and don't touch anything.' 'Don't bother,' would have been more like it; Dooley's delaying tactics only emphasized the irresponsibility of the whole venture from his point of view and its catastrophic appeal from ours. One look at the crumbling, horseshoe-shaped opening, with its graffiti-gouged blocks of Bath stone and protruding roots, said it all. A few paces inside and Combe Down's throaty darkness closed on the afternoon; dust curled forward around Craig Spillings where he'd already kicked an old sleeper to pieces, but his laughter fell backwards like something dropped into a well.

Two hundred yards further on, the tunnel's curvature snuffed out the last flicker of natural light, and with it a good deal of our high spirits. In places where darkness and silence appear to be absolute, noise and light are really just an impertinence. Even fifteen lanterns, held aloft, won't make much of an impression. Then the stone sky began to drip.

Dooley brought our glimmering procession to a halt and asked us in a loud whisper for an explanation of this phenomenon. 'Perhaps it's raining in Rainbow Woods, sir,' said an unusually inspired Craig Spillings, 'and this is, like, last week's rain tricklin' down through the cracks, or summat.' Twenty-nine nervous teenagers stifled a giggle and prodded each other, but Spillings checked us all with an expression of lunar seriousness. He looked up and so did we. There were the cracks; here was the water. A cathedral of sodden earth sat on top of us.

Towards the middle of the tunnel, the dark thickened and we smelt smoke, presumably from a fire built at one of the entrances the night before. A slow draught must have carried the rubbishy vapour deeper and deeper into the hillside, and now we inched along in its sour folds, closing ranks like so many penguins. At its densest, the pall of smoke made breathing uncomfortable. Bolshier elements at the front of the queue promised to 'pan in' the fire-raising culprit if they found him, and Peter Lillingston began to wheeze harmonically. Alarmed, Dooley urged us to get a move on. The file of lights dispersed again as a few boys broke ranks, and 3TD emerged from the pea-souper into the coldest stretch of tunnel so far, perturbed by witchy cross-currents from a works siding on our left. Ahead, I could hear Dooley checking on Lillingston, and Lillingston meekly protesting his health. 'All ri-ight, then. As long as you're sure,' said Dooley gruffly, and raised his lantern to attempt a head count.

Carey and I were right at the back, about fifteen yards or more behind everyone else, when we ran out of Gaz. The soft white glow of our lamp flashed a few times, as if signalling something desperate in Morse, and the low roar of the burner died away. Dooley must have counted us in before this, because he was already on the move again, apparently satisfied that all the torchbearers and their companions had made it through the smoke. Soon, the last swaying lantern had disappeared around the second and last bend in the tunnel. I shook the butane cylinder but it was quite empty. We stood in complete darkness.

Carey felt for my hand, the pulse of his fingertips quick with the fear of abandonment.

'Which way is forwards?' he faltered.

'This way,' I replied, and steered him left, into the works siding.

'How do you know?'

'I just do. Come on.'

'If we shout, they'll come back for us.' Carey breathed quickly, unsure whether or not to trust his invisible companion. 'I'm going to shout.'

'No, you're not.'

And he didn't. Instead, he opened his mouth in disbelief as I pulled him out of the main channel. Fear must have made him luminescent, like a heat island or reflective cloudbank, because I could easily make out the sweat in the cleft of his top lip as it merged with a fat droplet of snot. We reached the clammy back wall of the siding, where I let go of Carey's arm.

'I can't be friends with you any more,' I said flatly. He looked down.

'OK.'

'It's not that I don't like you,' I explained untruthfully. 'It's just that I want to be friends with Gregory Bray and Craig Spillings. And I can't be friends with them if I have to go round with you.'

There was a terrible, returning silence.

'Why?'

'Because that would make me like you. I mean, the same as you.'

Carey's eyes were all pupil, his orange hair a solar shadow. He looked through me, searching for an excuse to hunch his shoulders and splay his hands in nebbish exasperation. But I was implacable.

'There's nothing wrong with you,' I said. 'You're immature, that's all.'

'I am not.' Carey's voice was spectrally thin and high.

'Yes. You are.'

All around us the darkness heaved. For some reason, Carey could not take his eyes from my face – a transfixity that didn't explain itself until we emerged from Combe Down tunnel, with Carey's chilling 'How can you?' still ringing in my ears. I heard it as a plea, though it was also, as it turned out, an honest enquiry. The jeers and whistles from the other boys, already seated on thistly banks doodling in their rough books, faded abruptly.

'And where the hell have you two been?' Dooley asked, as I handed him the inert lantern. His voice was angry, but the frown that accompanied it concealed a mixture of surprise and relief. No one had missed us, I realized; either that, or we had not been gone long.

'Light went out, sir,' I said. Silence, again.

I looked back at Carey, who stood in the mouth of the tunnel like an urchin in a daguerreotype, his punched-in features astream with helpless tears. Slowly, he raised one arm and pointed it at me, dragging twenty-nine pairs of eyes in a leery arc from his face to mine.

'He can *see*,' he squealed at last, and I felt a shameful calm descend. 'Daniel can see in the dark!'

Secret Ambition

The prophet of fear and despair left me – a little rattled, a little chastened – at four thirty in the morning, with the beginnings of a conscience. I took two paracetamol and slept off most of it, but awoke after only four hours or so to the reproach of a brilliant morning and a scrawled message on the kitchen table: 'Tim. Thanks for the coffee. You fell asleep. I went home. Take care. Kevin. PS. Have washed up and nicked some milk.'

On the draining board were the plates from the night before, though not, understandably, the glasses, still mired in red wine and ash. (The kindness of strangers has its limits.) Clogging the bathroom sink, I found my shirt in a cold purple infusion of Surf and Stain Devil. Since there is no way I would have attempted to do this myself at such an hour, this means that somebody did it for me. And so presumably undressed me. Days could be wasted probing the shallows of a memory lapse like this, for which the only cure is a bath and a reminder of one's essential weediness.

By ten, my second quarter-century is well under way. As significantly, the oh-well sensation that life is after all complicated and that a false name is not quite a false identity – more of a safety precaution – has cut in where the painkillers didn't have the heart to. The pear tree and rose bushes wave to me from the back of the garden, like crowds in a silent movie. I step out from the kitchen into the light and feel deceptively wise.

Such a pompous feeling has to be acknowledged if one is to see through or past it. Life is complicated, principally because most of us have a vested interest in keeping it that way. As my boyfriend and I mealy-mouthed to each other a year ago, when we decided to open up our relationship, the complexity of love, desire and affection should on no account be denied, by which we meant, of course, the reverse – the simple urge to fuck and forget. Likewise, the simplicity of a pause for thought in a garden on a bright, sunny morning ought not to be mistaken for thought itself. Introspection is not insight, however many you've had.

As a rule, these moments of midmorning clarity are soon over, replaced by less oppressive realizations: the toast is burning, your flies are undone, you are being watched by neighbour Neville (dressed for the outdoors in cravat and waders). Today feels different, though, and I am inclined to blame it on this garden, which grows with such thorough and impossible conviction. Like a number of gay men, I grew up loving plants and trees because they seemed to reward affection and nurture. Put some beech nuts in a bag of soil, wait four months for them to germinate, plant them out in little pots, donate seedlings to indulgent local Parks Commissioners. Easy. The disappointing other side of the bargain is that some things grow without one's permission and mistakes can prove ineradicable.

When I bought my flat, with the deposit secured on my first lucrative contract as a production editor for *Media Weekly*, I didn't mind what grew in my garden as long as it grew. But since my father's death in '93, I've changed my mind. The

Russian vine is uncontrollable, tonguing its way through the bathroom window, and the Japanese knotweed positively sinister. Nor can their comic foreignness disguise the fact that my green fingers are an infantile fancy. My mother, when I see her for lunch in a little over three hours, will no doubt have bought me a plant for my birthday; last year, it was a marsh marigold, which shrivelled under a coat of mildew. Other items – flowering currant, Californian lilac, a hardy vine and a spotted laurel for the side return – have gone the same way, invisibly. What people notice in my garden, it seems, are the works of nature that came before me: the pear tree, the gnarled roses, the knackered plum, the sprawl of brambles at the back. They are only an inheritance, though. It would be nice to have earned them.

As it is, I am no more than their warden – sympathetic, custodial and non-interventionist. During the day, and especially now in midsummer, the follies of this feral democracy are plain to see: apart from the vine and the knotweed, my rosebuds are clustered with blackfly, and the leafy underside of the three ugly sycamores that border the garden on the right-hand side have become a breeding ground for billions of aphids. ('Just don't use any pesticides, man – they're evil,' my father advised, on his first and last visit. This from the man who wanted to smuggle an adder's nest into our home garden to control the local puppy population.)

Neville, I feel sure, disapproves of my cackhanded attempts to keep order in my seventy-foot plot. He claims descendancy from Dr Thomas Edwards, one of Brixton's early Victorian estate owners, and likes to think of our minor four-road enclosure to the west of the prison as an historical monument to those first garden suburbs along the Hill. 'This used to be such a desirable quarter,' he observed loudly when I first moved in. 'No hippity-hop music or pizzas. Did you know that John Lewis – *the* John Lewis – was incarcerated over the way for illegal development?'

Snobbery aside, Neville has a point. Windmill Road, so I've found, is truly a wonderful, desirable place to live: a red-brick, slightly weathered turn-of-the-century terrace, equidistant from Clapham's Abbeville Village – a *chi-chi* enclave invented by estate agents in the 1980s to attract chinless suits and their wives south of the river – and the friendly deep-time grind of Brixton, where all things come to those who wait, including one's own stolen goods (at Ray's Hot Sounds). Fortunately, most of our neighbours are Brixtonian, rather than Abbevillean, in means, spirit and ethnic mix; house prices are cheap, because we're at least fifteen minutes' walk from the nearest tube, and the local launderette is well attended, not so much for its ragged grey washes as for the gossip to be wrung out of the proprietress, Rula Zaniewski, a flame-haired sixtysomething Polish refugee (slight accent) who married an East End gangster in the 1960s and managed to divorce him ten years later without sacrificing any limbs in the settlement. Rula took over the Lyham Road Washeteria in 1973, lives with Carl, a handsome but severely alcoholic black plumber in his forties, and was the first person to congratulate me on moving in. 'You won't regret it, dahling,' she rasped. 'It's a lahvely spot. Lahvely people round here. Got a little gahden? Nice. Mind, I do not bother much with mine, 'cept what I put aht for the foxes. You seen them foxes?'

I hadn't then, but soon did. The previous owners – a theatrical agent and a mental nurse – told me to look out for them first thing in the morning, or at night, though after a week of self-imposed sentry duty by the kitchen door I gave up hope. Then, one clear evening, while lying tipsily on the long trestle my father gave me for a flat warming he never got to, I saw a sleek ochre-red twosome pour out of the drooping gooseberry bush which nestles beneath the old pear tree, and disappear over the wall. They paused once, perhaps surprised that I could make them out in the darkness, returned my gaze – ears cocked, eyes star-stippled –with the alert indifference of clever cats, and were gone in one bound.

Neville thinks our nocturnal tenants (they have a den beneath his shed) should be evicted. A shameless forager himself at garden centres and car boot sales, he resents the competition. 'Foxes are vermin,' he says. 'They slink into the city along disused railway lines and piss on my cabbages.' This is true. They also uproot bulbs and have ear-splitting sex in the springtime. There is little that can be done about them, though, now that they have colonized the area. Since the terraced back gardens of Windmill Road form part of a self-contained square of lawns, trees, ponds and shrubbery, the wildlife has any number of homes to choose from; turf the foxes out of one and they will decamp to another – Rula's, for instance. Not that Neville hasn't experimented with a novel series of deterrents. Convinced that the best of these would be lion shit, or straw from the lion's cage (anything that reeked of a more ferocious predator), he rang up Regent's Park Zoo and came home one evening with three sacks full of Bengal tiger bedding and panther crap. The cats for miles around were traumatized and the foxes unimpressed. Not a single cabbage survived.

The neighbourhood frogs, by contrast, do little to distress their human cohabitees, and even inspire a curious devotion among them. In theory, some should migrate, or at least leave my pond from year to year in search of new breeding grounds, but Windmill amphibians, so it seems, are generally content to sit on the lilypads and croak. A daily temperature of sixty to sixty-five degrees is needed to get them to perform, though the greenhouse humidity of the past two weeks has made them more vociferous. And their song, while not melodic, at least has the virtue of rhythm, which Neville, being a chorus master, values highly. He likes to 'bring them on', he says – even if 'bringing them on' simply means hanging around by the fence, drinking tea and pointing.

Neville is thinking about other things, of course, when he does this, including the passage of years, and what the future holds for an old-school bachelor who missed out on liberation, but it's a subtext of mood rather than matter, and one which barely intrudes on our banter. 'There's a good alto in the making on the second rung of the fountain,' he told me last week. 'And I rather fancy the chances of that handsomely marked basso nobile lurking in the lilies.'

There have been periods of silence, too. After the spring thaw, when the frogs are spawning, they are usually so preoccupied with sex and survival that there's no time for concerts. Next door's cats get wise to the first stirrings of pond life in early April, when the frogs themselves are too dopey to take evasive action, and the season of rut is soon the season of slaughter. My own experience bears this out. Several times, I've wandered into the garden after breakfast to find a row of tiny corpses crisping by the side of the pond, their innards knotted and fused with strings of spawn. Tinned food tastes better than common frog, of course, and the killings stop once the cats realize this, though not before a mass grave has been filled beneath the clematis.

*

Windmill Road has plenty in it, then, to attract the amateur naturalist: foxes, frogs, owls, woodpeckers, a dog with two wheels where its back legs should be. (This last yapping miracle of biotechnology is the devoted companion of Olive, a frail black lady who lives a few doors down with her warring twins Martin and Earl, joint proprietors of a dodgy lumber and hardware store in Streatham. Martin reversed into the 'fucked-up mutt' a few months ago, and Olive insisted on an expensive prosthesis; the car went, the dog stayed.) We're also just a stone's throw from Brockwell Park's out-of-time rose gardens, Norwood Cemetery (the last resting place of Mrs Beeton) and Clapham Common, where, the pious neighbouring Council claims, a pair of kestrels has nested for the first time this year. (Like they planned it.) Not that the area's exotic ecology, or any of its off-beam markets, mildewy shops (Morley's – 'four floors of exciting shopping') and clubs, can begin to explain why I bought my flat.

To find that out, sadly, one has to go to the usual filial insecurities to do with love and dependency, which seem to afflict even the most contented of children (once they've grown up). Foremost among these, I suppose, is the desire to find a station – a partnership, a career, a location – that exceeds one's parents'. That station may be rich or poor, risky or staid; its only value lies in the proof it offers of difference. And on any other day I'm sure my parents would have been delighted to hear about the editing contract and the flat-offer, but Dad, worst luck, was on his way back from the Royal United with the oncology consultant's report when I rang, so the celebrations were cut a bit short.

Big decisions, like buying a flat or a house, must also satisfy your innermost promptings – the ones you can't tell your insurance company about. Most people call these grubby urges 'subconscious desire', which mistakes surface complexity for deep division and lets everyone off the hook. Whereas the point about subconscious desire is that it's usually a fully conscious ingredient of our lives that we'd just rather not own up to. For example, I bought my flat, so I maintained, because of a nesting instinct – a piece of sentimental nonsense approved by everyone who heard it, including my boyfriend. I bought it, in fact, for more predatory purposes: to have somewhere to bring people, naturally, and because the Woolwich estate agent Colin, with whom I'd seen at least ten properties and enjoyed a number of telling pauses, let his hand drop down behind me one day, gave my cheeks a squeeze and fucked me in the vendors' bathroom. He said the property might benefit from a second viewing and I agreed. (The idea that I might be able to sign a contract on this kind of chance encounter and guarantee its recurrence appealed to me.) Naturally, I never saw him again after that, but put in an offer anyway: at £56,000, the place was a steal.

So for subconscious desire read 'secret ambition', which gets a little closer, I think, to describing our inability to tell ourselves, never mind anyone else, the truth. Gay men and women understand this kind of self-imposture very well, since most of us learn about sex while lying about our inclinations and, even after coming out, find it tricky not to carry on pretending in some capacity – as a squaddie, a leather master, a whipping boy, a suit. (I still find it impossible, though mine may be the last generation to feel this way: there's talk about lowering the age of consent again in the next term, and queer visibility in soap operas means that 'gay' school kids are now healthy individualists rather than loners.)

Yet secret ambition also gestures in the direction of something more abstract, for which nameless need there is no workable definition, only a sense of menace that grabs you by the throat on dark nights when the radiator strikes thirteen. Men with beards will tell you that it's illimitable desire, that it's the ego, that it's greed. For me, though, it's waking up on a day like today to find that your lovely garden has become a rebuke to the rest of your perfectly manageable but unlovely life. It's what's left unsatisfied when a lot of luck has come your way, and you still feel guiltily cheated. It's the thin, distant, growling wave of suspicion that, whatever else it turns out to be, it's bound to be your fault.

*

The first person I see on entering the Krishna Temple restaurant in Soho Street, on his own in one of the window seats, monitoring the ebb and flow of dahl as he pushes it unenthusiastically from one side of his plate to the other, is Connor. He is wearing a hangover uniform – unironed, don't-bother-me green polo top and khaki-coloured jeans – not unlike my own (except that my shirt's blue and full-length), has removed his black earring, and is frowning into the specular limbo-land of the sheet-glass in front of him, counting the shoppers, squinting at his reflection. Two tables further in, a pert and upright lady with grey hair and flared nostrils heaves her head back and sneezes into her salad. She gives a tight little sigh, looks around in vexation and then back at her fouled mixed leaf, as if to say 'Did you see that? Isn't it typical?'

The frustrated actress in my mother has never found it easy to be part of a crowd without drawing attention to herself. Put her in a train carriage or bus full of shoppers and she soon begins to notice things. 'Hasn't Battersea changed?' I once heard her say to an Asian guy with piercings and upper arms you could drive around. 'Look at all these trendy new boutiques. I remember when Arding and Hobbs was the only big shop for miles!' (She doesn't; born in Highbury, my mother probably never even came south of the river until I moved here two years ago, but, like all transient liberals, she harbours a secret longing for authenticity.)

I went through years of being embarrassed by this behaviour: the incessant low-level commentary in the cinema, the inspired visits to the loo at the end of the intermission, the habit of robbing others of the chance to appreciate a beautiful sunset by pointing it out. Frankie Schumacher, in her quietly venomous way, used to put this down to 'Jane's real deep insecurity, y'know, Daniel? A fear of silence?', which was rich coming from Frankie, and as a carping adolescent I was only too happy to agree with her. Things got bad when I went to university, and the mother–son line went dead for a couple of years until my boyfriend pointed out that dealing with shyness by talking to strangers and refusing to be intimidated by social custom was actually rather an intelligent solution to the problem.

It still drives me mad, of course, because the sneezing and the sighing is *so* contrived; and because it is *so* difficult to hold my mother's attention, always assuming that she has yours. Arguments are not a good idea, since the serious contemplation of another point of view makes her fidgety and tearful. But that's the need for reassurance speaking; that's what thirty years of marriage and sudden widowhood do to you.

Connor hears the door swing shut and looks up; he smiles broadly and ironically, draws a finger across his neck. This could mean any number of things: that he's been chucked and is feeling like death; that Kev has been rushed into St Thomas's for an emergency circumcision; or, more feasibly, that, of the thousands of faces on the gay scene, mine is the one he is least surprised to see. I give Connor a friendly wave, and he turns away to renew his contemplation of Soho's groovy troops in their Day-Glo stretch-cotton and beltless denim. Life strolls on.

'Ooo-oo!' My mother hoots twice from the middle of the room. Her right hand is raised in a brownie salute, fingers wide apart. Two aged hippies, to her left, smirk in a superior fashion and sink their teeth into some flapjack. There is a sharp crack as one of them hits a nut.

'. . . and wait for you to turn up!'

Her voice comes into range as I sit down. Without pausing, she repeats the sentence at high speed in a slightly louder whisper, a comma of elastic saliva flexing away in the corner of her mouth. She is dressed, as usual, in a close-fitting blue-and-white top with a cream skirt and flat brown shoes. The light colours are carefree, but I notice a flutter in the voice, nothing to do with her characteristic volubility, and she seems thinner. Her eyes move quickly, her smile brittle with suppressed fatigue.

'. . . and so I stayed with Maeve last night, which was nice – well, she wanted me to – and then the train was delayed this morning, so by the time we got into Paddington I thought I might as well come straight here instead of going to the Venice exhibition and wait for you to turn up! And here you are. And I've just sneezed all over my salad. Not very nice, is it? Well, it wasn't very nice to begin with. Still, there you are.'

The lights go out for an instant, and she is borne far away on a current of nervous, arrhythmic conjecture. She has started eating without me.

'So!' – the lights come back on – 'How was the big day? Can't believe you're twenty-five. *Can't* believe it.'

We embrace awkwardly across the table, both aware that I

have been listening to myself listening in order to check the temptation to shout out 'Stop! Please! No more!' I scan the floor for gifts, but there is no foliage in sight. This could be a sign that I have outgrown presents and reached that age of dignified self-sufficiency at which no one 'makes a fuss'. Or maybe all that stuff about Maeve, my schizophrenic second cousin, and the Venice show was meant to remind me that I alone do not merit an expensive day-trip to the capital. 'Fuck off to the sodding Canalettos, then,' is my mental comment. Until a gentle hoot surprises me.

'Ooo – and I've got something. In case you thought I'd forgotten.'

'You know you didn't have to,' I mumble.

'Oh, but I like to. Twenty-five's an important one. Of course I don't *have* to. I know that . . .' A squeezed-out sports car parks on the underside of my mother's salad spoon. 'Anyway,' she gulps on a windy intake of breath, patting her chest and looking up at the pattern-plastered ceiling, 'I was married at twenty-five, as you know.'

'Meaning?'

'Not meaning anything. I just was.' She rearranges a radish and looks at me, then quickly away. 'Really, I don't know.' A limbed blob gets out of the driver's seat and slithers to the bottom of the spoon, where all the other reflections meld like mercury. Behind us the café door opens. 'I can't think what I did to make you so critical. I can't say anything, can I?'

'That's not true.'

'You weren't like this with your father. And he never–'

She stops, pulls the V-neck of her top together, remembers that it doesn't gather like a normal shirt, and lets go. 'Cared' is the unuttered word. She wants me to infer Dad's dereliction of duty as a father: his incapacity to remember birthdays,

31

anniversaries; his infidelities (much hinted at, never discussed); his selfishness. Except that all I remember are instances of practical generosity and silent pride: that trestle table, on which he painted and scraped away for thirty years, the donation of meagre proceeds from an exhibition to offset my journalism college fees, repairing a blackbird's wing with a makeshift splint made out of a cigar packet, porridge on a winter's morning.

My mother recomposes herself; she is waiting now for a gesture of apology, some recognition from another that this is all still hard for her.

'I was. I was just as awkward. And I'm sorry. Let's not–'

'Oh, I don't mind. You know me. Say no more.'

She gives the grainy dressing at the bottom of her bowl a desultory stir and breaks, at last, the strand of mucus connecting both her lips with the tip of her tongue. In a final once-over of the restaurant and its diners, her eyes rest briefly on the beatifically unhurried bald girl at the till, and on the queue of disgruntled customers waiting to pay.

A young, smart-alecky laugh rises above the gentle prod and ponder.

'Is that someone you know?' my mother asks innocently. She nods at the window table where, half-turning, I see Connor being joined by Kevin, shorter, hairier and richer than I remember him, in suburban tennis shorts and a vest. Kevin leans on one elbow, cupping his chin, and jiggles the car keys with his free hand. He has registered my presence, raised one eyebrow and made a wry observation. Connor meanwhile, amused and animated, is busy scribbling something on a napkin. I am on the point of going over to defuse the tension, maybe utter a few tart pleasantries, re-establish the restaurant as a neutral zone, when Connor holds up the napkin with a cross-eyes grin and mischievous titter. It reads, in an American combination of upper and lower case, 'NiCE oNe TiM'. Seconds later, Kevin holds up another: 'Yeah, Nice'.

My vision blurs momentarily with that orange-hot flush of shame which is four parts low-grade self-pity and one part remorse.

I turn back to face my mother, who wears an expression of effortful good humour. 'They must have got you mixed up with someone else,' she says brightly, a note of ostrich-like confidence in her voice carrying over the general hubbub. Connor cracks up at this, drags himself to his feet – he is taller today – and saunters out of the restaurant with a frowning Kevin in tow. Outside, their laughter has a vitreous, bottled quality to it; they look back once more and shake their heads. Kev wags a single finger in elaborate mock-admonishment.

'Well, it's none of my business,' my mother mutters. 'Very strange behaviour. That's all I can say. Why didn't they just say hello?'

'They're friends of friends,' I reply lamely. 'I've met them a couple of times, but I can't remember their names, and they obviously can't remember mine.'

'Obviously.' A pause. 'Interesting couple, though, aren't they?' she adds, in the manner of a nice lady determined to admire an obscene tribal fetish. 'Attractive, too, in a funny kind of way. I thought so. Especially that thin Danish-looking one. Mind, he needs to put on weight.'

'The other one's Greek,' I offer pointlessly.

'Really? Looked more Italian to me. You know, the South.'

'Whereabouts?'

'Of course I don't *know*. I just thought he looked Southern. Or Sicilian.' She looks up warily and strokes the side of her nose. 'Aren't you going to eat anything, dear?'

'No.'

'Not hungry? Not even a sandwich?'

'No. I had breakfast.'

'So did I! But that was hours ago. Still, I expect you got up late.'

'Something like that.' Late rising, I recall, was the cardinal sin of my adolescence. During the school week, if I had not stirred by seven o'clock, the hoover was dispatched to rouse me; at weekends and on public holidays, I had a reprieve until eight-thirty.

My mother has momentarily disappeared from view and is struggling with something between her feet.

'Can I help?'

'No, dear,' she chirps, all sprightliness again, and hauls up onto the rickety postformed table a large oblong package in brown paper. 'Here we are. I kept it down there because of the size. Didn't want people staring, you know. But I got some funny looks on the tube, I can tell you! I'm sure they all thought I was a terrorist – with a bomb.'

'Probably.'

The intriguing idea that, minus the 'bomb', a tube full of strangers might still have suspected my grey-bunned mother of terrorism – 'she looks the type' – is enough to distract me for a moment from the package itself, which is two and a half feet long and deeply mysterious. Her arms folded high on top of it, Jane Rathbone looks at me with the slightly superior amusement of an Alice, forearmed against all filial sarcasm and loss of appetite by her own unassailable common sense. She gives a little hoot and a chilly laugh, not altogether unhappy to prolong my discomfort; after all, she knows what's underneath the brown manila, whereas I do not – a cache of withheld information as powerful, in its way, as a cache of arms. A measure of our mutual suspicion.

My mother lifts the package again – and hands it to me. I feel wood through the paper. Heaviness. Hollowness, too. A lid, possibly.

'It's too big to open here,' I stammer. 'I'll wait until I get home.'

'Oh, go on with you,' she chides, missing the point. 'If I can carry it halfway across London, surely you can unwrap it.'

I set it down gingerly on my side of the table and sweep my palms, like Geiger counters, over the top surface. The hippies to the left have mopped up their last crumbs and are trying not to show interest, though they and I are both drawn by the same mystery. Clearly – almost clearly – it is a box. But if it is a box, what does it contain? And why does whatever it contains have to be contained? The same simple stupefaction beset me the first time I heard my parents making love. We'd just been to see *Star Wars*, and, too excited to sleep, I'd crept upstairs in the small hours to have a pee. The bathroom door was shut; I could hear them inside. A whole universe of concealed possibilities was suddenly manifest and unreachable.

'Not a plant, then,' I manage, at last.

'Not a plant. The others didn't do too well, dear, did they?'

My fingers dock on either side of the box, and a propulsive, manic energy jerks them to life. The sound of tearing paper fills the restaurant, and my mother's painstaking italic dedication – 'To Daniel Rathbone, with all my love, on his twenty-fifth birthday, 1995' – is ripped in two.

Hunter

My optician was politely baffled. Various kinds of myopic deterioration were not unusual at my age, she agreed, but a specific gain in visual acuity was rare, and the kind of feline capacity I described belonged, frankly, to the realms of science fiction. Her air of put-upon nonchalance behind the old-fashioned desk betrayed the fear that I might be hoaxing. I had a test, which told me what I already knew – 'good eyesight, certainly, and no signs of anything amiss, but nothing extra-ordinary' – after which I persuaded her to switch off the illuminated letters on the far wall. A buzzer sounded and the panel went dead.

'Now,' she said, arms folded, looking down, 'what can you read?'

'All of it,' I replied, and rattled off the seven lines with just a few pauses over the smallest V and U to put her at her ease.

'That's very impressive, Daniel.' She unfolded her arms and took off her glasses. There was a small, fringed lamp between us that belonged in a 1950s hotel reception. She looked at me levelly, one thin eyebrow half-raised, and turned it off, too. For a moment, the memory of light flared darkly before me. Upstairs, at street level, I could hear the assistant taking an appointment over the phone ('We'll see you next

Tuesday, then, Mr Cousins. Yes, on the corner. Can't miss it.')
In the blacked-out room, I awaited further instructions.

'Well, to my eyes,' she began, hesitantly, 'this is night. I
mean, I can't see a thing. There's a chink of something from
the stairway around the hinges of the door, but that's about it.
What about you?'

'Pretty dim,' I said, 'but it's improving. You're getting quite
clear now and the panels are glowing. They're kind of orange
– the orange you see when you shut your eyes. And everything
else looks like a movie flashback shot through a blue filter.
You're biting your nails.'

Her hands jerked away from her mouth.

'Now you're smiling and pinching the bridge of your nose.'

She let out a tense, garden-party laugh. 'There's no hiding,
is there?'

'Not really,' I agreed. 'But don't worry, I don't go round
telling people what they look like in the dark. It's best not to.'

'I'm sure that's so.' She coughed.

'Though it's surprising what you do see,' I went on, 'in the
cinema, when the lights go down. Or in one of those Haunted
House things at the fair. Or in – you know, whenever you think
no one's watching.'

I emptied my mind of anything more shocking than furtive
glances, grimaces of frustration and absent-minded nose-
picking, though for a sixteen-year-old to talk about concealed
activity and not mean sex must have struck the kindly Dr
Greene as the height of facetiousness.

Sex was, of course, on my mind – it was Wimbledon
fortnight, apart from anything else, and every other close-up
on TV had the eighteen-year-old Boris Becker straining his
buttocks in pursuit of his second title – but it was not, just
now, at the front of it. I knew, and felt, that it was going on all

around me, in the backstreets and the bushes of Victoria Park, by the canal, behind the bus station, in the dark corners of the Cellar – a tatty nightclub for underage drinkers where I'd made a bit of a fool of myself the night before: but the more I saw of it, somehow, the less I noticed, or wanted to see. Subconsciously, perhaps, my night vision had taught me to observe a strange etiquette in respect of the hidden world it revealed. At any rate, I was wilfully oblivious to the obvious.

The intercom fizzed to life and announced the next patient. In the background I could hear Prince on the receptionist's radio, smooching his way through 'International Lover'. Lorna Greene fumbled for the lamp.

'No, I'm sure you'd make a very good spy,' she said primly, 'or a pilot, maybe. Though I suppose radar does most of the seeing for you up there.' I thought about this for a moment while she pressed a switch on the intercom and Prince wooed us with a request to place our legs in an upright position; a guitar twanged and cut out.

'Couldn't do that,' I said. 'Not good with heights.'

Dr Greene frowned, her shoulders sharp as an Anglepoise. 'Headaches? Bright flashes? Any trouble sleeping?'

'No trouble at all,' I lied. 'I just wanted to know if there was anything wrong elsewhere that might explain it. I'm not in any pain.'

She shook her head briskly – professional shorthand for 'Yes, there's an explanation somewhere, but if it's too specialized for me to know or care about, really, why should you?' – and got up.

'Then don't worry,' she said, making her way to the door. 'If it ain't broke . . . .'

On my way out of the optician's, I met the next appointment standing at the top of the stairs in Hitchcockian silhouette. His face was crumpled with confusions – the face of one to whom the debilities of old age are a perpetual affront. He flexed his fists as I passed by, and a pair of blind blue eyes rolled lawlessly in their sockets. 'You're *very* tall!' he cried out softly, before beginning his descent. From inside the consulting room, a once-confident, martial-sounding warble drifted upstairs like thin smoke: 'That young man, Lorna – so *tall* – gone now, yes . . .'

* * *

When Carey and I first emerged from Combe Down tunnel, his tears were treated sympathetically as tears of fright: our light had gone out, and Carey had panicked. Nigel Dooley, always good in a crisis, put a consoling arm around his shoulders and led him a little way down the track, telling him not to be upset, or embarrassed, because no one liked the dark really, and that we were sensible just to have kept walking. Watching Dooley minister *in loco parentis*, I felt a pang of jealousy. I wanted his arm around my shoulders, too; my head at least near, if not against, his chest.

Among the excited onlookers, it was soon agreed that Smacker had cracked up, 'gone mental'. Craig Spillings crossed his eyes, thrust his tongue inside his lower lip and began to drool. It was also agreed that a nutter's word carried no weight when it came to bionic eyesight, which meant that I had to submit to being blindfolded with Spillings's tie and bundled back into the tunnel, where an adjudicatory posse cast around for a suitable test site. The torches were switched off and a voice in my ear told me to describe the roof of the tunnel about twenty feet ahead. Hands groped my face to remove the tie and I looked up. Then I turned round.

An amateur chess-player, blinded by possibilities, sees everything and nothing on the board; a professional selects his square at once and moves to it. While my classmates' eyes rattled silently from the top of the tunnel to the bottom and from one side to the other, I picked out Gregory Bray, standing four paces to my right against the wall, glancing sideways at mind's-eye assailants, and told him what I could see: a hole in the roof from which roots struck out like talons; rocks, mortar and yellow-black earth scattered around a wide area on the floor; more stones threatening to fall from the age-swollen ceiling. I hoped that in his own way – not, of course, by breathing 'no shit', 'fuck me' or 'you creepy little cunt, Dan' – he would be impressed. That he would see the same blue shimmer of forms and open mouths as me. Instead, he switched on his torch, scythed us with a few swipes and said: 'We'd better get back, or Dooley'll go ape.' Bray spoke with that easeful authority, not found in more than one in one thousand adolescents, which permitted him to stop the party and stay cool. I realized, with a shiver along my temples and down my back, that he was doing me a favour; thirteen is no age to gain a reputation as a freak. 'Yeah,' I breezed back, 'time to go.'

Taking his lead from Bray, Spillings played down the results of the eye test to the rest of the class, waiting idly on the inner slopes of the cutting. 'Professor can see a bit, I s'pose,' he half-yawned, 'but I ain't creamin' myself over it. He's still a lanky git, in't you, Dan?' A number of voices agreed on my behalf, which seemed to put everyone in a good mood, and we started for home, this time overground.

Carey and Dooley remained in silent conference at the head of the group for most of the return journey, but when we got back to the changing rooms – half-flooded thanks to

Bruce Hartt's ministrations with mop and bucket – Carey went straight to the secretary's office and rang home. A short while later, from the contained riot that was the music block, we saw Carey loping towards the gates, head bowed and fists clenched. I feared the worst: accusations of bullying, a summons from the headmaster, the bitterest of inter-parental recriminations. Perhaps, if I'd had the makings of a real thug in me, I'd have laughed the whole thing off and made good my pledge to join the Spillings–Hartt axis, spitting, smoking, ogling posh girls from the High School and kicking in the bus shelters on the Bear Flat. In practice, though, my flushed cheeks and inability to meet Gregory Bray's gaze showed that I had lied to Carey in the tunnel – that I valued my good name above any fashionable alliance. In practice, too, my fears of the pillory turned out to be groundless. No more was said about the Combe Down incident; I never mentioned it to my mother or father, and there were no letters home or solemn debriefings by concerned teachers. Carey kept quiet; my night sight faded from view.

I was just a lanky git.

Two terms later, on a weekend 'orienteering' trip to Twr y Cwm, a spartan cottage in the middle of the Brecon Beacons where generations of hardy Lyncombe pioneers had learned how to follow glaciated contours and live off cold baked beans, I was unexpectedly rechristened.

The lay ceremony took place on night manoeuvres in the surrounding uplands, as the five of us in Group C, or 'Death Squad' as Spillings styled it, took a wrong turning at a cross-roads and found ourselves hemmed in by spruce trees at the end of a sheep trail. Overhead, roiling thunderclouds absorbed the stars one by one. We retraced our steps to the mid-forest junction, which now seemed to offer six rather than four potential exits, and gathered round a wrathful Spillings, bristling inside his Peter Storm kagoul, staring at the ruined threads of a 'treasure' map. It began to rain, hard. Within seconds, the map was pulp. Spillings looked around helplessly for the yellow checkpoint and tag that should have pointed the way back to the cottage. 'It ain't 'ere,' he raged. 'Hartt's mob've fuckin' nicked it, I swear. The gurt twats.'

The fat splutter of rain on plastic sealed us all in a clammy gloom. I squelched my outsize wellington boots in the mud and peeked out of a parka porthole at Gregory Bray – bareheaded, bare-legged and drenched. Leaning back against a tree, he stood with his torch upturned to illuminate a high funnel of falling dashes. Some private inkling of pleasure coaxed a smile onto his face, and the beam swung down into my face.

'I think,' he began slowly, 'that the Prof should help us out on this one.' Bray scratched the inside of his thigh where the wet hair had begun to form fan deltas, and I felt my balls stir. 'Because if hunter-eyes hisself can't see us right, no one can, and we'll be here until they send out a search party. If they send one 't all. Won't we, Dan?'

'Yeah,' Spillings agreed, sarcastically, 'and we'll still be 'ere when you tell us what the fuck you're on, Bray, you wazzard. Some hunter Dan'd be. I seed 'im in games las' week – couldn't find 'is way from one side of the goal to the other. 'Splains why we lost 'n all.'

Bray said nothing, but straightened up and walked over to Spillings, who flinched, afraid that he might have gone too far. Unencumbered by boots or leaky waterproofs, Bray looked oddly invulnerable; a faded T-shirt stencil of the sprinter Alan Wells clung to his ribs. 'Up to you,' he said quietly and disappeared uphill into the trees.

On the face of it, this was the least promising of the paths, because we knew our cottage to be near the bottom of an incline, not the top of a hill. But two years of cross-country training had given Bray a sure instinct for the lie of unfamiliar land. We had left the cottage by a minor estate road leading north-west to the uppermost reaches of a mountain stream that flowed south. Our instructions were to follow the course of the stream downhill and turn east at a waterfall on to a series of winding paths, in which we were now stuck. Rather than wait for Death Squad's gloomy troops to pick the right trail, Bray had worked out that if he went up, rather than down, he was bound to rejoin the road eventually, and that the road – however far up he joined it – would lead him home. Spillings had yet to reach the same conclusion.

'That's the wrong way, Bray,' he screamed after the winking sabre of torchlight. 'We want to go down, you knobsworth, not up. You're goin' the *wrong fuckin' way.*'

The determined figure in white stopped and called back, indistinctly, 'You tell 'em, Hunter. Use those eyes of yourn. Race you back.'

Spillings turned on me, red in the face, one arm raised threateningly. His acolytes, a couple of dough-boys from the Twerton estates (Bath's own skid row), fell back in anticipation of a beating. The rain began to roar.

'It's over there,' I said quietly, so that Spillings had to reach up and yank my head out of my parka. 'What,' he spat, 'is over where?' and gave a handful of hair an interrogatory twist. At school, this would have been a painful and humiliating gesture; here, in the middle of the Brecon forest on a stormy night, it felt cowardly and slack.

'The path home,' I shouted, smacking at his fist with my torch so that the batteries rang on the knuckles. Spillings

43

yelled; I yelled louder. 'It leads back the way we came and then does a U-turn towards the cottage. The checkpoint's over that way, too, but hidden halfway up a tree on the right – by the last team, I expect. Their idea of a joke. OK?'

Spillings blew on his hurt fingers and looked at me askance.

'Bray doesn't know all this,' I went on, 'because he can't see as well as me, but he's got the right idea. If he climbs up, he'll hit the road and then all he has to do is run downhill.'

A lull in the storm appeared to amplify my words; thunder crackled away in the valley. 'And in case you're wondering,' I added, with Bray's advocacy ringing in my ears, 'the reason I didn't say anything before now is that the whole object of this shitty exercise was to follow the map, which *you* were reading and which *you've* fucking destroyed. So *you* can either take *my* word for it that the cottage is a stone's throw over there, or you can stay here until you *drown*.'

The two dough-boys eyed each other nervously as I stamped past them. Behind me, I heard the words 'mental', 'stuck-up' and 'poof' repeated a number of times before the first sheet of lightning overruled any further objections. To the south, as I had predicted, beyond the dazzled stockade of spruce and conifer, the cottage blared like a comic caption. Ten minutes later, we skidded round the last kink in the U-shaped path to be greeted by a gleeful Greg Bray doing a rain dance under the porch. 'Hunter's back,' he called inside to lazy cheers, and fell over, grinning.

*

Carey Schumacher did not accompany us on that trip to Wales. He had been looking forward to 3TD's weekend at Twr y Cwm for more than a year – in a school of twelve hundred boys, the waiting list could be longer – but failed to pay his deposit, and so forfeited his place. This he accepted uncomplainingly, to the relief of members of staff long acquainted with his mother's shrill letters and personal calls. More impressive, from our point of view, was the subsequent revelation that Schumacher had in fact embezzled the deposit to pay for cannabis to be supplied by his father, who was planning a 'surprise' visit in the summer.

The long break came and went; I celebrated my fourteenth birthday and was packed off to Bordeaux on a French exchange with an anvil-headed monster who carried a knife and kicked my shins under the kitchen table. The bruises were eventually spotted by his psychiatrist father, and I was questioned. Did I fall over much? Had I told anyone about this? Would I like to discuss it? 'C'est simple,' I replied. 'C'était votre fils.'

My mother was sure that I'd 'filled out nicely' in France; after a little prompting, my father was sure, too. But the test, I knew, would be the first day back at school. Six weeks is a long time in the school diary – long enough to make classmates curious about seeing each other again, though not, perhaps, long enough to bury the deepest resentments. Last year, I'd grown several inches and acquired a new voice. This year, no one noticed any real differences in me except for my crew cut and exposed ears. My voice still cracked when I laughed; my canines fired off at right angles; my shoulders sloped like coathangers. No: this year, our astonishment was reserved for Carey Schumacher, or what had become of him.

When he answered his name at registration there were gasps. A few weeks 'checking out Scotland' with his estranged parent had turned freckles and milky breath to volcanic stubble and halitosis. His hair was greasy and long, the dyed black fringe sticking to his forehead in clumps like seaweed.

The perky treble voice had slipped and broken itself in a hundred places, and the already taut skin on his face looked sore where cheekbones threatened to rupture it. Microfibre legs dangled from a huge black donkey-jacket and terminated a mile away in size thirteen boots. There were fields under his fingernails.

Mrs Adadiche, the biology lab assistant, took one look at him and passed sentence. 'He'll end up at the magistrates,' she said, 'just like my Trevor.'

As if to reward her for her perspicacity, Carey boiled a frog alive the next day. In the few weeks that followed, he threw nitric acid out of the science block window, broke every chair in the art room to make a 'sculpture', and spliffed up twice in General Studies. More serious allegations, made in hospital by the woodwork master Gerald Noakes, whose stepladder mysteriously collapsed under him, were never proved.

'I shouldn't have let him go to Scotland,' claimed a tearful Frankie Schumacher in my parents' kitchen. 'He's an OK kid, really. I know he is. But he's impressionable. I can't get him to be *strong*.'

Gone, at any rate, were the former weaknesses: the questions about questions, the trumped-up enthusiasms for sport and music. The tracksuit was never seen again, and there were no more attempts during the lunch hour to break the six-minute mile. The clarinet was found in a canteen wheelie bin, and a secretly grateful choirmaster informed that 'dead music' was for assholes. In class, direct questions were answered with a curl of the lip; only now and again, in dismal mockery of his former self, the hollow-eyed scarecrow rocking backwards and forwards in his chair could be heard responding to imaginary oppressors with a barrage of whispered 'yessirs'. He stopped washing at Easter.

Among adults, such self-neglect would be seen as evidence of severe depression. But the privilege of the liberally reared adolescent is to be seen and not judged accordingly; to remain unhelped for what, it is assumed, he cannot help. It was in this spirit, presumably, that Frankie let her son attend school with matted hair, grey teeth and an upper lip that shook. The time for protecting him was over. She could not know, as I did, that Carey stood behind the telephone box on the corner of Lansdown Road and Camden Crescent, every morning, weeping. And if she had, what then? Carey's behaviour was disordered, certainly, but it posed no typical threats: he always made it to school, he didn't start fights or pick on younger boys, he never threw acid *at* anyone. He coped.

'Wait and see,' my mother counselled ungenerously, thankful that her friend's problems were not her own. 'I'm sure it'll all blow over.'

Frankie was hardly reassured. Carey had no good friends, spent hours every week in detention, and alienated even the most well-meaning members of staff. 'He shows signs of life,' wrote an exasperated Nigel Dooley in his end of year report, 'though not, perhaps, as we know it.' The findings of this document were made public one afternoon when its parental addressee paid the headmaster's office an unscheduled and very audible visit. Carey absconded for two days after that, and Frankie seemed to resign herself to the prospect of a fifth-form departure without qualifications. She foresaw years of painful humiliation while her son tried to claw back a few GCEs at the local technical college. There was, she confided in whoever was left to listen, not a glimmer of hope.

Until, one day, Carey asked for a flannel.

'I used the bathroom second this morning, and the soap was wet!' Frankie babbled excitedly.

The reason, I could have told her, had been hanging around Lyncombe's gates on Friday afternoons for months.

Karen Kale, younger sister of Sandra, the tart, was small and round with straggly blue-green hair; her eyes were brown and bovine, the lower lashes petrified in a stiff crust of eyeliner, her lips Banshee black. She hated school, liked The Smiths, loved chips, and spoke in a bitterly indistinct mumble no one except Carey could understand. The pair had met at Bath Computer Club, where a hard core of teen dysfunctionaries gathered at weekends to play Pac-Man and practise something called 'hacking'. (For the first generation of ostracized micro-nerds, remember, this was more than computer sabotage; it was sweet hormonal revenge.)

Frankie Schumacher declared the relationship a mystery. 'They spend every Saturday in that new shop in town, hot-rodding those IBMs,' she complained. 'Then they drift back and sit around all evening listening to this weird guy droning on about ten-ton trucks and what a privilege it would be to get run over by one. Jeez, it makes me feel old.'

She was, of course, delighted.

Karen's jowly recalcitrance would not have charmed many. It charmed Carey, though, or seemed to, and that was enough for Frankie. It also put *her* relationship with my parents on a more equal footing: having Carey securely attached (and with so little fuss) compensated her for the jealous pain of looking on while her art college coevals Jane and Philip reared an academic champion.

My parents were absurdly proud of me. From my room, I could hear them on the doorstep being calculatedly self-effacing about the latest grade prediction or piano exam success. ('I don't know how he fits it all in! I really don't! No, no. We just let him get on with it . . .') The irony was that the actual successes were all pitifully minor; by the standards of any real prodigy – the kind of hot-house product my father used to scoff at on *Young Musician of the Year* – I was remedial. But by the cosy standards of a middle-class county comprehensive, I was doing well enough, I suppose, impressing teachers, coming second or third in local piano competitions, and writing poetry which Iain Bachelor, the ineligible bard of the Hat and Feather pub, said showed promise.

I had never been so miserable.

The secret ambition behind my success was blushingly obvious to me: I didn't have a girlfriend – and didn't want one. More particularly, I didn't want anyone to find out *why* I didn't want one, and so worked hard at things that would distract everyone's attention – my own included – from the real source of interest, which nestled between the legs of the 1985 All England Schools Cross-Country champion.

In the run-up to my O levels, I continued to pass off high marks in tests and essays as sheer luck-of-the-draw, mindful of what had happened to Carey two years back. This time round, no one was fooled. Because, as I soon discovered, the sin of trying too hard is as nothing compared to the sin of trying too hard to conceal how hard you are trying.

'What d'you put then, Hunter?' asked Gregory Bray, after our English Literature O level paper. He looked hot and upset. It was June.

'What for?'

'That bit 'bout whatsit – "What is a Thane?" '

'Oh, that. I don't know. Probably left it out.'

I finished packing my bag and straightened up. Bray clocked me, took a breath and let out a derisory snort.

'Yeah. Reckon.'

He punched open the West exit door. My heart skipped a

beat as I followed him through. It was eighty degrees outside. Away to my right, beyond the school's potholed tennis court, a dormer window on one of the houses leading down to the Bear Flat had become a white-hot SOS. The air smelled of baked nylon mixtures and disinfectant.

'What d'you mean?' I said.

'Like,' he turned on the gravel path and snapped, '*reckon* you don't know.' A dust devil toyed with some leaf litter; above our heads, a classroom of younger boys started yelling.

'Why d'you always make out you an't got the answers, when you 'as?' he demanded. 'Not's if I'm going back in there to change anythin'.'

My tongue began to fur with panic. Greg's face betrayed no loss of temper, but his voice was all wrong – dry, bitter, constrained. I closed my eyes against the heat and tried (too hard) to forget about my arms, which seemed to hang robotically in space.

'I don't. I mean I haven't got them, the answers, whatever,' I heard myself whining. 'I honestly don't remember if I–'

''A' least the rest of us only lie when we don't know something,' Bray interrupted. 'You, though, you lie when you do. Like it's all a big secret. So important. You ain't that much better'n us, Hunter. Like I fuckin' *care* what a Thane is. Like I'm so thick I can't see you scribblin'.'

He took a step closer. His lips hung slightly open. He gave his shirt a nervous scratch and I caught a whiff of deodorized sweat. There was the faintest rash along his jawbone where he'd shaved.

'Sorry,' I said vaguely. 'I hate exams. They make you cagey.'

Greg stopped scratching and waggled his finger in one ear.

'Yeah, well,' he murmured. 'They're all over now. Thank fuck.'

This should have been a good sign. He withdrew the finger and inspected the tip before reinserting it briefly.

'Anyway, I won't be back 'ere for my retakes.'

'Don't be daft.'

'Not jokin'. I won't.'

His eyes met mine and drifted away.

'Probably won't need to do any,' I wittered, as a second wave of panic swelled nebulously behind me and threw us both into shadow. 'I mean, they're hardly going to fail you on a point of information about Scottish feudal hierarchies, are they?'

Greg's eyes darted back.

'About what?' he asked incredulously.

I gulped. 'Look, the point is – the point is you'll be all right.'

He laughed and started to walk to the front gate.

'Oh, I know that,' Greg said, taking off his tie and stuffing it in his trouser pocket as the sun came out again. 'It's you I'm worried about. The crap you talk sometimes.'

He swung round and pinched a fold of cheek so that my eyes had an excuse to water. 'What would you do without me?'

*

The Cellar was packed that evening. A few over-eighteens lingered by the bar, but the stroboscopic dance floor and black-painted alcoves were otherwise filled with swaying fifth-formers, celebrating the end of the exams and, in many cases, the end of inglorious school careers. Posing by the door, Robbie Benson, the club's macho-camp proprietor, demanded ID from a stream of bug-eyed sixteen-year-olds. ('That's no good, my lover. No, your library card hasn't got your – no, it *has not* got your age on it. I could lose my licence.') He let us all in.

By eleven o'clock, I was drunk. The crowd on the dance floor and in the squalid front-of-house area by the entrance and toilets had been joined by drinkers from the local pubs, including the Old Sulian (a biker's dive) and the Devvy (a rugger-bugger hang-out). They made for a mixed bunch with one purpose: the quest for a late licence. I leant unconvincingly against a wall by the Gents and stared into my lagerless pint glass.

'You don't want to stand there,' rasped a stubbly Sulian, as he careened out of the Gents. 'If that Robbie sees you, 'e'll 'ave you, standing there like that. Loiterin'.'

As he did up his flies, another man – younger, less drunk, but with the same moulded leather trousers and white T-shirt – emerged from the toilet and put his arms around the first man's neck. I looked past them, past the crescent bar, past everyone, including Carey and Karen wedged together on a stool, and fixed my gaze on the back wall. Carey interposed a hands-up salute between my gaze and the wall, and pulled a face. I nodded and raised my glass, though I had nothing to toast them with.

'Ooh,' said the second man, with a slow blink. 'I think we've been given the brush off.' Turning to go, he smiled and blew a kiss. 'So wise, some of these young ones. So wise and so young.'

I smiled sickly and watched them walk to the bar.

The music was loud, with a lot of Wham! and Sister Sledge ('We Are Family' appeared to be on a twenty-minute loop). People one would never have imagined dancing were writhing and stomping, their hair plastered to the sides of their faces, shirts unbuttoned to the waist and re-buttoned out of sync.

Craig Spillings, in tight white jeans and baggy black shirt, had Karen's polyandrous elder sister in a grinding embrace under the glitter ball; even Karen and Carey had loped on to the floor for a miserablist rendering of the evergreen 'Relax'. They stayed well apart for the whole song and then curled their lips at each other as it ended, as if to say –

'That was crap, why did we come?'

An arm flopped around my shoulders, and a head with short, black hair curling slightly at the nape leant tiredly on my shoulder blade. Both arm and head were familiar. Beyond the bar, blue forms gathered and separated in the darkness, prowled about the tables, felt for each other.

If I looked to my left, I could see that the arm emerged from a white shirt sleeve; at chest-height, I fancied the shirt half undone. If I looked to my right, I could see the arm itself, ridged softly by a single vein, its dark hairs paddling in feeble currents of air from the nightclub's one ceiling fan. The head was not looking up at me, but talking to the waist. As it communed, I caught sight of a line of dry skin on the underside of the nearest, raw-red earlobe that I wanted to moisten and taste.

'That's what old Carey's sayin', innit?' the head murmured. 'He's sayin' ''That was crap, I ain't dancin' to crap like that.'' What d'you reckon?'

'Definitively,' I said.

The head swivelled upwards; the arm rotated slightly without bothering to withdraw. The revealed face watched me seriously while I leant down to say something friendly to it, and its big eyes, sleepily intoxicated at first, widened into focus as I thought of better things to say and do.

The lips drew back from not quite straight teeth.

A whole body, not mine, lurched backwards and sloshed

beer onto the floor. The body was steadied by passers-by, who laughed.

'Christ,' it blurted. 'Hunter's drunker'n me.'

Far away, in a world of blue forms and flashbacks, Carey saluted me again and slowly shook his head.

The face in front of mine was pinkly furious.

'You need your fuckin' eyes testin',' it said.

The Slope

One of our hippy neighbours hums approvingly. His raggedy pal, still brushing flapjack off the front of a filthy smock, leans over: 'That's a nice piece,' he rumbles. 'Lovely inlay. You want to look after that.'

On the table before me, nestling in a crater of torn brown giftwrap, is an antique writing bureau, about the size of a large bread-bin, its marbled grain smooth as Danish oil. I'm afraid to touch it lest a thumbprint turn it to fingered toffee. Two inch-wide bands of dark and light mosaic, one each side of the box, have been meticulously repointed. Some of the new mahogany tiles that make up the mosaic brackets are slightly brighter in tone than the others, and a tiny strip of veneer around the rear hinges has come unstuck. Otherwise, it's a flawless object. The brass plate in the centre of the lid bears my name and a stern Miltonic inscription: 'The mind is its own place.'

'Well?' my mother chirps. 'Do you recognize it?'

The polished surface and nameplate reflect us both in vague silhouette, all form and no feature.

'Yes, I do. You've had it cleaned.'

'Of course I had it *cleaned*,' she squeaks. 'It was in such a state, I had to take it in to be *cleaned*. But it's all there –

solid walnut, with the original marquetry. The man at Great Western said it was one of the best he'd ever seen. The little knobs on the inside are ivory.'

I'm frowning. My plastic seat has become bruisingly uncomfortable, and I have not said thank you.

'That's a lovely piece,' our smocked friend repeats. 'Yours?'

I smile weakly. 'Kind of. Well, it belonged to my father and my mother's had it since he–'

'It's Daniel's, now,' she interrupts, looking straight at the grubby duo. 'He used to write on it when he was a little boy.' She swivels round and begins to fold the wrapping paper with the vigour of a Dickensian aunt. 'I remember you asking me if you could have Daddy's writing box when you grew up. Don't you? That's why we kept it. Philip bought it and then wanted to get rid of it – you know what he was like. But I said no, the writing box is Daniel's. When he wants it.'

'It's a good slope,' the hippy says thoughtfully, a remark my mother instantly construes as provocation.

'Oh, I *see*,' she says, too quickly. 'I see what you mean – yes, it *does* fold out into a slope, you're quite right. But I don't think that's what it's called. You see, it's a secretaire, or so I'm told. Edwardian, I believe.'

The smock shakes his head.

'Dunno who told you that. Secretaires was desk-sized, fixed, with drawers. Proper furniture. Writing slopes – boxes – was portable. Popular gear with Victorian gents doing the tour, y'know, a bit like laptops now. Fact, I sold one last week. Not as nice as yours, though. That's worth a few hundred at any auction, that is. Maybe more – you should get it valued.'

My mother's eyes narrow. 'How interesting,' she almost spits. 'You clearly know more than the man at Great Western. I hope you won't mind my asking – do you deal?'

'Yeah, got a place in Battersea. Workshop off Lavender Hill.'

He gets up, trails a dry finger along the edge of the box and toys with the silver key. Hesitating, he turns back to his table to leave a tip, which could be our cue to go, but isn't.

'So,' Smock says, turning again, 'your dad's dead, is he?'

'Yes.'

My mother's mouth drops, like the ramp of a ferry.

'Recent?'

'No. Two years.'

He considers this. 'Not very long though, is it?'

'No.'

The directness of his enquiries throws me – the way it might if a station tannoy stopped announcing trains and asked you out for a drink – but my mother, who made the mistake of mentioning Philip in the first place, is in full command of the situation's potential for outrage. She looks away dramatically, then glances back at me to make it clear that she is just – but only just – under control. Her tongue swipes her lips and she breathes in quickly. She shakes her head an inch to the left and to the right; rolls her eyes; shuts them. A shiver of disgust ripples through her, as if the memory of some ancient indignity had returned to haunt her.

Sadly, the whole performance is lost on the Battersea dealer, who leans on a chair directly behind her, while his friend ambles off to the Room Lets and Sits Vac noticeboard.

'Miss him much, do you?' Smock asks.

'Quite a bit.'

He nods. 'Yeah, well. Nice to have something to remember him by,' and laughs uncertainly.

'What about you?' I ask, not thinking what I really mean by this as I open up the box.

'Dunno,' he murmurs.

A thick scent of beeswax diffuses into the air. The box unfolds to form a sloped writing surface, made of green leather and embossed around the edges, with pen tray and inkwell at the top. The upper half of this slope – the inner lid – lifts up again to reveal the main cavity, which has enough room in it for, say, half a ream of A4. The compact design conceals another secret, however. To the right of the inkwell my fingers feel for a catch which I know used to unlock a compartment under the pen tray. I find it, press it, lift the lid and slide back a slat behind the well. Wedged inside this niche is a sheet of rolled-up paper. I'm about to extract it when –

'I nearly forgot,' my mother says quickly, delving into her bag and producing a small blue envelope addressed to me. The slat snaps back into place. 'Here we are. This came for you the other day. No idea who it's from – I didn't look closely.'

I put the envelope in my back pocket.

Late sun tilts across the floor and into the box. Smock's arms clutch the back of his chair. 'Dunno,' he says softly, once more.

*

Her last words to me, at the entrance to Tottenham Court Road tube, are: 'As long as you're happy and well.'

We have not said much else since leaving the Temple restaurant. She has given me the writing box and done her best – and I have disappointed her by being so reserved. I can see by her movements – the tucking of wisps of lichen-grey hair behind her ears, the air of anxious probity with which she zips up a thin fawn jacket – that she has our lunch marked down as a failure. I'm sad about this, though the angry scepticism of her parting shot, typically, leaves no room for such an admission. If I am happy, it's more than I deserve; and if I'm not, I bloody well ought to be, considering my upbringing.

I stop for a coffee at Libertines on Compton Street, a once characterful diner languishing – or thriving, according to your point of view – under new management. The old place served tea that tasted of nails, its walls dunly streaked like the haddocky lungs of the locals. Now it is all got up in a pert cerise and staffed by pretty boys who take one look at you and say 'Can I help?' as if they mean, well, probably not.

I perch by the window, and try balancing the slope on the banquette next to me, but it slides off. I try again. It slides off again, hitting the window with a loud crack. That's it; it'll have to go.

My coffee arrives with the kind of bill you pay in monthly instalments. The aspiring male model who delivers it sees me scowling, and utters the dread pleasantry, 'Cheer up – it might never happen.'

'Then again . . .' I snap back.

The waiter, sadly, has not read my script for the end of our scene together, and doesn't laugh, applaud or vanish. Instead, he looks frankly bemused. He is about my age and height, and – now that I bother to look – ordinarily attractive, with fair hair, pinkish skin, a wide mouth and ears that stick out. Doubtless we share a few beliefs, too, not the least of which is that it costs nothing to be civil. He walks away.

Despondency, in my mother's world-view, is not a psychological flaw. It is something much worse – a lack of gratitude.

*

On my way to the Tulse Hill amenity site – the dump – it occurs to me that this is the most important illusion of parenthood: that a child's future happiness may be shaped by a good start in life. It also occurs to me that, since children and adults have such wholly different conceptions of what it is to *be* happy (a difference established by sexual development), the only symmetry between the smiling babe-in-arms and the contented grown-up must be a broken one. In most cases, one has nothing to do with the other. The same goes for talent: early promise in one field or another is a poor indicator of adult capability. Failure and disappointment, on the other hand, are continuous. We are unhappy as children and as adults for exactly the same reason; we wanted something and did not get it – justice, love, the job, more custard.

Or we wanted something, and the thing turned out to be different from the want, like this stupid box I'm about to throw in the crusher.

Of course I feel wretched that my mother has spent money having it French-polished and engraved; then again, she only spent it in order to feel less wretched herself. Both of us are troubled by our associations with the slope; neither of us wants to shoulder any responsibility for them.

The day my father brought home his 'great find' from the auction house on Walcot Street was the first time I heard my parents shout at each other. I was eight years old and money was tight – perhaps not as tight as my mother would later claim, but certainly in short supply: the local education authority had just reclassified my father's job as a part-time teaching post, which meant a significant cut in an already meagre salary. This put paid to any thought of sending me to Widcombe Boys, the private school with smart grey uniforms and Latin, and forced on us a number of austerity measures my mother couldn't wait to implement: the cancellation of a camping holiday in Cornwall, pocket money (£1 a month) frozen at 1977 prices, liver three times a week.

'Christ, Jane, it's only money,' my father said feebly, after he'd told us how much his bargain had cost. (He lied; it had cost more.) 'Y'know, it's not like we're about to starve, or anything.'

We had only just started our lunch, but my mother got up from the table, went to the sink and started drumming her fingers on the draining board. The dull brown box rested mutely by my father's plate.

'How much did you say again, Philip?' she asked.

'A hun–' I began loudly, before deciding it would be better to let my father answer the question.

'Yeah, a hundred. I don't know, more or less. A hundred and ten, I think, in all. Christ, man, it's worth more. Even I can tell that. Look at the inside. Look at the fittings. I can use it in the still-life class.'

The basement kitchen darkened. Our stringy, nympho-maniac cat slunk in from the passage and collapsed on a bed of old *Observers*. My mother winced horribly, her fingers stilled now on the rim of a patterned bowl.

'That's as much as you give me for housekeeping,' she said, acidly.

'Hey,' my father remonstrated, appealing to me across the table. 'Hey, that isn't fair. Look, man – Jane – if you need more, just ask, yeah?'

'As much as you give me *all month*,' she added, her voice rising like a fire siren. I was excited: privileged to be the witness of an adult quarrel, and nervous of the outcome. 'Well,' she went on, 'a hundred and ten pounds may not be much to you, Philip.'

My father groaned and shuddered.

'But it makes a big difference if you know what it's like to be without.'

He screwed his eyes shut and I slunk lower in my chair, pretending to be absorbed by the ads on the back of a Shreddies packet. If I collected ten Superman tokens, I read, I could exchange them for a lump of kryptonite in a key-ring. Twenty would get me a figurine of Marlon Brando as Jor-El, and thirty – a blue leotard. To the side of the packet, I could see my father running his hands through fly-away brown hair. He smiled at me.

'Laugh away, I don't care. Where I grew up, a hundred pounds would have been a lot of money. Repeat, a *fortune*. When I *think* of it. We didn't even have running water!'

The tension eased slightly. My mother's chattering internal demons had drowned out the specific grievance and steered her back to their favourite subject: respectable poverty, her parents' sacrifices, the war, a scholarship to grammar school. Art college. Duty.

'No electricity!'

'I know.'

'One bed.'

'It must have been very hard.'

'No – ' my mother wobbled slightly – '*meat*. At the week-ends. Not like this. Imagine, *never any meat*.'

I caught the glint in my father's eye as he suppressed a second smile, and pressed the tips of his fingers together. 'No running water?' he backtracked. 'Is that right? Highbury must have had its supply for years and years. You're sure you don't mean you had no *hot* water?'

Something smashed on the wall behind me. Bits of bowl (one of my father's, from the early 1960s) rained down onto my shoulders.

'You don't know what it was *like*,' she shrieked, and ran from the room, slamming the door.

We could hear her in the passage, not upset enough to climb the stairs but determined to bring matters to a tearful conclusion. There were a few more you-don't-knows and you'll-never-understands while my father and I picked up the fragments of shattered pottery and finished eating. Then a sob leaked through the keyhole – 'I wore the same vest to school for five years: that's how poor we were' – and we laughed once, guiltily, a snigger of complicity that sent my mother howling to the back door. Her last exclamation was lost in the crunching-open of locks and shaking of door jambs. My father sighed and scraped a thread of spinach off his front teeth. A passing lorry made my thumb-pots rattle on the basement window sill.

'Shit and derision,' he muttered suddenly, jerking his chair backwards. On the garden threshold, I heard my mother's victorious 'Ah!' wilt into the 'oh . . .' of chastened alarm, as he caught up with her.

Never before had Philip responded to any of her goadings about money and class. Never before had he even listened to them. What could he do about where he came from? He was, it so happened, the son of Hampstead philanthropists who ran the Working Men's College on Holloway Road; she was, it turned out, the daughter of a tailor educated there. As far as he could see, that was all there was to it. Inside this coincidence of origins, Jane Moorcock nevertheless found much to resent.

'You keep saying I don't understand, but what am I *supposed* to understand? What's the big fucking mystery?' I heard Dad bellow, his voice cracking with frustration. 'What do you want me to do, Jane – give you less? Give you more? What? What is it you want?'

The back door closed. Inside the house again, my mother's words were lost in echoey snivels and sobs. I could sense – I could see – her standing in the corner of the damp passage, by the rake and rickety Swingball, rolling and unrolling the hem of her pullover.

*

Eight years later, after my O levels, I decided to spend the summer in romantic withdrawal, confined to my attic room, wallowing in my botched pass at Gregory Bray and writing poetry.

By then, Dad had exhausted the anti-functionalist possibilities of his great auction-house find: he'd drawn it, filled it, collaged it with other paintings and wrapped it Cristo-style in newspaper and string. He'd done everything except write on it. Seeing that this was the case, I put in a bid for it, and custody of the slope passed effectively to me.

In this trove I stowed letters, short stories, suicide notes, ideas for plays and novels, a birthday card from Greg ('To the Prof, from Greg. All the best, weirdo') and dozens of poems. These were the result of some ill-advised encouragement on the part of Frankie Schumacher, who'd read an early effort ('Collusion in G' by D. A. Rathbone) and, smitten with its incomprehensibility ('I am the hedge of bone . . .' etc.), decided that I should join the Hat and Feather poetry group, run by Iain Bachelor, who looked like Brahms, or God, but sounded like Peter Lorre.

Here I was warmly received, as the scion of an admired teacher. Most of the group, I discovered, were graduates of my father's art foundation course at the City Academy, and spoke reverently of 'Phil's tremendous energy'. To have trashed his son's work then would have seemed impolite, although in truth nobody's writing was ever seriously criticized, because it was all so obviously bad. People came instead to read their work, gossip and get plastered. Frankie downed pints of cider and invited comely students back to her house to try out her loom; Iain shuffled about with unsold armfuls of his quarterly magazine, *The Ninth Wave*; and I drank shandy while forty-something women with sleepy eyes and husky voices told me what a wonderful man my father was.

As a sign of special favour, Iain decided that summer to publish two of my shorter verses (from a long sequence, called 'Fugue'). This must have nettled Frankie, inasmuch as her own poetry – a sort of Christina Rossetti-flavoured rock gothic – had so far failed to impress the same editor. I stayed up all night fiddling with slivers of poor man's William Carlos Williams, and worked for weeks on twelve lines of cloudy imagism ('Painting in Water') which eventually won a prize at a festival in Frome. All of these poems were written on the slope. All were read out at the Hat and Feather. All were admired.

Something about the ersatz bohemianism of the group disagreed with my parents, however, neither of whom ever attended a Monday reading. My mother bore, I knew, a personal antipathy to the 'strong' women in Bachelor's circle, several of whom she suspected of having slept with my father, on the grounds that they had posed as models for his life class and looked too pleased with themselves when talking about yogic 'positions'. 'Fancy,' she said to me one day, while wringing out my father's grey Y-fronts, 'paying all that money just to sit up straight.'

What Dad's aversions to the group were I couldn't quite make out – perhaps, if the gossip was true, he feared an awkward encounter. Certainly he read little poetry himself, but liked to think of himself as a connoisseur when it came to the actual books. In our spare bedroom, which doubled as a studio, was a damp box full of volumes (including a tatty first edition of Yeats's *A Full Moon in March*), which he claimed to be restitching. In an effort to speed up the process, I filched a small, feather-frail edition of the *Rubáiyát of Omar Khayyám* from the box and showed it to Frankie.

'I thought I could get this bound properly and give it to Mum and Dad for their anniversary,' I told her. 'What do you think?'

Frankie was taken with the idea.

'I think that would be the neatest thing, Dan,' she gushed. 'And I can get it done at the cattle market. Tina – you know, runs the Friday leather stall? Uh-huh. She'll do it. She can do this. Otherwise it gets kinda pricey.'

'I knew you'd know someone,' I said.

'Yeah, well, Tina's cool,' Frankie replied, thumbing through the little book with one hand and holding her pint of Strongbow at a perilous angle with the other. 'And say, Dan,' she whispered conspiratorially, with that lustreless illumination of the eyes that accompanies all bad ideas, 'why not stick one of your own in on a card? The one you read in Frome – we'll get it printed. Like a postcard. Yeah, do a series – we'll do an edition!'

On closer inspection of my published *œuvre* (three twelve-liners and a brace of haiku), we decided that an edition would be premature. A card with 'Painting in Water' printed on it (unsigned) seemed like a nice touch, though, and the re-bound *Rubáiyát*, in soft brown calf with a speckled rice-paper fly-leaf, was duly presented on August 11.

My parents, enjoying a lie-in with the morning papers, were impressed. The minor trespass of entering the studio and rummaging through my father's effects in order to get the book was noted but not enlarged upon: it was in no one's interest to draw attention to other volumes I might have chosen to restore (such as the Yeats, or the copy of *The Joy of Sex* I'd found, with annotations). Instead, I was congratulated on my thoughtfulness.

'Hey, that's great man,' enthused Dad. 'And well done for remembering. Christ knows, I nearly didn't.'

'No indeed!' my mother laughed aggressively. 'It's really a lovely present, Daniel. You do think of such clever things. Not like me, of course. I'm – we're – very touched. Aren't we Philip?'

'Yeah, really am. Knockout.'

She took the book from my father and read the title aloud: 'The Ruby Art of Omar Karum. Oh! Translated by *Edward* Fitzgerald.'

Then, as she turned the first pages in wondering incomprehension, my card slipped out on to the bed covers.

'Is that something?' she said, patting the duvet near my father's groin. 'Was that – a card? Oh!' Her voice sagged. 'It's another poem.'

Dad picked it up and shot me an enquiring glance.

'It's one from the group,' I fished vainly. 'By one of the group.'

' "Painting in Water",' he mumbled, and started to read.

I sniffed, sipped my tea while perched on the cane rocking chair in the corner, and half-listened to Mum telling me about their planned twenty-first anniversary break to Alnwick – 'a bit of a long way to go for a weekend, but fantastic scenery and lots of castles. And Lindisfarne, of course, the Holy Island. Bird sanctuary, now.'

Dad put down the card and let out a long satisfied yawn. A flicker of suspicion interrupted him mid-rictus. He frowned.

'It isn't one of yours, then?' he asked, waving the poem.

I shook my head. The yawn resumed.

'Thought not,' he sighed contentedly. 'Doesn't half remind me of the kind of stuff I used to write at your age, though.'

'Oh?'

'Yeah. Puddle poetry, you know – treading on your reflection, getting wet in the rain. The usual.'

I tried to concentrate on this revelation.

'I didn't know you wrote, Dad. How long did you—?'

'Just for a bit. It was only a passing phase.'

He rolled his shoulders until they clicked, and chuckled at the memory: 'Pretty terrible it was, too. Not good at all.'

We laughed, and I went downstairs to practise the piano.

* * *

At the exit to Brixton tube, my ark-sized heirloom is spotted by Jake, one of the station's Special Brew vagrants, who staggers down the steps towards me, one hand pointing, the other feverishly ironing his clover-print shirt with a can of lager. Nick and Luke Rizzi, the cheeky twin florists at the top of the steps, call after him – 'Jake! Oi, Jakey, yer girlfriend's on the phone. Jay-kee!' – and clutch their sides. My way is blocked by a softly ruminating pensioner, who stares rigidly at the advancing, lazy-eyed prophet.

'Pandora!' Jake screams. 'Pandora's a curse, mun. Don't fuckin' do it.'

Overbalancing, Jake half-trips and slams into the pensioner, who grabs hold of the central handrail and manages, somehow, to stay upright, with Jake's carcass writhing at her feet. Her many bags are split and spilled; oranges, tomatoes, mushrooms, three overripe pineapples and a head or two of cauli bobble past me into the ticket office.

'Awah dis,' she wails. 'You're drunk inna broad daylight.'

In an instant, her despair takes a nasty turn. Jake is having problems getting up, and she has begun to prod – to kick – him in the stomach with irresistibly sensible flat, brown shoes. 'Bounce mi down, mash op mi shopping. Listen to me nah, man, is wah wrong wi you? Chuh. Com out mi way, gwey from mi, bwoy . . .'

Other people have collected one or two of the oranges and tomatoes, and are helping Jake, spitting and growling, to his feet. He still has hold of the can of Carlsberg, but its contents have been dashed onto the tiled walls. All the people helping each other are old, I notice suddenly. Not old, perhaps, but over fifty. Cool, pneumatically muscular black guys in brilliant white trainers and yellow vests cruise past on the other side of the rail, confiding in mobile phones. The number 2 bus screeches to a halt at the lights ten steps above me, and I shuffle around a crab-pool of scrabbling hands and squashed fruit to get to it.

Jake is standing again and shouting as before: 'Pandora's a bitch! I've seen the box. She's a fuckin' bitch. You wait. You WAIT!'

Lurching towards the hop-on ramp, I clout a small child stepping off the bus with the edge of the slope. It feels bad: the loose strip of veneer at the back of the slope snaps off. The vehicle moves away as I fall into it, almost ramming the conductor, who steers me – because my arms are full – to a seat. Behind me, strong enough to rise above the splutter of acceleration, I hear the child's belated klaxon-cry. A young mother makes a 'tsk' sound at me from the seat opposite, but I cannot speak. Or look back.

*

Twenty minutes' walk from Tulse Hill bus stop and the smoky heat of the afternoon has dispersed, though my blood is still racing and I hear myself muttering peculiar obscenities whenever a kind face walks past.

As I near the dump, I am overtaken by two chortling, seam-bursting men in their forties striding along the road with a fridge-freezer wedged between them. By pitiful contrast, my forearms are tired of their load, and I flinch at the skinniness of biceps that fail to fill the rolled-up cuffs of my shirt. Way ahead of me now, the men's laughter ricochets from house to house like pebbles rattling in an empty cylinder. Curtains twitch on either side of the street; kettles, I know, are being boiled behind partitions, cat-flaps flapped, surfaces wiped.

When I reach it, the dump seems very small, as if its high walls had themselves been crushed into a ragged block of aggregate and razor wire. Three massive iron hulks, their jaws agape, fill the middle of the yard. Upon these unlikely altars, local residents cast their offerings: gardeners bring logs and trees; decorators hoick sacks of loose plaster; couples unload hatchbacks full of ratty carpet and underlay. All are busy about their destruction and happy in it – disposal, not acquisition, being the least arguable exercise of taste here, where every-thing and nothing is beyond repair. What some consider derelict, others invest with hope: the fridge-freezer so recently abandoned has already been adopted by a young couple, who want to know what's wrong with it.

Around the hulks, amenity site workers sweep diligently, answer questions, direct the softly spoken to the recycling bins, and hurl any escaped detritus back into the crushers. Children assist, picking up twigs and shoes, tending the rusty jaws like pilot fish. One little girl stands guard at the end of a line of broken baby things – a buggy, a bashed-in stair-gate, a bag of soiled clothes – while her tall, stiff-jointed father bins each item with a series of convulsive jerks. By the time he reaches his daughter, he has established a rhythm, and turns back from the Portakrush 2000 ready for another armful. The little girl eyes him carefully. He scoops her up.

It would be just as unthinkable, I suppose, to pitch the slope in among the sycamores and smashed kitchen units. Too public. The longer I stand at the entrance though, the more attention my unwanted antique, bearer of accumulated debt and tension, and of puddle poetry, is likely to attract. ('That looks like a find!' says a friendly driver, on his way out of the compound. 'You done well there!') Startled to attention by the sudden activation of one of the hulks, I slip behind a car to reach the wall where the worn-out washing machines, fridges and cookers are stacked, and shove my birthday present inside a doorless oven.

I am so relieved by the ease of this despatch that I am nearly out of the yard before I remember the nameplate.

'I'm so sorry,' I explain to a perplexed site officer, who has started closing the gates, 'but can I nip back in? I've left something behind.'

Back in front of the oven, like a chef turned safe-breaker, I remove the slope and find, to my faint annoyance, that 'Daniel Adam Rathbone' comes off rather easily, with one stab and levering twist of my front-door key. Several cookers further down, I can see the jerky father watching me with interest. His daughter tries the lids and doors of every contraption against the wall, testing a fridge seal here, banging a grill there. She sees me get up, and stops.

'What have you got there?' is her frank demand.

I smile back. 'Nothing, really. I think this lot is done for.'

She looks at me seriously, not blinking.

'Daddy, what has that man got there?'

'I don't know, darling,' replies her father, with his head inside a tumble-dryer. 'Go and have a look. Ask nicely, now.'

But I am already going – all but gone. It's two miles home, and the long July shadows lick my shoulder as I pad down the street.

*

'Daniel!'

Windmill Road in the early evening is smacked awake by a familiar voice. I turn my key in the lock and glance behind me. It is Neville, wearing his shapeless corduroys with a white shirt over a dark vest. He folds his arms and leans back against the bonnet of a clapped-out Ford Fiesta, looking serenely triumphant.

'Daniel,' he cautions, pursing his lips. 'You have skips under your eyes. Are you still hung-over?'

'Could be, Neville,' I reply, feeling it. 'Tea?'

'Dear boy. I think I might. It's all been *too* exciting.'

'Oh? Good run-through?'

He waves a hand irritably.

'*Jamais, jamais*. Ghastly Verdi-gurdy. Silly poofs in the second choir can't reach their top As. No, no – I've been out shopping.'

'Something nice?'

'Something and nothing. I've bought you a fountain for the pond. It was on offer in Peckham market, and I couldn't resist.'

'You bought me a mug already.'

The hand waves again.

'Pshaw. Anyway, I popped in at one of my old haunts on

the way back, did a little beachcombing and picked up a treat for myself. Can I show?'

He giggles and scampers round to the boot of his car.

'What,' he crows, delving inside with both hands, 'do you think of this? Isn't she a beauty?'

He holds up the slope.

'Didn't cost a penny – I got it off a scrap heap!'

A catch in my head clicks open, a slat slides back, a roll of paper falls out. I'm always forgetting something.

Neville sniffs proudly: 'It's solid walnut, you know.'

Music for Babyface

Neville Clute FRCM has what my piano teacher used to call a 'fine inner ear'. In a good year, he can earn three times his chorus master's salary doing sessions arrangements at short notice, sometimes overnight, for the major labels – Sony, WEA, Columbia, Warner, East–West. He hates the music, and feels frumpish delivering his meticulous scores to cashmere-clad executives half his age, who are 'all love and no lunch'. Stevie Wonder he likes; last year, 'Stevland' called him from LA and thanked him for ten seconds of 'sweet strings'.

Conversationally, though, Neville is deaf. Once started, he finds it difficult to stop. Now, for instance, as he brings a mug of over-sugared tea to his lips, his buffed cheeks and sloping forehead glisten with decisive tension: to drink or speak? He cannot help noticing my kitchen's raw plasterwork. What did I have there before? Anaglypta? And how did I get rid of that? By hand? With a *scraper*? Tsk.

The convenient thing about Neville in this kind of mood is that he is impossible to distract, which means you don't have to pay much attention to him, or even stay in the same room. While he talks, I play back two messages in the smoke-soured lounge: one from my mother shouting goodbye in Paddington Station, the other – more alarmingly – from Carey, announcing his arrival tomorrow, three days earlier than planned. The software launch in Earl's Court has been brought forward. He would like to hook up. He would like to stay.

'But it's not a problem,' he brags. 'I can get a room at Brown's. I guess I should have written, you being so formal 'n' all, Daniel.'

The tape whirrs. There is a three-thousand-mile gulping noise, a kink in the deep-water cable that takes a moment to right itself.

'What was that?'

'Nothing,' I tell the machine, expecting flight times and patting my back pockets for a pen. 'Get on with it.'

'OK,' Carey agrees, his voice brightening mysteriously. 'So, I have news, Daniel, though maybe you already heard it . . .'

He pauses on the brink of confession. Whatever it is, I can't write it down, since the faint crackle in one pocket turns out to be neither pen nor pencil but the half-crushed blue envelope, dry as an honesty seed-case. The torn postmark is for the day before yesterday.

'It's no big deal, really. You'll han–' manages Carey, just before the tape swallows the rest of his message.

In the kitchen, Neville enlightens my table about the best way to use a steam stripper if you happen to be asthmatic. A roar filters through the wall from next door, where someone is watching football. I open the envelope and scan its contents.

'Bless you,' Neville says suddenly, appearing in the doorway as if summoned, with the slope under one arm. 'What's the matter?'

I look past him.

'Just some home news.'

He fidgets.

'I see.'

A trail of cobwebs, detached from the ceiling rose, drifts down between us. Neville burbles another blessing and moves forward impulsively. A schoolfriend has been hurt, I tell him, recoiling slightly, and he condoles, dabbing with a free hand at his cheek as though I had slapped him.

'I'm sorry. Truly.'

He looks down vaguely, and backs out of the frame into shadow.

The letter is in fact from Norman and Liz Spillings, to whom I may have said hello at a school concert years ago, but do not clearly remember. It tells me that their son Craig – Death Squad's unvanquishable leader – lost control of his Tornado two weeks ago on a routine flight over the Brecons, and 'cracked his head open' while ejecting. I might have seen the news. I did, but missed the name. Just – missed it.

The memorial service for friends and colleagues is this week. 'Come if you can. We'd like you to,' the note says, with a curious lunge. 'People you know will be there.'

*

After all those mugs of tea, Neville was supposed to have peed at least once. This would have given me a moment or two alone with the box – enough to unlock it, spring the catch and retrieve the *other* sheet of paper rolled up in its front compartment. Because I feel sure that I have seen that piece of paper before and written on it. (And if I wrote on it, I probably put my name to it – teenagers sign everything.)

When Neville finds the sheet, as he is bound to, what will he think? Never mind what it says – as if any poem or love-letter could be that embarrassing – what will my name say of me, the slope's last owner? The coincidence of my being in the dump at more or less the same time as him will look suspicious because of my silence. I should have come clean, I now realize, as soon as he produced the box from his car boot: 'If I'd known, Neville, I'd have given it to you,' I could have said.

In any case, he didn't pee. Not after three full mugs. And then Craig's death intervened, which made him feel unwanted. So he has hastened away, with the slope and the note inside it, and I am left rinsing the last of last night's blood from my white shirt, planning my next move, listening out for my neighbour's front door, calculating the risks.

Neville is never in on Saturday evenings. He either visits his spry nonagenarian parents in Burgess Hill – which means he could be away for the rest of the weekend – or goes to a concert. 'The Sixteen' are singing Poulenc at St John's, Smith Square tonight, so he could well be there. Either way, he will be gone for at least three hours – plenty of time for me to hop over the garden fence and climb in through his bathroom window. The slope will be in the front room, on top of the baby Broadwood or the drop-leaf table in the bay, already covered in scores and manuscript. These will have to be put back in the same order when I close the box, though that's a detail he might not notice. No alarms, no problems. Say ten minutes, there and back. Fifteen, if the window sticks.

At seven o'clock, I hear the tap-tap of polished soles on bare boards marking out Neville's passageway, a squeak and judder, the sombre clunk of a dead bolt. Devious instinct tells me to wait another twenty minutes, to allow for forgotten car keys, money, glasses.

In the basin, I slop my cotton shirt from hand to hand, its folds slimy as liver, and count infinitesimal windows on planes inching across the skylight. Behind one of them, soon, will be Carey Schumacher, his head full of smart codes and software acronyms, cushioned by business class. I think, too, of the RAF's lost birdman – Craig Spillings – in terminal free fall, his face battered by reefs of cloud. Like rain crawling up a train window, I can see the blood wriggling out of the gap in his teeth and over his lip, clogging the nostrils.

But Carey just circles – circles and yawns.

★ ★ ★

As soon as I realized I was not going to be sick, I turned off the cold tap, stared in the mirror, wished the reflection's huge nose smaller, and tried to remember my mother's advice.

'Say you're quite happy with them. But just ask if – if there's a breakdown, or a report, or something.'

'It's not an election, Mum. There's no recount.'

'You don't know that.'

'I do.'

'All right, all right. You know. I don't know anything.'

She stirred an emergency ration of sugar into a mug of milky coffee and stared at my father, slumped over the table with his head in his hands.

'I don't want to make a fuss,' I lied.

My mother squeaked. 'Then don't make one! Heavens, Daniel, they're only exams. And you did very well. Six perfectly good O levels.'

'You make it sound like a maternity ward.'

'I would have been delighted with six! So would your father.'

Dad winched his head upright.

'How many?' he said in a horrified whisper.

'I once got three per cent in geometry,' my mother

laughed, 'and that was for writing my name at the top of the paper: Jane Abigail Moorcock. Three names. Three per cent.'

'You can't do an O level in geometry.'

'A school certificate, then. Whatever they were called. Maths, RE, Latin, biology – I was last in all of them.'

'I don't believe you.'

'I remember my father saying to me, "Don't worry, Jane. When I was your age, I'd been in the shop for three years." Since he was *twelve*. Never sat an exam in his life. Made *all* our clothes.'

The supposed virtue of my hereditary imbecility failed to reassure me. Improvising uncertainly, my mother pointed to a foreign news headline from the *Guardian* – 'Lake of death kills 1,500 in Cameroon' – and reproved me for my lack of wider perspective. ' "Teams of French and Israeli rescuers are flying in to help",' she confirmed, before turning the page. I snorted. Volcanic catastrophes were to be expected in such places. A C in English Literature was not.

In the dingy green school toilets I prepared a little speech about disappointment – how I knew it was in vain to argue with the results, but couldn't quite believe, etc., etc. My joints melted in the approach to the duty master's office. On a desk in the corridor, a pile of blank detention registers proclaimed the criminal year ahead. Above them, Lyncombe's most famous old boy looked down moistly on generations to come, his polished frame improved by the graffito carving: 'Arnold Ridley – Tosser.'

To my relief, the master charged with sorting out the results and congratulating – or grief-counselling – prospective sixth-formers was Nigel Dooley. As I knocked and entered, he gave a rat-a-tat laugh, nearly a shout, and stood up quickly to rummage for something in his tracksuit bottoms. Above the drawstring, I could see a strip of tanned stomach with a few elastic scorch-marks, below it an unexpected prominence in the oatmeal grey fabric. His desk was covered in examinations syndicate printouts and official correspondence, a magazine or two thrust to the far side.

'Disappointed, Professor?' Dooley asked, fishing out a packet of cigarettes and a lighter. My sinuses prickled in momentary confusion.

'A bit.'

He sat down and tapped a cigarette on the desktop, looking now for an ashtray and strewing a second layer of papers over his magazines in the process. He smelt, pleasantly, of coffee and smoke.

'Ri-ight, let's see. The examiner was probably drunk. Or in a bad mood. Maybe you tied up your answers in the wrong order.'

I sniffed and looked down. 'I don't want to make excuses, sir. I know it's not the be-all and end-all. I just thought–'

'In a year, no one'll give a toss, Rathbone. You passed most of them, anyway. Spare a thought for the poor buggers who didn't.'

He picked up a stripy green slip with not much on it.

'Your mate Bray – though I shouldn't be telling you.'

'No, sir,' I said, and waited.

Dooley leaned back so that the chair creaked.

'Sat five. Failed four. And guess what?' Dooley smiled sadly. '*He* won't be up here wanting an explanation. That's him done with. He'll probably sign on next month. So count yourself lucky.'

I felt my cheeks burn and recalled Greg's vow not to return for retakes. In anyone else, it would have sounded defeatist; in his case – and more so in retrospect – it was somehow ennobling, a presentiment of failure that mocked the vanity of success. Besides which, tactful remarks from Dooley about difficult papers and 'the surprising spread of results' quashed any further appeal. I thanked him and left, stopping just a few paces on at the admin office to say hello-goodbye to the secretary, Cynthia Leggett.

Cynthia's response would be significant, since her universal pleasantness comprehended different shades of meaning, depending on what she'd heard or learnt that morning. If, for example, she returned my greeting with a woolly chortle ('Hillo-hillo! Daniel-Daniel-Daniel! Nice-summer-been-anywhere-nice?'), then all would be well: my Bs and Cs were indeed of no consequence, and raised eyebrows from secretly delighted peers were all I had to fear. But an indulgent smile, with one hand adrift in the folds of her plum cowl, would be the end of me, as it had been of countless applicants for junior teaching posts – signifying her pity, their disappointment and, at some obscure level, comeuppance.

Her chair was empty, a cup of coffee left to cool among piles of envelopes and in-trays. In the distance, toilets flushed. Soft soles tripped pitter-pat along the corridor, and stopped; another, heavier footfall from the opposite direction clumped to a halt outside the door. Inside, I shrank towards the window, looked around vaguely for means of escape.

Then, in the stale hush of late summer, Mrs Leggett, an admiralty wife with an even keel despite trying circumstances (five sons, one absent husband), gave a joyful shriek. The shriek dilated and bore other shrieks; words began to cluster around it –'oo,' 'ew it,' 'ould do,' 'olutely arvellous'. Further ecstasies were stifled by an embrace and answered by a familiar, accented rumble: '. . . I wondered if it was, like, a mistake . . .'

Dooley opened his door six yards away.

Trapped in the school office, I watched a wasp hurl itself against the smeared pane, tumbling away like a tiny jet in an air pocket. The window was open half an inch at the bottom. I grasped the sash and jerked it upwards. No one in the corridor seemed to hear or object.

'Glasses suit you, Mr Schumacher,' Dooley boomed. 'They give you a studious air. Well done, lad.'

'I'm kinda surprised.'

'Don't be.'

Carey's silence flooded the building. Of course, I wanted to see what he looked like with glasses – foolish, I hoped – but since that would have meant declaring myself and offering congratulations, I ducked down and rolled over the sill instead. In pursuit, the wasp swung angrily at what should have been glass and sailed off into inexplicable freedom, trailing a song of victory higher and higher, fainter and fainter as I picked my way free of Lyncombe's rosebeds: 'Eight As, eight As! Oh Carey, you *must* be thrilled . . .' I ran to the gates, silently cursing.

Back home, my mother took a firm, if less jubilant, line. 'What did I tell you? It's all luck of the draw. Now ring him up and say well done.'

'Brilliant idea,' I snarled. 'I say, "Well done," and he asks me what I–'

'And you tell him the truth!' she interrupted, arms thrown wide apart in exasperation. 'It's not the end of the world.'

'It fucking well is. I'm retarded.'

'Excuse me?'

I repeated myself, louder.

My mother snapped on a pair of Marigolds and banged our immersion heater with her fist. Upstairs, in bed with a headache, my father moaned at us to leave off. The voice of conscience hissed from the sink: 'With language like that, Daniel, I'm not surprised you only got a C.'

So I dialled the Schumachers and spoke to Carey who, not for the first time, surprised me. 'It's weird, is what it is,' he said, and clicked his tongue. 'Eight As and suspected diabetes. Whaddya think?'

*

I think two things. First, Carey was being kind – a kindness I cannot pretend to have acknowledged with much grace. How many times – in the Cellar club, when those daft results came out, throughout the sixth form, much later at the crematorium – has this alternately sombre and fluttering misfit seen me squirming in a tight corner, and resisted pity or ridicule? Friends should not have to be so sparing.

Second, as my eyes adjust to another tight corner and the blue-sight I cannot switch off switches on, it seems to me that Carey was wrong, not just about the diabetes, which turned out to be myopia, but about weirdness in general. 'Weird,' so the scene – the room – in front of me suggests, is a category of experience that transcends the 'inexplicable'. In fact, most things that happen to, or afflict us, defy explanation, however well they may be described. My night vision, for example. The pupils superdilate, so more light gets into them. (That's just a matter of good ocular reflexes.) There is a reflective layer in one eye – my left – which bounces light back through the retina and gives me another chance to register the image. In nocturnal animals, this layer is called the tapetum; in my case, it's a fluke. A deformity. Why it's there I have no idea.

Far more weird, infinitely less describable, are the trivial things in life – how we hang our curtains, what colour we paint the bedroom walls: matters of taste which, though nominally inexplicable, are soon said to 'explain a lot' once events take an unusual turn.

As they have in Neville Clute's cellar – where I am now cowering.

Its layout is familiar. Like mine, Neville's basement is about thirty feet long, ten feet wide, and follows the hallway out to the old coal chute under the porch. Unlike mine, it is selectively padded, with some . . . unusual furnishings. A steep wooden stepladder leads down from the passage entrance. In an emergency (I think this qualifies), a thin and terrified person might hide behind it.

Above me, Neville's key grates in the front door. (I was out of the front room with the slope's scroll safely in my hand when I heard the first turn, but too far away from the bathroom at the back to make a dash for it – he'd have heard my boots on the kitchen's chic slate tiling.) Now, with the second turn, a voice – two voices – clarify on the threshold and the passage light switches on, a half-second too late, surely, to show the cellar door under the stairs being pulled shut from the inside.

I look at the bit of paper in my hand and wonder at the insanity of the last two hours. It isn't a note or a shopping list. There is no betraying signature. It's just an indistinctly Xeroxed photo of me as a toddler, which I've seen a hundred times before – maybe even copied myself in a fit of extreme adolescent narcissism. It would have meant nothing to Neville. It means nothing to me. I left it in the slope nearly ten years ago.

It raises the question: What am I doing here? Why did I think it was a good idea to break into my neighbour's house? How, if he finds me, am I going to defend myself? And what, Christ knows, will I say about all *this*?

'I'm glad you like the fireplace,' I hear Neville call from the front room. 'It was walled up behind a lot of plaster board. Fancy wanting to hide something as beautiful as that! Of course, it was covered in rust – covered – and the flue was blocked. So I rang the Gas Board, had it unblocked, spoke to some friends and they all suggested Hammerite for the restoration. The tiles are reproductions – can't help that . . .'

'Hammerite?'

A cultured voice, deep but youthful, interjects, his smooth query stemming the flow.

Excited, Neville fusses with glasses. He is on his feet, near me, standing by the bookshelves and piano – probably keeps a bottle or two stashed in those wall-length music cupboards. His companion creaks in the 70s leather recliner by the window table.

'Metal paint,' Neville says, clearing his throat. 'You put it on metal – railings, ranges, fireplaces. It's an industrial-strength varnish.'

'How interesting,' purrs his friend. 'A DIY expert. I wouldn't have guessed. You're full of surprises, aren't you? The self-improved man.'

Neville laughs nervously, takes a few steps towards the bay so that a cast of dust exhales downwards through the floorboards. 'Oh, hardly,' he twitters, too flattered to regret the other's insincerity. 'A few tweaks here and there. A little redesign. Some minor conversions.'

Another creak from the chair, masked by a broken titter.

'But plenty of original features, yeah?'

I feel Neville flinch. Like one of Dooley's stray polysyllables, the 'yeah' gives his companion away. It doesn't fit. At some point, the young man's voice has been re-keyed; shaped so as to conceal either flat, 'ow'-shaped Middlesex vowels, or an expensive upbringing – probably the latter.

I'm assuming he's rent.

Neville recovers: 'Ha! Yes.'

'In perfect working order?'

'Ha.'

He might be that strange Cambridge philosophy graduate who made a documentary about being a prostitute. Best friends with a nun and popular with his teachers, the programme claimed.

' 'Cos they don't make them the way they used to.'

'Indeed,' Neville agrees, his voice soaring. '*Laudator temporis acti se puero. Multa* something *anni venientes.* I think.'

There is a sullen pause.

'Take your word for it.'

Neville's beam fades, disappointed.

'Horace,' he sighs to himself, brushing a world aside.

'Steve,' says the creaker, and clunks his glass on the table. 'But I can be whoever, you know. Within reason.'

The boy's voice drops low, hums through the rising water main to where I'm stowed behind the cellar steps, breath stopped.

'Where d'you want me?' he says. 'Upstairs?'

'Actually . . .' Neville begins, but his voice, hoarsening, trails to a shivery full stop. Nothing happens for a little while; someone shifts their weight; Steve cajoles inaudibly.

There is no contact, no clasp or leading gesture – none that I can hear, none that I can imagine. The silence between the two men is cautious rather than erotic, invested on the one hand with professional restraint and on the other with a humbled rage, the unguessable frustration of years spent watching. In the luminous dark, I seem to see once more the thermal profile of a young boy, his head distinguished not by tumble-weed hair but by a bubble of snot expanding and contracting with each short gasp. I peer closer at this inside-eyelid phantom, and find him altered. The boy is a balding man with shiny cheeks, a sloping forehead and two pinches of coarse nostril hair. He wears a cravat.

The front room door opens; footsteps sound in the passage, no more than fifteen feet away. There is a shuffle and a scrape at the bottom of the stairs. For a moment it seems as if they will both ascend, and liberate me. I urge them upstairs, my eyes shut and jaw clenched in hopeless petition. The first step of the staircase gives a groan under the weight of one foot. Affably, Steve assures my older, wiser, sillier neighbour of the absence of rules (apart from the cardinal one: even chat costs). A birdlike electronic pulse scatters the silence; Steve waits, his mobile phone clicks off, and Neville clears his throat.

'Anything?' he says, disbelieving.

'You name it,' returns Steve, a note of genial condescension creeping into his voice. (What was it the TV prostitute said? 'The men I see are *lonely* . . . I honestly think they *deserve* someone like me.')

'In that case,' Neville at last announces, 'I'd like a kiss.'

A long, yawning beat. And an embarrassed laugh.

Neville steps back off the stairs. 'Is that all right?'

Steve leans against the wall. The cellar door has a keyhole, but it's choked with dust and lock-rot. I can't see much through it at this fine angle except two leathery legs, nearer and heavier-set than I'd imagined, one straight, the other drawn up to advertise a sculpted fly.

'Anything except,' Steve half-laughs. 'Horace, the boyf'd kill me. Fair's fair. He has to get something I don't give out. No kissing.'

A hasty chortle greets this explanation. 'I quite under-stand,' says my neighbour in his best Joan Hickson, the elastic sigh unshockably attuned to domestic mishap and global catas-trophe. 'Well,' he reflects, 'I suppose it won't harm to show you. Come on.'

They leave the stairs and walk towards me.

My heart bouncing, I swivel on the top rung and slide, tumble down the ladder, cramming myself behind it and crouching in a pouch of darkness. Three or four too-small, too-noisy cardboard boxes share my exposed priest-hole. (Why didn't I take my shoes off?) The cellar door opens. A hand reaches in and turns on the light – which is mercifully low, maybe forty watts, and hangs by a bare flex at the other end of the room. Still it blinds me. Eel-like, I curl into the shadows.

Neville says 'After you,' his mouth dry.

Steve steps in and descends awkwardly, front-facing, five of the ten rungs. I am looking at his booted feet, up at his squeaking calves and thighs. He is wearing a blue-black bomber jacket with a fake furry ruff. I had pictured longish, dark hair, but it is fair and ultra-short, revealing a single pierced ear (the left), his whole upper body slighter than the legs would suggest. I cannot see his face. I can only hear him breathing. Long breaths, teased out between pursed lips.

He stops on the middle rung and puts a hand up to steady himself against the underside of the stairs. Neville waits aloft.

'What do you think?' he calls down anxiously, after a minute.

Steve stumbles down the last five rungs and onto the rubberized matting that covers the lit portion of the cellar floor. He treads carefully between objects – between instru-ments – fixed and suspended, like an underwater trapeze artist. He has seen rooms before, perhaps, but none like this.

In the middle is an old iron-frame upright piano, a Rud Ibach, with its lid removed. (Neville told me he'd sold it to get the Broadwood.) Where the candlesticks would have been on the front panels, two pairs of handcuffs now dangle; on the fold-up music stand is a score – and a copy of *Alaska Men*. Arranged in a horse-shoe crescent around the piano are chairs for string players, with bows riveted to the floor rising up through the middle of the seats like lightning rods. Two violins and one viola, attached by wires to the low ceiling, their strings gutted and lolling, brush against the fronds of four or five whips hanging alongside them.

'OK . . .' Steve replies, in a strangled voice.

'OK?' Neville sounds hurt. 'Is that all?'

His back still to me, Steve passes a perceptibly shaking hand over one of three hugely modified piano stools. An extended, disinvolved trombone slide links the legs together to form a fixed pew.

'You . . . sit on these?' he asks, pointing to their moulded peaks.

Neville gives an indecisive shall-I-shan't-I squeal.

'With practice, yes.'

'OK,' says Steve, nodding his head. And 'OK' again, as he inspects the small brass section at the back of the room, its tubes, valves and mutes bracketed to a torn leather bench. Beside it, a Marley's Ghost tangle of chains and rigging spills out of a skinless kettle drum.

'It's an ensemble,' Neville explains, flustered, not entering. 'Or at least, modelled on the idea of one. It started out as the Brahms Piano Quintet.' He swallows guiltily. 'Then I got a bit carried away. Chamber music is so sexy, don't you think? Sexier than sex, really. Anyway, I had this idea years ago – to build a sort of erotic sculpture. And I've just, sort of, let it accumulate. I – I – I don't know why.'

'OK . . .'

'It's just a piece of fun. I hardly use it.'

Steve puts his hands to his face, takes another deep breath and turns round, digesting what he has seen, pulling at the skin of his white cheeks so that his eyes' red under-rims are exposed. His colouring is Nordic (South African maybe, which would account for the accent) and naturally pale. The eyes themselves are a beautiful white-blue, but the greyish skin around them has begun to sag. He looks tired.

'I have to say–' he says. And stops.

Distracted by the pulsing of veins on Steve's neck and temples, it takes me a few seconds to notice the slow, un-hinging of his mouth, and a few more to work out the object of his appalled gaze. He moves away from the hanging violins and peers into the recesses of the cellar. There is a clinging shape behind the cage-like rungs of the ladder; something distressed and voiceless; someone *kept*.

Me.

Aghast, I put my one finger to my lips and plead with him, silently, hands together, not to give me away.

'What?' Neville asks. 'What is it?'

Steve's frog-like eyes roll up and down, track right to left. He stoops suddenly and, at the bottom of the ladder, picks up the crumpled sheet of paper, the great non-secret of the slope, which I dropped in my haste to be hidden. *It's nothing*, I want to shout. *It's only an old photo*. But to him I dare say it's something else, this Xerox of a toddler, found in an orchestral sex-pit – now with footprints all over its face.

'What? Tell me – what?' Neville says, frightened.

Not giving me another look, Steve lets the photo slide

from his hands, charges the stepladder and pushes Neville over at the top. There is a toppling crack and a thin, painful cry. The escort's boots thunder down the hallway passage. 'I wasn't here. I didn't see anything,' he shouts, wrenching the door open to address his parting words to the whole street.

'And I don't do fucking psychos.'

*

After a while, Neville got to his feet, turned off the light and lumbered into the kitchen, where he sat for hours, talking to himself and blowing his nose. When, finally, he climbed the stairs to bed, I emerged from the cellar with the remaining shreds of babyface tucked in my wallet, and tiptoed as steadily as I could to the back door. On his kitchen table, I couldn't help noticing an open First Aid box and a pile of tissues. In the garden, the birds were singing up-tempo, ambient Stevie Wonder. I slept for an hour or two, and dreamt things I am relieved to have forgotten.

By nine, I am wide awake again, alert as only the truly sleep-deprived can be, standing on my own doorstep with a cup of tea in my hand, watching the neighbourhood stir.

Normally, as the day grows in confidence, the treetops quieten. Not today. Today, they are clamorous and irrepressible, magpies shrieking in refractive nests, beaking bits of foil and flashing their tail-blue insanely. Today, the sun at the end of Windmill Road is the kind of sun which only prolongs beginnings. How could its brilliance lessen? How could it ever have been less? It surrounds you wherever you go. Wherever you walk, you find yourself walking towards it, frowning and smiling. Olive and her sons, Martin and Earl, have just floated past on their way to church. They were smartly visible for ten paces and are now lost in the solar flare. All over London, kids dare themselves to look directly at it for more than a second, then sway groggily.

Because of my condition, such bright light can be painful: I have to squint more than most. Today, I'm squinting so hard I hardly register a tall, suited young man in front of my decrepit wooden gate, until the taxi which flashed him into existence flashes out again. He may, a minute ago, have been helped out of the car – if there was one – by the driver. He may have tipped over-generously and said goodbye with unusual warmth. He may have been standing there, grinning at me, for much longer than that. Shielding my eyes with one hand, I find myself envying the lean but muscular frame, solid shoulders and immaculate dress. The suit is light grey worsted, cut sixties style, with a cross-hatched blue stripe; it shouldn't match such slick-and-trim red-brown hair, but it does. The tie is turquoise blue, the shirt white. And the smile, so dazzling the magpies have already hatched a plot to steal it, goes with everything, even the dark glasses.

'Daniel, take a shower,' Carey says. 'I can smell you from here.'

Even the white stick.

Part Two

Bond with Aliens

The other girl stood at the far end of the same corrugated bus stand and leant against its cold iron post, arms folded. Two young men, with narrow shoulders and prognathous grins, ambled past. One of them took a cigarette packet out of his breast pocket and shook it invitingly at the girl with folded arms, who smiled a refusal. Jane turned her head so that they wouldn't tease her, and heard laughter as she pretended to scan the horizon, where the clouds hung like burning flags.

A green bus with a curved grille bumped over the bridge at the bottom of the high street and began to chug uphill through haze and chimney-shadow towards the Old Palace. As it neared the stop, Jane saw that the first three letters of its silver-on-black number plate formed the word 'YOU'. The confident girl in front of her sprang up the three steps to the driver's seat, greeted him in a low voice she couldn't quite place and asked for South Avenue, the Gastard turn-off. 'The same, please,' Jane said, and glanced at her fellow passengers: a stony-faced old couple, a young woman in a spotted scarf with two string bags full of shopping by her side, and three lads at the back (not, she thought, students), their legs proprietorially splayed. The audience, though sparse, made her nervous. She wished she had not worn her best jersey woollens, or tried to curl her hair. The old couple looked sceptically at her two suitcases. The young woman blinked slowly and, sighing, produced a waking baby from behind a seat. One of the lads, the middle one, his face not quite visible in the grainy darkness beneath the glowing rear window, drew his legs together and sat up. Jane took her ticket and fell over the suitcases.

The driver stopped the bus, which had begun to turn. Jane started to pick herself up, blushing and laughing, but felt her left leg caught. A brass latch on one of the cases had bitten into her tights and laddered them. She knelt down and tried to disengage the material. It wouldn't separate. There was no more polite laughter in her, and her eyes filled.

She heard the words 'big and clumsy', without recognizing the voice as her own. She yanked the nylon from the snaggletooth of the latch. A pair of hands helped her up and she allowed herself to be lifted. 'Enjoy your trip?' called the driver. 'Loved it,' said the girl from the bus stop, and guided Jane to a seat. Their chivalry untested, the three lads – already halfway down the aisle – returned to the back of the bus.

'If we could afford taxis from the station, like the staff, there'd be fewer injuries,' Jane's rescuer whispered. 'Shame about those tights. And that graze, too. Never any iodine when you need it.'

Jane stared at her companion. The accent was American and the auburn hair explosive with natural curls. She was shorter than average, but well fed, even voluptuous, with none of the scrawny tightness that made Jane's big bones stick out so at the shoulders and hips. The eyes, an unbudging hazel green, were lashed like Betty Boop's, the face round as a March moon. She wore a long yellow print dress with open-toed sandals.

Maybe she's too big to feel the cold, Jane thought ungenerously, and touched the red spot on her knee, which stung.

'You're just in, right?' the other girl asked. 'I thought so. It's a custom round here – you know, don't help anyone with their bags *until* they've maimed themselves. Then bear down on them in a pack.'

The American nodded over her shoulder at the back-seat boys, and Jane felt the peculiarity of being complicit with a foreigner in the comedy of rural Englishness. The yellow dress sighed to itself. It looked home-made, and was daringly cut, with a low neckline and ruched bodice; somewhat theatrical, too – the garb of a comic shepherdess – as though its wearer would rather startle strangers than seduce them.

'I don't know your name,' said the American girl, presently. Jane told her, laughed and shook free a hair-pin. Her fringe lolled over her face.

'OK, Jane. I'm Frances. Pleased to meet you.'

'To meet you, too.'

'Uh-huh,' Frances said, firmly. 'Well, Jane, just be on your guard, that's all I'm saying. The locals are pre-tty desperate. You know. Any excuse.'

'I see,' said Jane, tucking the pin back in.

The bus swerved to avoid a motorcyclist roaring out of a gleaming hospital forecourt to the left. The driver swore and blasted his horn, but the boys at the back cheered. Inspired, one of them started boasting about his new TW9 – new, as in 'retuned' – the one he'd got off that Yank at the Colerne base. His friends grunted, like they'd heard it before.

'We don't want,' Frances said, leaning closer to Jane and lowering her voice, 'any more Catherine Bannons.'

Jane coughed. 'Why not?'

Frances fluttered a hand on the shelf of her chest and took

a deep breath. She looked pityingly at Jane and then, once more, behind her.

'Cathy Bannon was a catch who got caught.'

Jane looked blank.

'With a farmhand from Melksham,' Frances explained, rolling her eyes. 'Yeah, her first. Quite a fuss – and he was German, which didn't help. Anyway, she was on the next train back home after the jani– the caretaker found them. So what can I say? Peel them peepers. You ain't safe.' She blinked and frowned. 'Middle one's cute.'

A twenty-year-old with bowl-cut brown hair, shiny cheeks and elbow patches, solid as a milk churn, glared at the back of Jane's neck, as the bus left Chippenham and began its climb towards Corsham Park. Heavy sunbeams strafed the aisle. The sky was purple-red and the beech trees behind the estate wall had begun to turn. On the other side of the road, where thistly meadows stretched as far as Biddestone and the Long Barrow, Jane saw some scattered figures picking at a hedge, pointing at inaccessible clusters of fruit and sucking their fingertips.

'But we're cosy in Monks,' Frances rattled on. 'Curfew after eleven thirty, strictly no trousers. Who needs them? Life's busy enough.'

Jane smiled to herself.

'Oh, and watch out for the guys in ceramics – the kiln kilt? – Don Muir? He keeps hawks. Hey, at least *they* only go after mice.'

By the time the bus reached Corsham – a couple of streets with some subsiding mews, four shops, a garage and a post office – Jane had a lively impression of the various roads to ruin converging on her new home. Forewarned against the predations of the Academy's tutorial sculptors, printers, painters, potters, textile workers, musicians, caterers, cleaners, gardeners and rogue farmhands, she looked forward to an equally lively account of her fellow students on the long walk to Monks Park, the women's halls of residence – but was disappointed. According to Frances, the 'other guys' were merely 'wild' or, at best, 'outrageous'; Frances' room-mate, Hannah, had a 'stash', and, last year, Pete Zender, a twenty-six-year-old ex-copper temperamentally unsuited to still-life, had told Howard Hodgkin where to stuff his egg. Otherwise, everyone was pretty much in line – and passionate about Art. They were part of the radical tradition, the principal had said. Living and working together as members of a community. Teaching, learning.

When the bus stopped at the South Avenue gate, it was almost dark. Behind them, on Corsham's main street, there were a few lampposts, but the Gastard road was unlit. Conkers and their half-grenade husks lined the potholes of Monks Drive itself, and a black duckpond lay opposite the park gates, to which a sign had been affixed: 'Less speed, moorhens.'

Frances took one of Jane's suitcases – the one with the offending latch – and staggered ten yards before dropping it.

'How many bodies you got in here?' she demanded, lifting the case front-on with both hands and waddling ahead. The road surface was slippery with mulched leaves; wind rattled the hawthorn borders.

'No bodies,' Jane replied, 'just things to cut them up with. Scissors, shears, knives, a saw – my dad lent me a lot of things on the equipment list. Crewel needles, palettes.' She paused. 'He's a tailor.'

Frances was impressed. 'That makes sense. I thought your knits weren't high street – and now I know.' (Had that come out right? She hurried on before Jane could answer.) 'I guess the saw is an extra, huh?'

'Important tool,' Jane said breathlessly, the weight of her case pulling her down one side of the canted lane towards a ditch. 'Or was before I came along. Dad used to make wooden legs for some of the hopalongs up Whitechapel. Course, they're all metal and plastic now.'

A low-hanging branch swiped at Frances' face and picked at her dress. The wind gave the sopping horse-chestnut leaves and stems a tentacular life of their own. Both girls stopped, while Jane, taller she now saw by a good three or four inches, helped Frances disentangle herself. Once freed, Frances began to pant with laughter. 'Jesus,' she sighed. 'He couldn't just use it to put up shelves.'

It hadn't occurred to Jane, who blushed. He must have done, at some point, she supposed. Obviously. But he'd told her about the legs and the old boys when she was a very little girl; when she saw her first veterans in the ration queues off Holloway Road. They called it the peg-saw.

Frances smiled. 'How old are your folks?'

'Dad's fifty-eight,' Jane said. 'My mother died when I was little.'

Around a bend in the lane, the canopy of chestnuts cleared suddenly. Not more than two hundred yards away stood Monks Park, a fine Georgian mansion at the end of an approach over imperfect sward, with a row of windows lit up above the pillared portico. The students' huts lay to the east, a relic of the estate's occupancy by the Ministry of Supply.

At the main door, Frances introduced Jane to the warden and caretaker, Dougall Voss, who asked why they were both so late, and Jane explained that she'd had to help out in her father's shop until after lunch. (Frances waved the question away: this was her second year; she wasn't a kid no more; she knew her first class – nine-thirty with Helen Odish. Right?)

Voss tried hard to be stern, but his youth undermined the attempt. He was perhaps the same age as Jane, twenty-two or less, and leanly dashing, with reddish hair cut close at the sides, then built up in waves on top. He told Jane that she'd have to register tomorrow at the Court, and instructed Frances – whom he called Frankie – to show Jane her room. There were plenty of girls upstairs in the common room if she wanted to introduce herself. Breakfast in the refectory at eight.

Frances tweaked his lapel. 'You're looking very smart, Dougall,' she complained. 'Too smart for the Pack Horse.'

'Goin' to the flicks in Bath, aren' I?' said Dougall morosely, brushing at his jacket and picking hairs off one shoulder. 'That *Dr No*'s on, y'know. James Bond 'n' tha' – at the Beau Nash.'

He looked embarrassed, and Jane felt for him. His 'office', where the three of them now stood in uncomfortable proximity, was a tiny storeroom, not much more than an alcove, behind the main staircase on the way to the back toilet. If you wanted to use the loo Dougall had to get up to let you pass by. His room had a child's desk jammed up against a damp wall, one shelf with a few paperbacks on it, some cards pinned to a cork tile, and various mops and buckets. He slept downstairs, in a much larger, colder room, stacked with art supplies.

'Are you going with anyone nice?' Frances asked meaningfully.

Dougall checked his trouser pockets for keys, and wrapped himself in a blue woollen scarf. 'No,' he mumbled, and put out the light.

*

It was cramped in Dougall Voss's Austin. After *Dr No*, on the way back to Corsham, Jane had to share the back seat with a card table they'd picked up from a junk shop on the way in.

Dougall liked cards, and was glad James Bond liked them, too. He didn't know how to play, but Pete Zender had promised to teach him – poker, whist, a few tricks maybe.

'You be careful,' said Frances at the mention of tricks, and laughed knowingly. Annoyed, Dougall accelerated along the village high street towards the turn-off. He sliced the car into Monks Drive at twenty miles an hour so that the wheels span in the mud.

Jane gave the rear-view mirror a furious stare, hoping to catch the caretaker's eye. She hated show-offs – especially show-offs behind the wheel. Dangerous driving wasn't clever; it was frightening, and silly films like *Dr No* only made it worse. In fact, Jane thought, films like *Dr No* gave men the wrong idea about a lot of things, besides going fast down narrow roads. That woman with the knife in her swimsuit, for instance. How ridiculous. Hands completely unmarked. Couldn't catch a fish if you served it to her on a plate. Not much of a voice, either.

Dougall stopped the car.

'What was that?' he said, and they listened.

The engine ticked softly to itself; the trees washed in and out of earshot.

'Nothing,' said Jane, crossly.

But she listened, too, and could soon make out a faint creaking sound nearby. Strange spluttering noises, unsettled laughter. Ahead of them, Monks Park rose up like a face lost in the deep glass of night.

'I don't hear anything,' Frances lied.

And still the creaking – of what? A weather vane? An open gate? – called to them.

'That – there,' said Dougall.

There was no ticking any more. The Austin's motor had

cooled into silence. The dark listened to them, listening to the dark.

'There!' he repeated, and leapt out of the car in time to be knocked over by three scarved men who dropped from the branches overhead, thrust grinning faces up against the wind-screen and pelted off down the lane.

Another prankster yowled for help – and yowled again. He had fallen badly, ten yards or so in front of the car, and couldn't stand.

'Right,' said Jane, and clambered out over the driver's seat.

Frances sighed, suffering a little in her thin summer dress and open sandals. The cold air had begun to pinch. On the road, the fallen student let out more groans, and Dougall went back to the car to fetch a torch from his glove compartment. It glimmered feebly; Jane impatiently suggested turning on the headlights instead.

In their smoky brightness, her practical anger vanished. The casualty, she now saw, was a nervous-looking young man of meagre proportions in a huge Harris jacket and flannel trousers. He lay in the mud, like a stubborn crease. His mouth worked against the pain.

'Ankle,' he said, loudly.

'Idiot,' replied Jane, and had a look at it.

With Dougall's help, she got him to stand on his good leg and hopped him to the Austin. He smelled of beer, but not unpleasantly. Dougall said that he'd better drive him back to the men's halls.

'Shouldn't I see a doctor?' said the young man, preciously. 'I think I've broken it. It may need pl–'

'It's a sprain,' Jane said, flatly.

'Bloody Rathbone,' Dougall muttered.

Frances and Jane stood in the lane and waved at the

reversing car. As its yellow eyes retreated, a softer, massier light – not quite light and not quite shadow – surged upwards to suggest the immense outlines of the horse chestnuts. With the Austin gone, the creaking returned, and a flock of bicycles sang gently from the treetops.

* * *

The programme began at 8.30 p.m. There would be a queue, and we'd have to be near the front of it – no further down the street than Dewhurst's the butchers – to be sure of our seats on the left-hand side of the auditorium. For such an important film, seats in the middle might be acceptable; but not even the first showing of *Aliens* would induce the committee of Bath Schools Film Society to sit on the right, where plump young Tories from King Edward's, the local boys' public school, wore stripy shirts and planned dinner parties during the intermission.

A half-hour wait in the October rain had made us less fussy. The film was more popular than we had anticipated, and our politely shuffling progress no match for the hair-flicking blondes from the Royal School for Girls, who stood athwart the queue, gazing with wounded disbelief at its length, before pushing in ('Jeremy? Hi! Can I just . . . ?') at the front. By the time we reached the box office, we were soaked. My fawn cotton baseball jacket clung to me like wet strudel; Carey's boots and fatigues squelched with every step; and Karen Kale's many morbid dyes had unfastened all over the carpeted lobby. Greg Bray, for whom neatness had become an article of faith since landing a weekend job in a sports store, closed his umbrella and gestured despairingly.

The fat man with the high voice and drifting toupee who

took our tickets laughed at Karen and Carey: 'Arr, come to see your relatives, 'ave you, my lovers? Well, best 'urry up – you're on in five minutes. Aisle two, row L, turn right.'

Inside the Beau Nash ABC, a fifties fleapit with moth-eaten drapes and threadbare plush, the Friday night audience screamed as the lights went down. I found row L and decided to take the seat nearest the wall. Carey and Karen would follow, and Greg could sit on the end. To encourage the idea that my lunge in the Cellar had been a prank, I tried not to position myself anywhere near Greg in committee meetings or during screenings, and was distressed to note that this was fine by him, since he had begun – with understandable success – to prefer female company. That night, though, without turning to look, I knew that the chemical fragrance at my side as I sat down was his. It was lemon-scented aftershave – and Carey only ever reeked of patchouli.

The Morse crackle of the screen gave way to the King Cone ad and a chorus behind us of 'lick me, bite me, any way you like me'. I hummed along and so did Greg. 'As long as you love me, it's all right.'

'You having one?' he said, getting up as the tray-bearing usherettes tramped down the gangway and the ceiling spots came back on. I nodded. Karen and Carey shook their heads and made quiet retching sounds.

'No E-numbers for me,' said Carey archly, wiping his glasses with a pinch of filthy shirt. 'But don't let that put *you* off.'

Greg trod on Carey's toe and edged to the end of the row. He was almost out when a voice from the King Cone chorus described us as 'fucking hippy shits'. Carey and Karen, used to this kind of insult, exchanged tired looks. This is what you get, they seemed to say, when you mix with the great washed.

Greg, immaculately turned out in blue check shirt, brown jeans and trainers, was stung but made no reply. He got the ice creams, sat back down and whispered something to me about the charming company. I agreed feebly, and inhaled as much of his citrus odour as I dared without sniffing audibly. Behind us, the beery comedians from King Edward's also sniffed, wafting each other's farts along the row and cackling about the vintage. 'Chernobyl compost, excellent,' said one toothily, and then – with a smack at the back of Carey's shaggy head – 'nine out of ten hippies say they prefer it – oh, *sorry*, hippy, sorry!'

There was a time when Carey would have let this go, too. But academic success and romantic stability, the proof of his resilience, had made him fearless. The carillon of giggles in row M died away. Carey swivelled and put a finger to his lips. Then his hand moved to his army coat pocket.

In profile, he looked nobly ascetic, the high brow bordered by veins which forked at the hairline. It struck me, too, how smooth Carey's skin had become over the summer, like a layer of skim plaster. There were other blemishes, of course – the smell, the pallor, the hair (still black, but with a smoulder of ginger at the roots) – and a general unearthliness, as of a long shadow at midday, which made people (including the Edwardians) wary: Carey knew that he would never be popular.

Yet such self-awareness, notably distinct from the usual adolescent self-consciousness, commanded attention and respect. Three years of isolation had fostered unsuspected genius. Within two weeks of starting A level computer science, the alcoholic maths master and former code-breaker Ned Burridge declared Carey 'off the scale'. (It took Burridge four days, every year, to work out the timetables for 1,700 boys and sixty members of staff; as an exercise, Carey did them one afternoon, with seven variant schemes attached.) When Carey proposed me as Film Society Chairman, his surprise backing conferred honour on an otherwise faintly ludicrous candidate. Most impressive of all, he appeared to bear his former tormentors at Lyncombe no ill will, though those green eyes surely knew too much. Where the pupils had once jiggled in terror, they moved now with planetary stealth behind Joe-90 specs, replete with the knowledge of all that we, his hard-working peers, could never hope to achieve.

The lights dimmed again. The censor's card flashed up on the screen. And suddenly, uncoiling from his seat like one of the film's universal predators, Carey rounded on the enemy.

There were ripples of concern from the rows around us, and I started to my feet. I sensed – or could I see? – a hundred Friday night couples on the other side of the cinema patting each other's thighs in anticipatory reassurance. But right next to me, the special effects were well under way. Blocking out the cosmos of the titles, Carey stood in silhouette with his arm raised. In his fist, he held a short knife. He stabbed the air, twice, before lunging across the back of his seat, apparently sinking it into the neck of the toothy boy behind, who said 'ffff' and dropped his ice cream.

My hand got to Carey's forearm just as he withdrew the knife with a snarl and a yank, as if it might take root in the sinew.

Greg curled forward, crash-landing style, to assist my scrambled dash over the seats, and Karen, still as a child who wants to make herself invisible, put both hands over her eyes. In the mottled blue of the darkened theatre, I could see a few open mouths, sucking in airborne plankton, but no advancing forms, no offers of help. The stabbed boy, from whom a confusion of smells – beer, sugar, hair gel, starch and sweat, shit and dried semen – seemed to emanate, tried steadying himself with his left hand, fingers gnawing at the armrest in spasm. His right hand moved ineffectually to his neck. What had happened? How had he been hit? Was that shock-haired goon with the mad stare one of those tramps with dogs that hung around the Abbey churchyard? Did he have a history of assault and school refusal? A plan in life?

A smear of ice cream bubbled on the inside of the boy's lower lip. It distracted me, even as I knocked the knife out of Carey's hand and toppled over into row M thinking how good I'd be in a crisis.

I landed on my stomach, and wriggled towards the main aisle through a mess of wrappers and tubs and legs that kicked. Once there, with laughter crackling behind me and voices at the back of the stalls telling us all to 'sit down and shut the fuck up', I found the knife. It was pretty convincing, the size of a small Kitchen Devil. I put my thumb over the point of the blade and pushed. The blade vanished but you couldn't hear the springs.

'Not funny,' I said to Carey, and dug my fingers impotently into his bony shoulder. In the exit doorway at the top of the aisle I could see the fat attendant, dithering, patting his rug like a dopey pet.

Carey settled himself. 'Excuse me,' he murmured, prising away my fingers without bothering to look at me. 'I'm watching the film.'

In the spooky music accompanying the opening credits I heard only my own clunking sense of the dramatic. The stabbee in the stripy shirt rubbed his neck and slouched in his seat, knees drawn up into the small of Carey's back. Go on, I thought, with that marrowless 'excuse me' thudding in my ears – knife him back for real, why don't you.

I considered walking out, then sat down, faint with a formless humiliation, and tried to pay attention. I could feel Greg looking at me, his elbows planted squarely on the armrest so that I had to adopt an imbecile pose, with my shoulders drawn in and arms folded in front of me.

The huge screen moved slightly at the edges. I tried again, and nervousness made me swallow. Would I understand the plot?

As Film Society Chairman, I had to say a few words before each club screening, and the prospect of introducing *Aliens* at the Christmas party filled me with dread. My first film, Buñuel's *Le Charme Discret de la Bourgeoisie*, had been a cinch – a lot of arty nonsense about eating and crapping. But a fortnight ago, I'd run into difficulties with *Jagged Edge*. Halfway through my précis of what I'd airily called a 'low-concept thriller' I realized that, low-concept or not, the various strands of the plot were too tightly woven for me to pick them apart. And that, in the retelling, I wasn't making them make sense. In the glazed eyes waiting for me to wind up, I could see a mixture of boredom and pity. Just give us a flavour of what happens, they seemed to say. So I panicked and heard myself yelping 'and then . . . and then . . .' like a seven-year-old asked to describe his weekend. Anxious to get to the point, I missed it. In the margins of set texts, my annotations were always the same – 'remember this and *this*!' or 'don't forget, this is *important*!'

At the beginning of *Aliens*, Sigourney Weaver has a nightmare. She is lying on a hospital bed, freshly hatched from a plastic pod; there is an alien inside her. A prowling camera signals menace. She smiles at the kindly space doctor –

shoulder-buttoned for the future like a dentist from the 1970s – and falters. The blood drains from her face. She arches her back and screams; thrashes about; gapes at the tight drum of her belly as it swells horribly with the soundtrack. And wakes up.

Throughout the cinema, delighted girlfriends clung to their breathless swains and eeked for attention. Except for Karen Kale, who got up unsteadily, clutching her stomach. Carey followed her out.

'It wasn't that bad,' said Greg, sceptically. 'No blood.'

'You wait, it gets worse,' I said, adding without thinking: 'You can hold my hand if you're scared.'

The words flopped out with such looseness that my mouth refused to close. Their whispered echo diffused in the air like the spores of a disease. My eyelids throbbed. The screen, with its heavy industrial guns and robots, was an irrelevance.

Greg smiled quickly, froze, checked himself, and seemed to relax.

'You should be so lucky,' he said.

The entrails flew by for the next two hours.

*

After the film, Greg and I had a half in the Crystal Palace, where Carey and Karen had unofficial tenancy of the stools by the dumb waiter in the corner. They didn't turn up, although we did bump into Craig Spillings, the only boy in Bath still wearing grey slip-ons in 1986. I'd seen Craig twice since his defection to King Edward's that September: the first time, he was sarcastic about my results; the second, he grew maudlin, over his seventh Stella, about how he didn't fit in – apart from the rugby – and how he missed Lyncombe. (How's Greg, then? How's Smacker? How's you?)

'Oi, Greg! Hunter!' Craig called from the bar. 'The posh twats are looking for you. Something about Smacker gone ape.'

'He left,' I said. 'He stabbed a yuppie with a trick knife and Karen got queasy about the film. They both left.'

Spillings flinched. 'Yeah, I heard.' He paused. 'She all right?'

'I suppose so.'

'Yeah, anyway. Burns-Wilson swears he's going to put one on you. An' he will. He's fucking mental. Rich and mental, like his Dad.'

'What's his Dad do?' asked Greg.

''S a bastard barrister,' explained Craig.

The barman looked unhappy about this description and pointed at the door. Craig stayed to argue, while Greg and I drank up. After our warning, we decided to walk across the Abbey churchyard towards the bus stops in Orange Grove. The courtyard was desolate by night, its flagstones smeared with residue from the café tables, but it was well lit and sharp smelling after the recent rain. Of course, even a well-lit square has dark corners, which is where they were waiting.

I remember practically nothing about the attack. (Whereas Carey's earlier, joke assault is fresh in my memory – the animatronic jerks of his hand, the comic deliberacy of his aim.) But that's because nothing about theatrical violence prepares you for the real thing – the way people get hit in unglamorous places like the buttocks or ears; the way, even as you curl up into a ball against the railings, it all feels like a mistake.

Beyond making sure that I kept my head down, I seemed to have no part to play. There was no shouting, not counting a few well-enunciated obscenities from the Edwardians now that they'd got us out of the main square and into the Abbey's side return, and no preliminary baiting. The first punch (from

Burns-Wilson) was to the face, and it felled me. I heard shoes shifting, shelving, scraping, nuzzling each other, seeking position. A pair of laces had come undone; somebody's shirt-tail wasn't tucked in; lines of moss grew like hairy putty in the cracks of the stones. I put my hand out and grabbed a leg; it swung free. The unidentifiable roaring lessened. I saw four figures running off waving an umbrella.

That wasn't too bad, I decided.

The next thing I remember is sitting down on one of the benches in the middle of the square thinking: all my own teeth, still. No injuries down below. Tears that felt like an allergic reaction confused the facade of the Pump Rooms in front of me. I squinted without meaning to squint. My sinuses rang numbly.

I got up. It was getting warm north and south of my nose, and I felt thirsty. Where was Greg, I wondered. His absence struck me at first as an infantile fact – another balloon gone – then with a kind of idly returning panic, as if there might be a range of explanations for his loss, all of them evil, inevitable. I began to look for him in the shadows of the nearby streets, eyes averted and furtive. I loped around for a few minutes, circling back feebly to the cold benches. Deep down, I knew he'd run off, but didn't want to think about that. Deeper still, I thought: if he comes back now, I'll be glad. Glad if he comes back at all.

'Dan!'

A shout pounded the walls of the courtyard. A fiery blob came lumbering towards me through the bruised swim of my vision. Its limbs pulsed like something trapped in a bottle. It grew steadily, the clatter of flat footfalls snapping on and off, and slowed to a panting halt.

'Dan, what the fuck did I tell you? Where'd they go?'

'I didn't see.'

Craig bent over to ease his stitch, and motioned behind him to the blue light spinning outside the pub.

' 'S OK. Greg ran an' got the police. Said where you were. Landlord's 'aving an eppy 'cos he might get into trouble – Christ.' He drew a laughing breath. 'Make jam out of those shiners.'

I did my best to smile. The grey shoes weren't the white trainers I'd been expecting. Those came a minute later, when Greg joined us in the company of a surly, quietly disapproving officer.

'You all right, Dan?' Greg asked, nervously. He had a handkerchief pressed to his nose, some spots of blood on his shirt. We were silent while the officer said 'over' a lot into his walkie-talkie.

Craig heaved and spat through the gap in his teeth. Then he came forward, sat down and put a hand protectively round my waist, hauling my left arm across the back of his neck.

'Up we go,' he said.

Phantom Lovers

The day before I left home for Sussex University, my parents had a barbecue in the back garden. Frankie was there, with Carey, Karen and their sixteen-month-old daughter, Florence.

To keep Flo amused, I got my battered old toddle-truck down from the loft and emptied the slope of its poems and letters. The truck came with a drawstring bag full of alphabet bricks and dried moths, which Flo stuck on the ends of her gluey fingers and patted into the grass. When the moths were gone, Karen helped Flo transfer the bricks one by one from the truck to the slope, and back again.

'Where does the time go?' my mother wondered aloud. 'It doesn't seem – it could be just – well, days, just a few days, really – since we were all at Corsham together.'

She looked to Frankie for support.

'And no time at all since Daniel was born. And you had Carey, and came back from – from America. And now *they're* going away, too!'

Frankie frowned into her 'mint betty', a livid rum cocktail of my father's devising, finished with sprigs from a plant so rank not even the local cats deigned to pee on it.

'Doesn't seem possible, does it?' my mother ploughed on. 'Even starting their own – their own . . .'

Her voice trailed off, quenched by the hiss of meat and fat.

It was a warm evening. Below our boxy hillside plot – on one of the 'hencoop' estates built by Bath Development Corporation in the mid-1960s – the city's older terraces and mansard roofs glowed massively. Flo's pudgy fingers made long shadows, blotted out every few minutes by the hot-air balloons drifting overhead. Darkness fell and light returned as though the sky had learned to blink. Some ballooners, who couldn't have been more than a hundred feet away, waved at us and gave little screams of delight with each burst of the burner. The turps-scented smoke from our barbecue rose straight up to greet them.

Flo fell into the truck.

My mother tried again. 'No, but it really is. Isn't it?'

Frankie glanced up at me, sitting astride the first-floor window sill. Grandmotherhood had come early to her, in an unflattering range of henna tints and silver leggings, and she resented it. Her deckchair sagged; she grunted ungraciously through a straw.

'Is what?' I said, contemplating the drop from the sill, which was about twelve feet. When I was very small I'd jumped it, and sprained an ankle.

My mother sat beside the toddle-truck and picked at the grass.

'Amazing,' she said, teasing Flo with the letter X.

Karen – slimmer than I'd known her for a while, but top-heavy with all the feeding – leant over with a Y, vying for the baby's attention. From my vantage point, the two women looked like the mid-morning and mid-afternoon points of a dial, with Flo at noon.

The three generations hardly made eye contact, though where their arms interlaced in shadow an unspoken sympathy seemed to cool the memory of harsh words and unsought opinions.

While still a foetus, Karen's baby had been the focus of parental gossip, much of it predictably unpleasant. But when Florence Kelly Kale finally made it back from the Royal United Hospital, with her porthole-dark eyes and cirrus-light hair, there was suddenly no more chat about ruined youth, and a lot instead about the virtues of 'having them young'. Frankie Schumacher, harder to win over, declared Flo an unresponsive child ('she doesn't focus properly', 'her head's loose, I tell you') and hinted darkly about special needs.

'Go on. Which will you take? Mummy's or mine?' my mother coaxed, waving the X. 'Look at me. Mummy's or – mind the box, dear. You don't want to hurt your . . . no, good girl. Tha-at's it.'

Arms outstretched, Flo grabbed the brick and held it aloft; then gave it back, with a pout. My mother pulled down the corners of her mouth to make a sad face, and released them, laughing. Karen seemed pleased, too: a moment's play with an older woman meant more to her than the support of teachers and friends, on whose lips 'how are things?' and 'I'm so glad' somehow sounded so eager-to-be-gone.

Flo took both bricks and dropped them into the slope.

*

Frankie had called my mother in the middle of the night when she found out about the pregnancy, and got Carey – the son, the father – to drive her to our house. Five minutes later, we heard Carey being screamed at on the pavement outside and ordered home. My mother, crackling with static, wafted to the rescue in her brown Ann Summers nightie.

'I couldn't be on my own,' Frankie wept as the door opened.

'That's cool, Mom,' said a haggard Carey from the car. 'In six months we'll have company.' He tore off down the street, pursued by the flatulent echo of the exhaust. My mother shut the door firmly, and spoke to the quaking mass on the doormat.

'I want you to stop crying, Frances,' she said quietly. 'At once.'

I lingered at the door to my bedroom. The black-and-white checks of the linoleum in the passage squeaked as Frankie got to her feet. Her mascara and lacquer had run together. She looked like Alice Cooper.

'You were always unsympathetic, Jane,' she sobbed, reaching for the door. 'I could never get through to you.'

My mother's nostrils gaped. She slapped Frankie's hand down.

'I am *entirely* sympathetic,' she hissed, 'but it is *three* o'clock and Philip hasn't been well. I know it's a shock, but it's not something you can do anything about right now. It'll be better in the morning, you'll see. Carey will be all right. And so will Karen.'

'The bitch.'

'She is not a bitch.' My mother held up a warning finger. 'She's a perfectly . . . ordinary, nice girl. You've said so yourself.'

'I did? Come on, it was Karen or Borstal. How could I be pleased about Carey going out with one of the Kales? You know the rumours about that family. They all play the fucking banjo.'

'Honestly.'

'Swear to God. Ever wondered why Karen never speaks and can't look you straight in the eye?'

'You'll regret this.'

'Me? What have *I* got to regret?' Frankie lowered her voice incredulously. 'It's not my fault. I didn't *know* they were having sex. I thought they were upstairs watching *EastEnders*.'

My mother cleared her throat. 'Well, there you are. Have you seen it recently? Colin kissed his boyfriend last week.'

Dad thudded down the stairs, grey and drawn after a two-day migraine.

'Hey, hey, hey,' he said, in the vulnerable tones normally used to delegate the washing-up. 'What's going on?'

'Nothing,' my mother snapped. 'Carey's pregnant.'

'I see.'

'Sssshh. It's nothing to do with you.'

'. . .'

'Go back to bed.'

'All right.'

My mother led Frankie down to the kitchen. I followed in my striped dressing gown and made a small show of filling the kettle. Reflected in the window, the two friends clasped each other awkwardly.

Frankie unclasped suddenly and pointed a shaking finger. 'And how long have *you* known?'

'A week,' I said, which was the truth.

She looked at me with impotent fury.

'OK,' she said, beginning to cry again. 'I believe you.'

For a little while we were silent, until I said: 'It was an accident.'

Frankie banged the table with her ringed fist. 'You don't *say.*'

The breakfast spoons buzzed. 'All I meant was–'

'Well, let me tell you something–'

'Frances, stop,' said my mother tiredly.

'– about accidents.'

Frankie's earrings tinkled like far-off storm-warnings.

'There are accidents and accidents, Daniel. And there are excuses. Some situations in life have the *potential* to become accidents, but we try to *avoid* them by taking preventative measures.'

'You mean contraception.'

'Listen to him,' she snarled. 'Yeah, honey. Contraception. Condoms, the pill, prevention. Ways not to get AIDS. Foresight. The way if you and Gregory hadn't got those guys pissed at you, or even if you'd walked home another route, you wouldn't look like a panda now.'

'You're the expert,' I said, not quite knowing why.

Frankie's round face sickened.

'What do you mean?'

'*Sit* down, Daniel,' said my mother.

'No,' Frankie stammered, her eyelids twitching. 'I want to hear this.'

'Hear what?' I said. 'I'm just saying – you're the expert.'

The eyes narrowed. 'You got something to say?'

'No.'

'I sure hope not.'

My mother had been watching me closely during all of this, and now turned to Frankie, slumped next to her. And was silent.

'What?' said Frankie, blowing her nose. 'What, now?'

'Nothing.' My mother smoothed back her hair.

I made the tea.

*

Frankie sat apart in the underhang of the faded buddleia, and watched my father, across the lawn by the wall, talking to her brilliant son. Dad was asking him about his maths scholarship to Gonville and Caius College, getting the young genius's views on that guy in the motorized chair; whether he'd be taught by him, whether anyone *could* be taught by him, whether the guy could do anything, you know, physically, except drool. Though he had kids, didn't he? So yeah, maybe.

Dad prodded away at the coals with a paint-scraper, waving his other arm. Now and then, flames leaped up through the grill to singe his eyebrows and cauterize another stretch of the looped *montana*.

'Man, that's something else,' Dad enthused, nudging a blitzed chop. 'Jane, d'you hear that? About this new theory?'

'Yes, *very* interesting.'

'You heard it, then?'

'Yes,' said my mother, with achieved serenity. 'I'm listening.'

The chop joined others on a plate of char.

'I mean, like, *forget* Einstein,' Dad suggested recklessly. 'Hawkwind's gone way beyond all that. No boundaries, that's where it's at now – the No Boundary Condition of the Universe. I like the sound of that. Yeah. Break all the rules.'

He stood back from the forge, and wiped his forehead.

'Course, if you're talking about pushing back boundaries, then you get into the whole *aesthetic* of what space really is, I guess. Which is what art's been about this century, sort of. Picasso, Morandi. (Great painter, Morandi – get into him, man.) What constitutes form, distance, perspective.'

Carey managed the meekest 'hmm', and tapped his Bakelite rissole with diplomatic concern.

'Don't give him ideas, Carey,' my mother warned. 'Paintings with no boundaries – that's all we need. Where would we keep them? He's got the top floor of the house as it is.'

Dad ignored her – man, some people were so literal – and scanned the sky. Undimmed by years of innumeracy, his eyes glittered with speculative zeal. Surely the cold fusion of painting and physics lay within reach.

'So what does "no boundary" mean, then?' he asked. 'Like, space and time – they just go on for ever? Wow.'

Carey swallowed hard.

'Not exactly,' he said.

'Oh.' Dad dropped his head.

'But let's see . . .'

Carey tried to sound encouraging, like the special guest at a school fête when the prizes have run out.

'I think what *Hawking* means is that space-time is finite in extent but without an edge, so that it has no beginning or end.'

The lawn passed into shadow again.

'A bit like the surface of the earth or, uh, like that balloon, there.'

A red and blue British Gas planet sailed by overhead, its longitudinal stripes pulsing with thermal currents. The basket creaked; inside, a lone goggled figure refired the burner.

'Think of the Universe as a closed balloon,' Carey went on, 'only in four dimensions. Finite, continuous – measured in imaginary time, of course . . .'

'Of course,' Frankie murmured.

'Which means, uh . . .' He faltered, and fiddled with the arms of his spectacles. 'Actually, it's kinda difficult to explain.'

'Right, right,' Dad said quickly. 'I get what you're saying. I mean, we're clued into the same thing – though obviously, it's not my *field*.'

'Or mine,' Carey nodded, unable to conceal a hint of frustration at my father's category errors. 'I'm doing computer math, not physics.'

Despite several more tugs on the burner, each shorter than the last, the balloon directly above us appeared to be having difficulties gaining height. The long tongue of its shadow licked our party on the lawn, and we fell silent as it swung back and forth. To me, as usual, the shade distinguished itself from evening light only by its grainy blue cast, in which all flesh – faces, forearms, shins – glimmered suggestively. But the half-darkness had a more profound effect on the others, who seemed enlightened by its odd guarantee of confidentiality. Masks dropped, and I saw: Carey, stilled by the familiar sputter of escaping gas; my parents and Frankie, becalmed by long friendship; Karen and Flo, buoyant with answerable, biological need. I felt, too, a familiar twinge of envy, looking down. For good or ill, their faces radiated a truthfulness I wasn't meant to see, or share.

A breeze blew the low sun out from behind the descending balloon. Its sole occupant leaned out of his basket and shouted despairingly at other families on the lower slopes of Alpine Gardens. A woman yelled back: 'Don't go landin' on us, you bugger,' and the balloonist flapped his arms. People whistled from windows, pointing him towards Hedgemead Park, halfway down the hill. He was a hundred feet in the air at most and had to clear a bank of trees. My mother got up, shielding her eyes.

'I can't help thinking the universe was a lot simpler when I was young,' she said, 'before British Gas got hold of it.'

Karen produced a Polaroid camera and took a picture. There was a tangled thwack as the basket skimmed the crown of a Scots pine, followed by a chorus of 'oohs' and 'ahs' echoing up the hillside. Children were already clattering down to the park. In a few minutes, there would be sirens and neighbours shaking heads.

'Sure it was,' said Carey. 'It was much simpler. Want to know why?'

My mother turned to him with a broad smile.

'Entropy,' she said, stroking one of her earlobes.

Carey laughed with astonishment. 'All *right*.'

Dad coughed on a bit of sausage, and had to steady himself against the wall. Frankie snorted quickly into her tonic.

'Judith Hann was talking about it on *Tomorrow's World*,' explained my mother, and turned back to watch the balloon set behind the trees.

Karen took another picture, this time of Florence imitating the adults' thoughtfulness, standing arms adrift, head tilted to one side.

My mother bristled with the evening's first cold draught.

'Oh, you'd be surprised what I know,' she said.

*

At the police station, they took a wildly misspelled statement and ordered a squad car to take me to hospital. Greg, still dabbing at his nose, offered to come along, but Craig said, 'Nah, you've had enough excitement for one night,' and sent him home in a taxi. Then he turned to me, looked at my half-closed left eye and tapped the bridge of my nose with his forefinger. Threads of pain, like the whiplash crackle of an approaching train, fanned out across my forehead. I flinched.

''S all right, Dan,' Craig said, in a voice I didn't fully recognize. 'Not going to hurt you.'

The arresting officer held open the front door of the car

and I lowered myself in. Before I could object, Craig had got in the back.

'Mind if I come along?' he said to the driver, who searched for the right monosyllabic reply and settled for a shrug of the shoulders.

Casualty was unusually empty for a Friday night. A yawning houseman promptly forwarded me to X-Ray and I had some eye tests, after which the ophthalmologist, or whoever passed for one at such short notice, made a phone call. He explained to me that it was probably all down to bruising and minor vessel damage, but that the tests for my right eye – the one I could still see out of – had produced very odd readings, and that I'd need another examination in a week or so. For some reason this tipped me over the edge, and by the time I got back to Casualty, clutching my appointment card, no injuries to report apart from a hairline fracture in my nose, I was brimming with tears.

The waiting area greeted me with posters and paranoiac impertinence: 'Are you worried about Drugs?'; 'Worried? About AIDS and the law?'; 'Have you had your Flu jab? It's not too late!'; 'What is Hypertension?' But the harsh strip-lighting and broken vending machines only made Craig's fraternal concern more comforting.

He sat in the middle of the room with his feet apart, looking down at the floor, hands clasped, thumbs weaving and whirling. There were the usual ownerless copies of Car Hire Weekly on a low table next to him, and a couple of dark stains on nearby seats. (Dried blood, Ribena?) On the other side of the room, a young girl with a thumb mummified in pinkly blotched toilet roll had cried herself breathless, and now sat in her mother's lap, gulping. There was no one else in the room.

'So,' Craig said. 'Did they say anything?'

I sniffed. 'Not really. Everything's fine. Just bruises. Got to have a check-up, but apart from that, nothing. They gave me this.'

I showed him a night-patch for my eye. Craig nodded. Then he nudged me with his leg, inclined his head and smiled.

'Not the doctors,' he said. 'The posh twats.'

A cream-and-brown drinks dispenser whirred into life.

'The ones who hit you. Did they say anything?'

'Like what?' I said, stung. 'I hit the deck, for Christ's sake. How the fuck would I know if they said anything?'

'All right, all right.'

Craig bit his lip and scratched behind his ear. He seemed undecided about something, perhaps not quite sober.

'I thought they might have said something, that's all. At the start – called you a name, anything.'

'Why?'

'Well . . .' Craig squirmed. 'Maybe 'cos you were with Greg. You being so . . . close an' all. Nutters like Burns-Wilson–'

He paused, letting the inference draw itself slowly, like a thorn.

The shoe-smeared linoleum was suddenly of feverish interest. I stared at the reflected lighting and felt wet shivers of denial trickle under my arms and down the backs of my legs. My left, bad eye throbbed.

'They just jumped us, OK?'

'Right.'

Craig ran both hands through his hair and rolled his shoulders. His neck, effervescent with freckles, filled a large yellow cotton collar with a tie-button at the back.

' 'Cos nutters like Burns-Wilson,' he said again, ' 'ave it in for people like you, Daniel.'

My first name hung in the air.

'And if they didn't say anything,' Craig carried on, his words slurring as they gathered meaning and momentum, 'then I reckon you should. To Greg. Clear the air, yeah?'

I told Craig that I'd already given the police a statement, and he laughed. I asked him, in an old man's falsetto, what he found so funny.

Craig thought about that for a bit, and pressed his thigh against mine. Then, for the second time that night, he put his arm around my shoulder. I protested my ignorance of what-ever it was he thought I was supposed to say, but lost my thread almost immediately. A whole lexicon of innocent, artful deflections shrivelled on my lips.

After a minute or so, Craig said: 'He can only say no, can't he?'

I was silent.

'To whatever,' he added, with calculated vagueness, 'you suggest.'

The absurdity, I thought, of asking Craig to make himself plain.

'Are you saying . . .' I began, and pulled at my shirt to free it from the dampness of my lower back. It struck me that my unlikely brother-confessor was not even being particularly insightful.

'Go on,' he said.

'Are you implying' – the idea was to make it sound like a mystical revelation – 'that I *fancy* Greg?'

Craig tried to disguise his snigger as a sneeze.

'You think I'm gay, don't you?' I said, with a stab at indignation – but my voice was so strangled only the middle two words made sense.

Craig sat up and looked at me as squarely as the gallon of

export lager swilling around his veins would allow. His nose had grown flatter and wider over the years, which suited the butcher-boy proportions of his face. He still smelled of the pub, with its peculiar half-life emanations of sugar, alcohol, fags and cheap aftershave.

'I dunno if you're anything until you try,' he said.

This was pretty flattening. The voice of youthful experience struck an especially scornful note – beyond the follies of the adolescent crush, new born to adult candour. I shrank from the nearness of Craig's leg, and tried to move his arm. So he caught my neck in a stranglehold, tight enough for me to feel the confusion of pulse and fabric.

'All I know,' he said forgivingly, 'is that you're mental about him.'

'Ow,' I said.

Craig interpreted this as a question and sighed.

' 'Cos, why else'd you hang round with him? I mean, I'm no fuckin' Einstein – and, yeah, you're both nippy on your pins – but you 'aven't got anything else in common, 'ave you?'

'I don't care,' I said, miserably.

'Yes, you do. You stare at him. I've seen you. Can't take your eyes off him at Film Club. Don't think I don't notice.'

'Been staring at me, then, have you?'

Craig laughed firmly. 'Nah, got past all that.'

He sniffed once, aware of having let something slip.

'Anyway' – a pause and a scratch – 'I don't fancy blokes.'

He bowed his head reflectively. The girl with the injured thumb left the room with her mother, who glanced back at us as she slipped out through the sliding doors. The daughter's descant drifted back to us, 'Mummy, why are those men . . .' and was cut off.

Craig lifted his face, grinning.

'Though I 'ad a phase, y'know.'

He crossed his eyes and touched the tip of his nose with his tongue. It was the cue for an enquiry I was too tired and sheepish to make.

'Yeah,' he drawled. 'Used to come on a biscuit an' that, with the lads at ATC – before I met Sandra.'

'You used to *what*?' I squeaked, suddenly awake.

Craig waved it away.

'Kids' stuff,' he said. 'You sit in a circle and wank on to a McVitie's. Last one to spunk up has to eat it.'

In the distance, an ambulance mocked and jeered.

'You and who else?' I demanded, jealously. Why the hell hadn't I joined the Air Training Corps? All those years doing drama and learning the easy ones out of *Forty-Eight Preludes and Fugues* when I could have been meeting like-minded patriots.

'Well, Greg for a start,' said Craig. 'Always took him ages – played to lose, I reckon. And Bruce, and a couple of tossers from Culverhay.'

I nodded, as if chatting on Monday morning about so-and-so's weekend, though it was a while before I could speak. The visibility of my affections – the invisibility of others' – was a humiliation of imponderable depth. I could see Greg dancing in a Welsh thunderstorm, Carey shaking his head from the heaving recesses of the Underground.

'Greg wasn't in the ATC,' I said.

Craig rubbed his chin. 'Er, no. Not officially.'

'Nobody ever asked me to join.'

'True,' Craig agreed, slowly, giving my neck a light squeeze.

'Why not?'

'Probably because we thought you was a poof.'

I frowned, and clicked my tongue as if contemplating a move at chess.

'Who have you been talking to about me?' I said, at last.

'Karen, mostly. At Sandra's.'

Craig looked away.

'And Carey?' I asked.

He shook his head noncommittally.

'Nah.'

I waited. The drinks dispenser stopped purring, and the ambulance wailed louder, nearer and nearer, swamping the forecourt.

'Genius, though, in't he?' Craig said.

'Yes.'

'Wrongfooted the lot of us.'

'Yes.'

'I like Karen,' he said, on a quick intake of breath.

'Good,' I said bitterly through my hands, anger welling up inside. 'And she likes you, I'm sure.'

Craig withdrew his arm halfway, pinching me on the neck, and kissed me. His lips were soft; he used the tip of his tongue.

'Tell you a secret,' he said.

*

The secret was that he'd been sleeping with Karen as well as her sister, his official girlfriend. He'd had to tell someone. He felt bad – bad about two-timing Sandra, bad about leading Karen on, and bad (no, really) about Carey. He could trust me; I'd had a secret of my own. What did I think?

I said that I thought Weston bus stop (just outside the hospital) was a bit public, and that it was time for me to go home and explain things – the eyes, the fight – to my parents. But they'd be in Bristol most of tomorrow afternoon, at the

Arnolfini arts centre, so maybe we could meet then and continue our discussion? Before he went, Craig made me swear I wouldn't ever let on about Karen, so I swore.

When he came round the next day, Craig told me straight off that he'd reached a decision. I prepared myself for the worst – last night was a mistake, I had to forget everything – and tried not to take in too many details of my soon-to-be phantom lover: the ginger-blonde hair flattened by sleep on one side, the thickness of the eyebrows and the lightness of the lashes, the gap in the front teeth, the pale width of his biceps jutting out of a blue and yellow tennis shirt, the erotic constraint of those awful Burton trousers with their uneven pleats. The white socks and grey shoes.

Then I heard him saying that he'd spoken to Karen that morning and that they'd agreed to stop shagging; that it wasn't right or fair, all things considered. And that Karen thought Greg was now definitely straight, so it probably wasn't worth me confronting him, was it?

'No.'

We spent the afternoon in bed.

I was all elbows and knees to begin with, but Craig ignored my mistakes, or perhaps wasn't aware of them, and turned out to be gratifyingly difficult to displease. I thought, during and after, of how it was I'd managed to overlook him so completely, and of how his ugliness in memory, as a podgy thirteen-year-old bully, made his adult bulk with its blue veins and sweaty embraces all the more appealing. I tried to make a mental note of the many firsts that afternoon, marvelling at each – the first deep kiss, the first stroke, the first taste, the first lick – and soon gave up. Someone was whispering in my ear, telling me not to think so much. That I remember, of course. That and the reply: 'Ouch, my nose.'

There wasn't much mess. We didn't fuck – the taboo was well and truly entrenched on that one, even by 1986 – but we did swallow. (Craig insisted that this was only practical, as my duvet was a receptive dark blue.) And then – when we'd washed our cocks, patted them dry and snogged in front of the bathroom mirror – we got dressed and agreed to do it again after Film Club. (See you, then. Yeah, see you.)

I watched Craig lope off through Alpine Gardens, his hands in his pockets. He didn't turn to wave, which was worrying.

On Thursday, I couldn't wait for *Babette's Feast* to end. As an incitement to lubricity, the film had been well chosen, though the slick truffles and trickling yolks of the last reel gave me an erection I was not confident enough to enjoy. Niceties of gesture plagued me. Would it be natural, afterwards, for me to 'ignore' Craig? Or could I risk a flippant greeting – a coded thank you, perhaps, for escorting me to the RUH? Might he find an excuse to stay behind and help clear up? Or would we have to leave separately and meet somewhere else? And where would that be?

We had coffee as usual in the sixth-form block, and there were plenty of jokes – sympathetic ones, mostly – at my expense. My left eye was open again, but the blueberries-in-custard marbling effect of the bruise had spread across my face to form a mask at which everyone – even Craig, from a distance – winced. Greg had a milder discoloration on one side of his nose, and a forced ease in his manner that unnerved me. He was with a willowy girl from the High School, who I remembered seeing in the row behind us at the cinema and who clearly remembered me. 'Melody' introduced herself with the news that our chief assailant from King Edward's, Tom Burns-Wilson, had been suspended.

'Let's hope it's from something nice and high,' I said.

Melody laughed hoarsely.

'Ha, ha, that's right – Gregory told me you were the funny one.'

Greg blushed.

'Don't say it like that!' he tutted, shuffling his feet, as though Melody's clunking insinuation were a love-token too generously bestowed.

I smiled and offered them the tray of biscuits. Melody declined, but Greg said 'Mmm,' cramming two digestives at once into his mouth. Above the noise of general chat I heard someone say 'You're *joking*,' (it sounded like Craig), answered by Carey's excited nasal protest, 'Am not, it's true,' and confirmed by Karen's growling mezzo. I stared ahead, dumbly.

'Wha'?' Greg said, his mouth full.

Melody gave her sporty escort a look of mild disgust, and tugged at his sleeve. They went out hand in hand, though Greg pursed his eyebrows at me enquiringly as he left. Carey and Karen caught up with them on the threshold and surged past, giggling and yelping, into the night.

'Oi, Zorro,' said a voice behind me. 'Got your horse?'

Stony-faced, Craig handed me the four cans of film we had to pass on the next day to a society in Bristol.

'Take this lot to the car, then, an' I'll give you a lift,' he said.

I ran to the parking lot inside the school gates and waited. The air was tense and acrid with the promise of an early frost. After five minutes, a solid-looking figure morphed out of the sixth-form building at the other end of the driveway and jogged heavily towards me, hands thrust deep into the side pockets of a padded jacket. His determined progress was ghosted with fiery pixels, like a badly tuned TV, so that I seemed to see

Craig not just as he was, but as – an instant before – he had been.

We drove the few hundred yards out of the school grounds into Alexandra Park, and stopped at the head of Beechen Cliff. Four hundred feet below us, through a gap in the trees, the pointillist contours of Bath glittered from Twerton in the west to Bathampton in the far east. In a room somewhere on the left-hand side of this map, Sandra Kale, the reformed tart and dental technician, glanced crossly at her watch.

I unclicked Craig's seat-belt and squeezed his thigh. He gave a contented snort, but his hands were unnegotiable and stayed fixed on the steering-wheel. We kissed and he relaxed, returning my kisses cautiously at first and then with unattributable intentness until, at some much later point, angled across the front seats like a mountaineer in difficulties, his head nodding in my lap, he snorted again and sat up.

I asked him what was wrong, but of course got no reply. Craig wiped his lips and pushed his sappy hard-on back into his trousers. Mine twanged foolishly in space a minute more. Stricken, I trailed my fingers over his crotch and was gently, firmly repulsed.

'That'll do for now, I reckon,' Craig whispered to himself while he started the car.

'Will it?' I said.

He laughed and shook his head as though dealing with a five-year-old.

'Yeah.'

Outside my house, he turned off the engine and studied my face, which was trying hard to save itself. My mouth made an odd shape. His voice, when it came, had a guilty, hopeful tremor.

'You don't think I'm a cunt, do you, Dan?'

'No,' I said. 'I think you're–'

'That's good.' He screwed up his eyes. 'Friends, then?'

'And a bit more.'

Still smiling, I groped for the door.

The next day Carey rang and told me that Karen was pregnant.

★ ★ ★

The balloon went down at about eight in the evening, and Greg Bray arrived a few minutes later, bursting with the news.

'D'you see it?' he shouted, punching the air with his fist.

'Oh yes,' said my mother, placidly. 'We all saw it. He only just missed the trees – I hope he's all right.'

Greg's ears went bright red and the cluster of spots on his chin, which Carey and I attributed to the hormone-scrambling excesses of weight-training, shone angrily.

'Not the git in the park,' he raged. 'Ben Johnson! The hundred metres – he's smashed the world record. There's highlights – now.'

Greg ran indoors and turned on the television.

'How do you get highlights out of nine seconds?' Dad wondered, as the Seoul Olympic stadium zipped to life and cheered from our sitting room. Flo clapped her hands and flung the letter F at Frankie.

Greg was transported.

'Look at that! Look at him go – ohhh, fuck. That's *beautiful*, man,' he roared. 'Nine point seven nine – ninepointsevennine. Now tell me that isn't fucking magic. Go-oo on, John-son! Yeeess!!'

My mother, tipsy after three glasses of boxed wine and

sentimental enough to pardon the bad language, put her face to the window.

'You know,' she said, pointing through the glass at an ecstatic Gregory Bray, 'it's so nice to have friends. And so nice that you're all so different.'

Frankie's eyes crossed. Dad left the barbecue in Carey's more capable hands and slunk inside to show sporting solidarity with Greg.

'Because the friends you make now' – my mother said to her dark, unlistening reflection – 'can be friends you keep for the rest of your life.'

She tidied her hair.

Her gloss on friendship, a typical mix of accidental truth and wishful thinking, was of course unanswerable; one by one we went in to join Dad and Greg, leaving her outside with Carey.

Like the teacher who extracts the sad promise of a visit from her favourite pupils, she must have known that the evening's intimacy was already a function of memory for its departing guests. Within twenty-four hours, I would be in a shoebox room in Falmer, sifting through flyers for the 1988 Freshers' Fair, and Carey would be packing for Cambridge, where Karen and Flo would join him in a few weeks.

Greg wouldn't be going anywhere, of course – not just because he wasn't a university candidate (he failed those retakes), but because he loved the city and saw no reason to leave; besides, he had a flat in Norfolk Row to look after, and a good job as a deputy manager at the Sports and Leisure Centre. 'I don't get it,' he used to say, when Carey and I were brattishly comparing UCCA choices in the common room. 'Why d'you want to go hundreds of miles away to university, when you can go to the one here and be with your mates?'

Guffawing, we accused him of being small-minded, though in fact his stranded vow of loyalty touched a nerve. What did our decision to leave Bath imply, if not that the friends we'd made there were no longer a good enough reason for us to stay? For Greg, it was different. For him, the fact of friendship had been decided long ago with a mature disregard for the inevitable betrayals of time. It was unexamined and irrevocable – a bond that claimed certain rights and privileges free of explanation. He'd left school early in 1987, after splitting up with Melody, and disappeared for two months. No one knew where he was; his mad, shouting father never returned our calls. Then, the day after Flo was born, Greg turned up at the RUH with flowers and a Get Well Soon card. I told him the same evening that I was gay – and that I wanted him, badly. He said, 'Not with the zits on my back, you don't.'

*

Karen put Flo in the carrier at ten, and Carey opened the front door. I clapped him on the back and kissed Karen and Frankie. Greg shook hands with everyone. My mother linked arms rather forcefully with my father, who muttered something about tennis elbow.

A chunky, uniformed figure lurched so suddenly from the shadows between parked cars that Karen nearly dropped her sleeping cargo. Craig Spillings apologized and adjusted his skewed tie.

'How's my baby girl?' he said.

Winter Sculpture

According to Jane Moorcock's terrifying, and ultimately persuasive, headmistress, Bath Academy of Art at Corsham was the 'only' teacher training college for her in the country. While most provincial art schools of the early 1960s still coaxed their students to produce pastiche Cézannes, Corsham bore aloft the standard of education-through-art, forged in the Bauhaus and decorated by innovators from St Ives to New York.

'It is years ahead of its time,' said Jane's headmistress, a former student. 'The Academy is full of genius-adventurers, as you'll see.'

But, as Jane did see, Corsham's adventurers were also curiously out of time, being for the most part straight out of Rider Haggard. Sculpture was taught by Claudia Minnelli, six foot tall with waist-length black hair, who seemed to spend most of her weekends back in Lake Garda defending her fencing title (Champion of Italy). Don Muir, who ran the pottery but also taught life-drawing, kept 'prize-winning' birds of prey (he'd lost a finger to an angry kite). And Rosamond Kelp had scaled the Andes after the war to help a number of undiscovered tribes with their weaving. She had the poncho and slipper-socks to prove it.

Jane was impressed – and by the middle of her second year,

slightly fatigued. Did they do anything trivial, these geniuses? Did they make tea, or unblock the toilet? Were they ever uninspired? Was it a coincidence that the Academy's best painter, William Scott, who'd taught there in the 1950s, was also the least exotic? (His influence told in Corsham's still-life classes, where you drew the same things every week: pots and pans. Maybe a fish-head, or a pear in season.)

The days were long – a four-mile trek to Beechfields every morning for classes, down to Corsham Court for lunch, back to Beechfields, then home to Monks Park balancing drawing boards, oil-boxes and thread-bags on the handlebars of a decrepit Hercules – and the work was hard. But hard work in such a setting had to compete with a sense of unreality. Seminars were conducted in the Chinese Room, stuffed with rosewood lacquer cabinets and eighteenth-century hanging silks. The huge gardens – the Academy's playground – had been landscaped by Capability Brown. There were butteries and farms on the estate; stable blocks, box-tree mazes, ha-has, lakes, meadows, fluttering paper-bark maples, oaks grave as distant thunder. At the invitation of the principal, the young Jacqueline du Pré gave cello recitals in the State Room. Philip Larkin and Ted Hughes read their poetry in the library. There were rumours of a vast wine cellar. In front of the Gatehouse, Lord Methuen's peacocks preened and fanned.

Too many of the other students, Jane felt, took all this for granted. How so many of them could spend so much time discussing art, agonizing with the tutors about Pasmore and Piaget and Montessori, analysing the beauty of flowing white light on the figure or the suppressed dimensionality of flat shapes, without hearing a satirical echo, was beyond her. Look around you, she wanted to shout. Be a bit grateful; stop *going on*.

But you weren't allowed to stop, not at Corsham. Because going on, no matter how dispiriting the process, defined the Academy's work ethic. It was essential to go on; cowardly to stop. And so the encouragement you received itself became discouraging, Jane found, as though to be aware of one's limitations in a particular discipline were a bad thing.

Everything mattered, at Corsham. Everything you did – and did wrong – was important: mistakes, botched drawings, breaking a mould, collapsing pots after hours on the wheel. 'Photograph all – *all* what you do, Jenn,' Claudia Minnelli trilled one day, as Jane struggled with the plaster on her chicken-wire armature. 'Sometime,' Claudia sang out, a smile mopping up her raisin-black eyes, 'the best idea – it come yarrs after you go wrong the farrst time. Yes, I mean it – yarrs and yarrs! This I know.'

Jane pointed out that no one she knew owned a camera, and was about to explain the impracticality of loaning out the Academy's one Kodak to each member of the sculpture class, when the Champion of Italy hissed, 'Ai, ai, ai,' at her, and swished away.

*

Jane Moorcock didn't really get on with the other students at Corsham – a state of estrangement she shared with Frances Schumacher, the daughter of a USAF medic on the nearby Colerne airbase. The difference was that Jane enjoyed her own company, whereas Frances – the victim of a lonely, peripatetic post-war childhood – did not. The light in Frances' room at Monks Park was on hours after everyone else had gone to bed, and she was usually the first into the refectory the next morning. At dinner, she killed conversations by smiling and staring.

Jane felt sorry for Frances, but found it hard to empathize. Her own upbringing had been secure. After her mother died, her father raised her in the absent parent's image, and she learned to be self-reliant. Kenneth Moorcock spent every day cutting and sewing in an airless Whitechapel rat-trap. The only time he raised his voice was in private frustration with customers who failed to settle bills. Jane drew, and stitched capably. At thirteen, she won a scholarship to Highbury School for Girls, where she was teased about living in a basement off the Holloway Road.

So far from being embarrassed by her father or her address, Jane was, of course, proud of both. But pride, if anything, intensified her humiliation, and distilled it into a kind of righteous anger. She blushed when taunted, incensed by the unanswerable volume of a mockery she didn't respect.

At Corsham, she was criticized and misunderstood in different ways – though it was always the misunderstanding that rankled. Jane knew, for example, that Claudia Minnelli had got it all wrong. Her cheeks burned not because she resented the (true) suggestion that her plaster bust was a dud, but because she saw no way of making it better. Talent marked you out early on, Jane believed, and it was a corresponding sign of maturity to acknowledge its absence. If it had been an etching – a medium she liked and worked well in – she would have been anxious to put things right. But this was sculpture, for whose forms she had no feel. And in which her lumpen offerings were as unwanted as the helpful comments and murmurous praise they called forth.

As Claudia moved away to hum approval over a classmate's shoulder, Frances Schumacher sidled up to take her place.

'Never mind, Jane,' she whispered deafeningly. 'I think it looks great – animal-birdy, kind of like a Frink. Am I right?'

Jane ground her teeth.

There was a spattered art magazine on her trestle-top, open at a double-page spread on 'The Frink Effect'. Frances's loud attribution was therefore unremarkable – and inaccurate, because the dome of Jane's 'head' looked nothing like anything by Frink. It was horribly indented at the back and again below the moue of the overshaped lips, as though an appalling cancer had gnawed its way from cortex to chin.

Jane's nerve-ends screamed at the consoling touch of Frances's hand on her shoulder. She picked up an encrusted, leather palette-knife and stabbed her ill-favoured handiwork in the eye.

'Yikes,' said Frances.

A drumbeat pulse in her temples made Jane reckless.

'I'm not going to be a sculptress,' she said with force.

Five of the other students in the studio looked up. The sixth, Philip Rathbone, the Giacometti-thin prankster who'd sprained his ankle falling out of the Monks Park horse chestnuts, paid no attention. At the far end of the army hut, Claudia smiled broadly and defensively.

'I'm going to teach *children*,' Jane went on, 'in a *school*.' The studio darkened with disillusionment. 'And how many schools does anyone here know with sculpture on the curriculum?'

She felt mean as she said it – insincerely philistine. The hairs on her forearm stood up, and she shivered. There was a nasty hush, broken only by the chink-chink of bottles in a crate outside the hut, which made Jane think of warm interiors and the distant, comforting clatter of an early morning London milk-round.

Frances walked over to the windows on her side of the studio.

'Is it just me,' she said, 'or has it got real cold?'

Still shivering, Jane joined Frances at the window and picked at a strip of wizened putty in the window frame. When she let it go, the chalky sliver carried on rattling. An invisible hand thumped other panes. The two girls stood still a moment longer, listening to the knock-knock of winter, staring out over two acres of fallow ground at the copse that separated Beechfields from the rest of the Corsham estate. The trees groped each other in bony clusters, sharp-edged against a quilted sky. In front of her, on the hut's cracked concrete dais, Jane noted a few skirling snowflakes. Absent-mindedly, she tapped a private greeting to the trees beyond.

But·when she looked again, they were gone.

The cloud seethed like water filling an airlock; it spread and billowed, and rushed at the two day-dreamers before they were even half aware of its size and density. They stepped back from the glass and put their hands up. At first, the snow slapped at the window with the lazy insistence of a child throwing wet sand. And then the glass was glass no more, but a slab of clay, as the blizzard buried the hut in its gross fury.

*

The wind was soon spent. The snow remained, falling fast and so thickly that snow and sky were limitlessly confused. Dougall Voss fought his way down to Beechfields in a tractor to deliver grit; by the time he arrived, the roads had closed behind him. Jane, Frances and all the other women were marooned in the men's dormitory.

This was entertaining enough for one night, but the weather worsened. It stopped snowing in the early dawn and the temperature dropped. Pipes froze and burst; the students lagged the rest with sheets and blankets. Then they ran out of blankets, and Frances's father made his first appearance at Corsham in an army carrier loaded with USAF woollens and boots – and three cases of fiery gutrot. It snowed again. It froze again. Insensible with cold, a hungry crow flapped crookedly from the copse towards Beechfields on the second morning, and fell to earth with a stricken 'caw'. The radio, like a voice from the past, said that the whole of England was cut off. It was the same in 1947, said a farmer. And then it was worse.

A lull of sorts came at the end of January, after three weeks of snow. For five days the skies were clear while hibernating locals peered suspiciously at one another in the metallic morning light, mistrustful of the sound of running water (which they knew meant flooded drains and leaking tiles and thatch). Armed with shovels and spades, villagers and students joined forces with Colerne servicemen in an effort to reopen the roads. The main stretch to Rudloe and Box Hill was soon clear, and everyone cheered the first coal truck in from Bath. Other hedged-in tracks, leading to hamlets like Rudwick or Chapel Chauster, were harder to unblock, being too narrow for a plough and so deep-set between fields that there was nowhere to offload the snow and ice which filled them. None of the outlying farm cottages in the area had telephones (most lines were down in any case), but smoking chimneys were a good sign. And Archie Grey, a veteran navy signalman holed up in Botleaze Grange, flashed a reassurance one evening with his torch. The coded message ran: 'All cosy here. Worried about Norcot.'

Less than a mile to the south of Rudwick lay Norcot End – a brace of quarrymen's cottages hemmed in by Norcot chalk-pit and the tumulus of Cat's Hill. Both were in a state of disrepair and slated for demolition by the county council, but only one was empty. To the other clung Miss Diana King, a retired schoolteacher, and her docile companion Mrs Imelda Tibbs (widowed). They were loners, according to the landlord of Corsham's Pack Horse Inn, rarely glimpsed except on Sundays: 'They bides 't home, an' they goes t' church. 'Tis all.'

Smoke could still be seen rising from Norcot End – but it was agreed that the two old ladies wouldn't have the supplies for a long cold spell, and the prospect of more snow made their deliverance a priority.

On the fifth day of the lull, the 'volunteers' were joined by firemen from Chippenham. A number of students, Jane noticed disapprovingly, had already slunk back to Beech-fields or to Monks Park after a day of digging and shovelling. Dougall Voss, of course, stayed, as did Pete Zender, Philip Rathbone, Jane and, perhaps less usefully, Frances. Zender was impressive, blithely lifting fallen trees out of the road while Dougall and Philip – pale and pinched – tunnelled away on either side. Jane helped at the back of the V-shaped team, clearing away glaciated rubble and spreading grit, which was itself half-frozen. She paid as little attention as possible to Frances' background gush about '*real* blizzards back home', but was powerless to deflect those questions that hailed her directly.

'Jane, the guys. Don't they look cute in their duffels?' Frances chirped. 'Kinda like the seven dwarves. Don't they? Jane?'

Pete Zender stood up and squared his shoulders in massive reproof. It was the kind of remark you could neither dignify with an answer nor answer with dignity. Jane kept her voice low.

'As long as they're warm, that's the main thing.'

'I guess. They're not waterproof though, are they?' Frances

said, patting a snowball into shape. 'Philip and Dougall look pretty darn wet to me.'

Jane cast another handful of grit on the advancing path and Philip Rathbone threw an accusing glance over his hunched shoulder, which Frances met with vacant sympathy. Along with the sweaters and boots for the rest of the students, Frances' father, Colonel Schumacher, had brought his daughter a man's waxed leather coat and oilskin gloves to keep out the cold. The coat was too long and the gloves too big; they would have fitted either Philip or Dougall, but the appropriate gesture had not occurred to her. On the contrary, as kin to their general benefactor, Frances felt obscurely entitled to the group's thanks.

The firemen, properly kitted out in all-weather donkey jackets, burrowed hard and fast towards the clump of trees separating the two cottages from Norcot chalk-pit. Where it passed the first huddled tree-trunks the sleeve of the track broke up into ruts and roadlike patches of grey, which at least looked navigable. Then, while they were still three hundred yards from the copse, in the mid-afternoon, Dougall noticed that the plume of smoke from Diana King's chimney stack, just beyond the trees, had disappeared. Yellow-grey clouds pressed down on the wintered canopy and threatened a storm. The leftover brew in the bottom of the group's enamel mess mugs turned to brown ice, and the digging took on a new, silent urgency.

At four o'clock, a wind sprang up from the east, chasing day into darkness; squalls of snow sought out cheeks and fingertips where threadbare gloves had given way. Jane was wearing stockings and socks underneath a long woollen skirt which smelt faintly, she knew, of old ladies, but the cold penetrated every layer, got under her (borrowed) Dunhill overcoat and fisherman's jumper, needled its way into goose-pimpled skin. After ten minutes she could no longer feel her feet inside her wellington boots. The weight of the moraine she carried out of the main path made no impression on her, and she failed to mark Frances' unannounced departure until Dougall, chancing to look back, made a stabbing gesture in the direction of Rudwick.

Jane turned around. There, in the middle of the elver-thin road, halfway up the white, undulating slope, she could just see Frances' lonely, tottering figure, disappearing into the storm. Dougall broke off from the right flank of diggers and took Jane by the arm.

'Where's she to, then?' he bellowed.

'Home, I expect,' Jane screamed back. 'Good idea.'

Dougall cupped his hands over his mouth, and shook his head, caught in the face by a spray of silicate flakes. He spluttered, coughed deeply, and Jane reached out to clap him soundly on the back. The boisterous contact surprised them both, made them shy.

'We should all stick together,' Dougall shouted, and instantly regretted the 'all'. He looked closely at Jane while she stamped her feet and pulled a dark blue beanie over her flattened curls.

In half an hour it was dark, and the 'fire' chief called a halt. There were torches in the truck parked outside the Rudwick Arms, but the snow was driving too hard for the team to make any headway. The professionals opted to sit it out in the pub until the wind dropped, and agreeably suggested that the students join them there.

On any other day at sundown, the light from the drawing room at Norcot End should have been visible through the trees, an eerie glow cross-hatched with trunks and branches.

That evening, the cottages were lit only by the sightless glare of the storm, in whose eye the whole of Wiltshire, it seemed to Jane, was one vast, rolling white.

During the fifteen-minute hike back to Rudwick, she found herself walking – leaning into the wind – between Dougall and Philip. Dougall was quiet now that the opportunity to be useful had passed – doubly reserved, perhaps, in the presence of the only female in college he admired, and a man he had already identified as a romantic competitor. His jealousy was perhaps premature. Unlike Dougall, Philip could hardly have been called a handsome man: he was tall and life-threateningly gaunt and his fine, sandy-brown hair, which had begun to recede in adolescence or even earlier, now clung to the sides and middle-back of his head much as samphire clings to an otherwise barren cliff-face. His eyes were a snaky green, his skin too taut and dry, with a hint of glass paper about it, to be called youthful. Worse, the open-necked shirts and straggly sweaters he wore retained the whiff of panatella cigars which he smoked all day long. You might have said he stank. And yet there were, undeniably, compensations. For Philip Rathbone had unusual charm, an ear for voices – particularly the young caretaker's guttural grumble – and an infectious, after-hours cackle in the pub that drew glances from other tables, where people often found themselves laughing in amazed sympathy. He was also, Jane conceded privately, one of the few genuinely talented students of his year. In class, you could tell from the grudging vacuity of their remarks ('not bad', 'coming on', 'hmm, yes') that Philip's teachers were impressed with (depressed by?) his facility. Don Muir lectured about the need to find the 'animate line' in life drawing. But the more telling bottom line was that, by comparison, Muir's own productions (on sale at the end-of-year 'open') were a lifeless soup of flowing contours and graded tints. At the end of a sitting, it was always Philip's charcoal ravings the models asked to see – to have. So he gave most of them away.

The wind eased a little as the rescue party neared the top of the rise that planed back towards Rudwick. The flocky snow grew thicker, settling in clumps on bowed heads and shoulders.

Philip stopped and looked jerkily about him. A filthy scarf swaddled his neck and a misshapen balaclava obscured one eye.

'Where's Nitty Nora?' he said.

Jane smiled in spite of herself. Frances had earned the nickname during her first teaching practice in a primary school in Bradford-on-Avon, where the local nit nurse had been pleased to pronounce the school free of infestation, with one open-mouthed, adult exception.

'Gone on ahead,' Jane explained.

Philip blinked. 'That's not like Nora,' he said slowly, gauging the seriousness of the situation. 'Not like Nora,' he repeated, 'to show initiative. Are you sure we haven't left her in a drift?'

'Yes.'

She held his gaze, a snowflake in her lashes.

'Sure?'

'Yes.'

This was how he did it, Jane realized. Other men fumbled with car doors, bought expensive tickets or flowers. Philip just talked rubbish until he got the response he wanted.

'Are you quite sure?'

'I'm absolutely positive.'

The balaclava twitched. Philip inserted a mittened finger into one nostril, wiggled and withdrew it.

'Nitty Nora,' he said, surveying the green end-product with a connoisseur's disdain. 'Nasal explorer.'

A giggle slipped out, which Jane quashed with a sigh. Why did one exhausted laugh have to feel so involving?

Since the first night she'd diagnosed Philip's sprained ankle and sent him home, Jane had played up to her reputation for stern commonsense. This she did in the romantic belief that it might ultimately attract a suitor of superior and disarming wit. It had never occurred to her that the challenge she represented could be taken up by the college clown, or indeed by anyone who enjoyed a chase.

Philip fixed Jane with his one, unmasked eye. Next to her, she could feel Dougall squirming, the ginger factotum sloe-lipped with cold, unable to make silly jokes or to share in them. She felt tired – tired and dimly responsible for at least one man's discomfiture.

They walked the rest of the way back to the pub in silence.

*

'Jane. Guys. Problem solved.'

Frances Schumacher hailed her friends from the bar, pointing triumphantly at three sleds in front of the fire. These were solidly built affairs, with low-set tubular metal runners designed to skim over, rather than cut into, the snow and ice.

'Nice,' said Jane uncertainly, stamping her feet, somehow unable to applaud the aptness of Frances's solution.

The work party, chilled through after a day chipping away at a glacier, wanted to defrost by the hearth. But the sleds, which Frances had rounded up from the landlady and her neighbours, formed a barrier to the flames. There they were, in a row, asking to be admired, negotiated, stepped over – and, rather quickly, moved out of the way.

'How about we send a couple of guys down the hill on these with, uh, emergency provisions?' Frances suggested, the unsteadiness in her voice growing as people turned away from the bar, and from her, with pints of Marston's in their hands. The men said 'cheers' a lot and lit cigarettes.

The rest of her big idea was tested on Jane and on the wizened landlady, who murmured 'arr' while Frances spoke, but seemed generally lost in a reverie of pint-pulling. The old woman pursed her lips as she drew the beer, head tilted to one side. And moved on to the pumps in the lounge bar, where there were ashtrays to empty.

'The snow's in hard layers, right?' Frances carried on, almost inaudibly, feeling Jane close at hand, avoiding eye contact. 'I thought . . .'

She paused, tracing a shaky curve on a beer towel.

'I thought that we could go out the back with a couple of bags of coal and bread and milk, nothing real heavy, and get a run down the hill, round the side of the trees, end up on Norcot porch. Buy us time – buy the old ladies time – before the guys open the road.'

Wandering over from the fire, cigs flailing from their mouths, Philip and Dougall caught the tail end of Frances' explanation. Philip made an inarticulate, sceptical whining noise, gestured at the girls with a pint in one hand, a Woodbine in the other.

'Thing is, Frankie,' he drawled, green eyes glazed with wry self-satisfaction, 'even if we get down there on those kids' things – how do we get back? Sleighs don't go uphill unless you have huskies. It's a nice thought, but . . . Say the four of us went – wouldn't that just make six people snowbound instead of two?'

His tone jerked Frances from her despondency.

'Thing is,' she replied, 'you and me're not eighty years old, locked in the Frigidaire. And if I didn't know better, I'd say you were chicken.'

She spoke in gulps, as if exercising a cramped muscle. Her round cheeks blushed. She pulled up the fastener on her waxed jacket.

'Makes sense to me,' Dougall said, slyly.

Fingers of smoke stroked the four students as the firemen at nearby tables turned to listen.

'Now wait a minute,' Jane started, and the room fell silent. She took a breath. 'We know that they have gas and paraffin heaters and blankets, don't we? They won't freeze. I mean, we'll have them out by . . . by, oh I don't know . . . by midnight. The wind's already down, and we can get started again soon. It's not far to go.'

A log spat in the grate. The burr of local voices started up in the lounge and, in the middle of a long, disparaging rumble, the words 'art student' were painfully distinct.

'Might take a bit longer, my love,' said a voice from the corner.

'All right, a bit longer,' Jane agreed. 'But they definitely have gas. A paraffin stove. Or an electric bar. We know that.'

'Arr,' said the same voice appeasingly.

Dim laughter from the other bar.

'I spec.'

At which point, Philip put his gloves back on.

*

The snow layer thinned towards the back of Norcot End where a blasted quince tree straggled over the kitchen door and gave it some protection. A few blunted depressions on the step suggested that someone had stood there recently, looking out.

Smaller, crisper trails, as of a foraging animal, criss-crossed the orchard garden and pattered away into the shadow of Cat's Hill, which rose beyond the far gate like a gathering wave.

The door was unlocked. Jane stepped inside and called out.

She swept her torch across the dark, spartan kitchen, and picked out the square table in the middle, the four saddle-back chairs tucked in around it, the inert New World stove (no pilot light) and humless fridge, the Bilter sink and draining board, the rickety dresser with its chipped Wicklow china. The roving beam discovered two plates and some cutlery in the sink. A swan-necked copper kettle posed on the stove.

Dougall found the light switch by the dresser and tried it. There was an angry buzz and a phut-phut noise from the ceiling fixture.

'That's that gone, then,' he whispered. Then, louder, playing his own torch across the four cracked panels of the door in front of him – 'Hello? Miss King? Mrs Tibbs? Anyone at home?'

He hesitated before opening it, conscious for a moment of the ordinary complexity of smells that define a house. Soaped tiles, stale breadcrumbs in the grain of a table, the metallic tang of boiled water, onion skins, spent lightbulbs and the ghost of gravy. Afraid, too, of what he might detect on the other side of the door.

In the sitting room Jane went straight to the grate, bumping into a small armchair and standard lamp on the way, and found it ash-clogged but cold. The scuttle was empty, apart from a few sticks of kindling. Yet the room was not quite without warmth, and on the stairs, around the front door, exuded by the doormat perhaps or trapped in the tassels of the lampshade, Dougall thought he detected the sweet, adhesive reek of paraffin.

'There's a heater on,' he said. 'Upstairs.'

Eyes of torchlight mapped the ceiling as they climbed, and darkness pursued them, welling up in the spaces between things. The banisters, unhinged by the passing light, were rungs of sclerotic bone.

'I'm not going any further. I don't want to,' Frances said, before she reached the landing. The smell of paraffin was stronger at the top of the stairs; the floorboards had more give.

A loud scratch and skedaddle made them jump. Philip and Jane stopped in the upper passage; Dougall and Frances froze on the staircase.

'I'm not going on,' she said again, her voice tiny and hurt inside the puckered hood of her coat, her face swallowed up. 'They're not here.'

'Of course they are,' Jane hissed crossly. 'It's nearly ten o'clock. They're probably asleep. Just – everyone – *shhh*.'

Philip waved his torch about. 'Asleep? After the racket we made?'

Jane gritted her teeth.

'If they're awake, then they're awake,' she explained. 'If they're not, and we wake them now, they'll have a heart attack.'

'Two old dears that haven't seen a soul in days – and you're worried about *disturbing* them?'

Jane's whisper was a bottled shriek. '*I'd* have a bloody heart attack, if you showed up in my room. Imagine the disappointment.'

'Man,' said Philip under his breath. 'You are so uptight.'

'Guys,' Frances interrupted. 'Guys . . .'

She put a shaking hand to her throat.

'I think . . . I think *I'm* the one having a heart attack.'

She slumped onto the stairs.

After a few seconds, Dougall said: 'Are you sure?'

Frances stood up to answer him.

'Like you want compelling evidence?'

'You were exaggerating.' Dougall shone his torch at her. 'Weren't you?'

Frances flapped her arms. 'But how do you *know* I was exaggerating?'

'Because you're still alive.'

'OK, Sherlock. So I wasn't having a heart attack *for real*. But I could have been. Jesus. What a girl has to do to get some attention round here.'

From the room at the end of the passageway came a clatter of objects. A soft thump and the rattle of a latch. The crash of something heavy falling to the ground – and voices, sudden conversation, muffled but urgent, reassuringly official.

'Right,' said Jane. 'I'm going to look in the bedroom.'

She glanced at Philip, fishing for support. He prodded her in the back.

'Off you go, then,' he said.

*

It was a small bedroom at the back of the house, the kind from which infants are abducted in fairy tales. It smelt of quilts and apples.

The babbling voices came from a Hacker radio which had turned itself on after being knocked off the window dresser. Its batteries were low, and the Home Service chatter, interspersed with polite audience laughter, kept cutting out. On the far side of an imposing wooden bedstead was a paraffin stove, as Dougall had predicted. A blue flame glittered feebly in the draught from the window. The bed was unmade, almost empty.

'Oh, but look,' Jane breathed to herself. 'Look who's here.'

She turned off the torch.

The animal flinched, haunches stiffening against the cold. Warily, it began the feline ritual of intimidation, pressing the eiderdown with its forepaws, arching its back. One eye the lurid colour of marsh gas lit up the fringes of an old-fashioned old lady's nightcap which had wound its way around the cat's cocked ears. The other eye was dull by contrast, like the rumour of glass in a dank, subterranean corridor.

'You poor thing,' said Jane, holding out her hand.

In an invisible studio, an invisible audience laughed.

The cat made no noise, but sprang at the gloved palm and struck it squarely with outstretched claws. The penetrative power of their grip surprised Jane less than the impact of the leap, which nearly knocked her over. She stumbled, her arm dragged down by the weight of the cat as it tried to lift its hind legs. While it scrabbled, Jane turned and screamed.

In the three-panelled mirror of the window dresser, she saw a wizened shape in a bonnet, hanging from her hand.

It seemed to be pleading with her, begging for alms. The two outer panels, which faced inwards, reflected the grisly scene in infinite recession. And in the murky background, a tall, thin man suddenly appeared, with luminous skin and sloping, Victorian shoulders. Jane was momentarily dream-bound, instantly recalling the anaesthetic struggle to awaken which had coloured so many of the dawns of childhood.

The cat bit her, hard, at the base of the thumb.

She hit back, and half-threw the animal at the window, where it twisted itself on the sill, mouth open in a grinning ecstasy of fear. It swung on the latchkey, yowled once, and was gone.

Next – torchbeams and pale faces, questions.

'Jane, look at me. Are you all right?'

Philip held her by the shoulders. The others huddled by the bedroom door, their breath steaming. The stove was dead, the radio silent.

'I think so,' Jane said, in a daze. 'There's no one here.' Her voice grew tense. 'Did you see . . . ?'

'I saw.'

Jane nodded, and frowned to avoid crying.

'She bit me.'

Philip took a pillowcase from the bed, tore it in half, and bandaged Jane's hand. The thin wool of her glove was torn and soaked, but he left it on.

'There's no one here,' she repeated.

'We're here,' Philip urged, gently. The others nodded. Frances took her left arm. 'And now we're going home.'

Not knowing why, Jane doubted it.

*

For a short while afterwards, the four college friends enjoyed a portion of fame and notoriety. Naturally, the mention of a black cat near Cat's Hill got the locals excited. Feral cats were not unknown in the area, but stories of an animal about the size of a puma laying waste to livestock had been rife a few generations back, and folkloric pride attached itself to the idea that the Beast of Botleaze had at last made off with two OAPs.

The mystery of Norcot End also impressed Claudia Minnelli, who, besides winning fencing competitions in conveniently distant locations, liked a good yarn. She invited Jane and Philip to dinner in the tropically warm conservatory of the principal's house, and listened, rapt, as Philip embellished an already ornate saga of spectral anthropomorphism.

The action, as ever, was elsewhere.

After her mains, Jane mumbled an excuse and went upstairs to the toilet.

Glancing down as she pulled the chain, she suppressed a gasp of horror. For wedged inside the bowl (and rising out of it) was a deposit the pagan ancients of Avebury could have set upright and worshipped.

The water swirled ineffectually; it filled the pan, and for a dreadful moment Jane thought it might overflow.

This was, she reminded herself, the principal's bathroom. It was carpeted. It had a new radiator. The tiles around the bath and sink were probably original William Morris. It looked out over the conservatory at a beautiful garden. It had works of literature under the window and pots by James Tower on a shelf. It was a sanctuary of achieved simplicity. With, at present, one major complication.

Downstairs, Claudia and Philip were discussing sculpture. Above their heads, Jane was looking at it. The foul water hadn't drained away, so she dared not re-flush. She looked into the night for inspiration.

A voice sailed up from the extension.

'I completely disagree, Claudia,' Philip was saying, with a studied emphasis on their tutor's first name. 'If you've had a good idea, you can have it again. You don't need to hoard everything. Not every scribble is significant. Sometimes it's just as well to have a spring clean. Y'know, get rid of all your shit. Throw it out.'

As quietly as she could, and fearful lest any sudden noise carry, Jane lifted the sash and peered into the darkness. The safety of a clump of rhododendrons was only a few feet beyond the conservatory, and no more than three or four yards from the bathroom window. *Throw it out.* All she had to do was pitch it high – high enough to clear the tendrils of wall creeper that suckered up from the sill.

She wasn't as disgusted by the texture, which was warm and dense, as she'd imagined. Sculpturally, it felt true to her, an honest piece of work. Hardly shaking at all, she divided it into two – two seamed sausages, half a pound each – and took aim.

'Unless,' Philip continued, 'there's an obvious way of incorporating it in something else, making it serve a new purpose.'

Jane wished he would make up his mind. She looked again into the night. This time it seemed to her that the bushes were an absurd distance away, the conservatory roof transparent with probability. Already she saw and heard the bone shake of glass, the raised faces and thumping silence, the babble of future generations in awe of her mythic disgrace.

A knock at the door.

'J?' It was Philip. 'J. You nearly finished? I'm dying for a pee.'

'On my way. Down in a sec.'

'Right you are.'

The door, unlocked, drifted open.

In the sink stood a characteristic black-and-grey Tower pot, its scored, *sgraffito* body extended by a pair of weedy arms. From the doorway Philip watched, fascinated, as Jane Moorcock tipped a huge turd into the mouth of the pot. And another. She punched out a sigh when it was done, and noticed the door. Both she and Philip were silent for some time.

'It wouldn't go down,' Jane said faintly, then, less faintly, 'You didn't see anything. Please. Go back downstairs.'

'I didn't see anything.'

'Give me a minute.'

In the conservatory, Claudia was serving the dessert and flirting heavy-handedly with Philip, taxing him with pottery *as* sculpture. If you made a closed pot, was it a ceramic, or something else? Was utility, as Claudia believed, part of the 'very problem'?

Jane entered the room with a case in point.

'Look!' Claudia crowed, pointing. 'Tower is like this. So beautiful. His pote has empty spess, but the spess is *what* the pote contenns.'

Jane tutted at the spokes of creeper she'd stuffed on top of the very problem. 'Isn't it marvellous? Like a torso, or a sea shell. Pity the frost got the jasmine – I suppose I'd better chuck it away.'

She opened the greenhouse door, stepped forward a pace and emptied her competition-standard blooms into the rhododendrons.

'Philip?' Claudia insisted. 'What do you think?'

Philip smiled and repeated the question. What *did* he think?

Back at the table, Jane poured herself another glass of wine.

He thought: I am in love.

Part Three

Anyway

September 25 [1989]

Dearest Daniel,

    Sorry to write so soon after one of your rare visits (which we really enjoyed) – you'll think I'm mad (if you don't already!). Anyway, I thought you should know that P's going into the Royal United tomorrow for a small operation. It's very routine, the doctor says (terribly nice, looks a bit like a young Sean Connery). I don't think we even mentioned it while you were here because the check-up was weeks ago and so we'd forgotten all about it by the time you got back from the Ballearics (spelling?!). P thinks the aches and pains were probably psychosomatic – he's got quite a big exhibition on at the Vic in December, and you know how involved he gets. Always up there beavering away. Anyway, it turns out that the hard knobbly bit on his neck we were laughing about *is* a growth after all, not an actual vertebra – some people do have extra ones, apparently. But it's perfectly benign and quite tiny. 'Ectostosis' (cyst?), I think the doctor said, whatever that is! Nothing to write home about, though a card would be nice if you have the time.

    I shall be on my own for a couple of nights, which I'm quite looking forward to. (No snoring!) Frances will pop round, I expect.

Hope term has started well. Perhaps you'll find some nice bits and pieces for your new house in Seven Dials. Would you like that writing box of yours? It's still here. You never remember to take it with you. I can also give you plates and knives, if you need them. It all helps . . .

Love,

Mum.

October 9 [1989]

Dear Dan,

Thanks for coming down. J appreciated it, as did I. Obviously the results are a shock, though the truth is I thought something was up, so maybe shock isn't the word. I'm sorry *you* found it upsetting.

The good news is that it's treatable, which means (not such good news) radiotherapy sharpish. Surgery's out because the little sod has suckered on to the spinal cord, but radiotherapy should nix it and everyone at the RUH is being v. blasé. They tell me it will probably frazzle the hair on the back of my head. ('Leaving what exactly?' – J.)

The point, Dan, is that, as far as these things go, I'm not doing badly. The tumour's slow-evolving and doesn't seem to have disseminated – at any rate, the white coats have poked about and failed to turn up anything else. I asked Mr Yea about long-term prognoses, and he was a bit cagey. It's not in the lymph glands, that's the main thing. The gist was (I think) that if we nobble this one, I'm in the clear, so we'll see.

Show at the Victoria Art Gallery still on for Dec 8 – come down if you want, bring a friend. No need to reply to this.

Best,

P.

PS. Congrats on article in local rag, which I read with much interest. Did you know I met T. Hughes at Corsham in '62? V. nice guy.

November 30 [1989]

Dear Dan,

Results just back so please forgive injured tone (and don't tell J I've written again). Well it looks as though the l.s. has its claws in deeper than we thought. It hasn't got any bigger, but it hasn't dropped off either. Where that leaves me I don't know, but I can't say I'm sorry to see the end of the cobalt rays. I'm fed up with looking/feeling like a roasted tomato.

Thanks for making it to show opening. Sorry Frankie was so off – she has been having problems with Carey. He's going back to States, but you probably know this.

P.

January 5 [1990]

Dear Dan,

Hope you enjoyed Christmas. I did: apart from anything else, it'll be the last time the securitate homeguard lets me eat meat as she has just put me on to one of F's complementary practitioner friends at the hippy shop. Went to see her for the first time yesterday and she introduced herself as Ben. I said: 'Ben, that's an interesting name for a woman. What's it short for?' She said 'It's not short for anything!' and screamed with laughter.

Ben's 'treatment' room is a beige cell in a basement off Pulteney Street with soothing pictures of trees – and two of those gruesome posters that are everywhere with silvery cats on them. Tells me she once went to art school, as if it's something you do when you're temporarily unhinged, which in her case . . . Gave me a bottle of lavender skin jollop for my neck, a speckled diet sheet with key concepts heavily underlined ('pressed vegetables', 'food combining') and charged me thirty-five quid! Assumed J would scoff, but not at all. Job's comforter insists I go back next week and is taking diet very seriously. I made my standard objection, i.e. everyone on vegetarian diets always looks so fucking ill, but to no avail. Three-bean soup again yesterday, so my life is wind.

Ben also advised me to 'visualize' the l.s. and keep a diary. I told her I painted – remember? And I write to you, so that takes care of the diary.

J is being a saint about everything and I am a resentful sod. For some reason at the moment I find I can only say nice things about her to other people, like you, and even then my repertoire is limited. She is upbeat as ever. Also, F said I was 'remarkable' the other day, which could mean anything. Unduly pink? Completely bald? At least the hair gene is on J's side, Dan, so you should keep all yours.

Sorry to go on.

Best,

P.

PS. J wants me to remind you about box, which has your presents in. Should we send it? Which also reminds me – I didn't thank you for the new Ed McBain. Brain gone as well, evidently.

January 26 [1990]

Dearest Daniel,

I am writing this short note because it is *so* difficult to get through on your house phone. No one ever answers it – you are always out! (As you should be at your age!) Anyway, this is just to say that P is *much* better, and I am – naturally – delighted. Also to say a proper 'thankyou' for all your cards – he has never had a 'correspondence' before (certainly not with yours truly!), and I think it has helped him calm down on bad days, although there haven't really been that many. Thank you all the same.

P thinks I have been taken in, but the diet really seems to have helped. Dr 'Connery' thinks so, too – so I wondered if you could encourage him (P) to continue as well? I know he listens to you.

Awful fuss being made about plans for a new Batheaston bypass. Thatcher and co want to run a dual carriageway through Swainswick, across Bathampton meadows to Bathford and on to Limpley Stoke. Can you believe it? Everyone is frantic – Bath council are in favour of course. There are just too many cars! Perhaps you could write something for the Bath and West Chronic? Just a thought . . .

Have you seen *My Left Foot*, yet? We did on Monday – quite moving, though I think it is probably exaggerated.

Love,

Mum.

Feb 4 [1990]

Dear Dan,

Remission confirmed yesterday. Yea looked so serious telling me, I thought to begin with he was saying that the l.s. had progressed to stage three. Was ready to hit panic button when I heard the words 'shrivelled' and 'negligible risk' in rapid succession and found myself being shovelled out of the door. Consultants, radiologists, nurses, reception – suddenly no one's interested in you. Technically, I'm not out of the woods for a year or so, but Yea slapped my files and X-rays on a heap of scrunched-up forms as though it was all over. Came home feeling very blue, slept ten hours, and woke up this morning completely light-headed.

The light is amazing over the city this week: cold, quartzy with watery-yellow tints, and most of the valley weirdly in shadow as if the sun were shining somewhere below the horizon. Went for a long walk with J to Beckford's Tower and on down past Langridge Farm. Do you remember going there as a little boy? You got stuck in the stream and J said it was 'quicksand'. You were taken with the idea and had a thing about *mires* for months afterwards, especially the black tapioca ones in Tarzan films.

J and I had a good talk, which we don't often. She is a very strong person but paradoxically not a confident one. I have put her through it over the last few months and am taking her to Venice for long weekend. (To avoid arguments over £££, she thinks we are going to Minehead!)

Can you think of anything you need? I made about £3000 on the Vic exhibition, what with all the sympathy sales, and I'd like to buy you something. You've been a tower etc.

Best,

P.

February 15 [1990]

Dan,

Here I am in sunny Truro, planting trees and freezing my nuts off. How are you? I bumped into your Mum last week and she said all about your Dad. I am really sorry and glad it is sorted now.

I am engaged! Scary.

Greg X

Dearest Daniel,

Guess who I saw in Millets the other day? I don't go in there at all normally, but the weather has been terrible since we got back (while we were there, too!) and P and I both need waterproofs. Anyway – it was your friend, Gregory, snooping about in the tents. It was so nice to see him. He asked after you and he said you hadn't been in touch. He has got a new job as some sort of conservationist – in Cornwall. His skin has really cleared up and he is getting married. He is such a friendly character – I can just see him climbing about in the trees.

Talking of chance encounters, P and I went over to F's the other night and who should be there but Carey, who has put on a lot of weight and was very quiet all evening. He is taking a year out from Cambridge and going to America soon. We had a nice (rich) meal, but it was an awkward gathering and F looked drawn. She is so worried about C, who has been depressed and on drugs, etc. His eyesight is alarmingly bad, he says (tho' quite cheerfully) – and he asked after yours! I said it was fine as far as I knew and we laughed. He told me you used to be adamant that you could see in the dark. Well, we all like to feel that we are special in some way. (I suppose part of growing up is realizing that you're not.)

We didn't talk about it, but I do not think he sees anything of Karen. What happened to her? I know she was with the father for a while – not a nice customer, I think. But C is young and has life ahead.

Such a poor letter. P is upstairs combing his hair, singular. It has grown back very coarse and red. Most peculiar.

Love,

Mum.

PS. Will you have to pay poll tax? P did not make as much from the exhib. as he had hoped, I think – and we are strapped after Venice jaunt!

February 17 [1990]

Hi, Daniel!

I have been meaning to write you for some time now, but things have been screwy for all of us – J with P and me with Carey. Well I just wanted to say how wonderful it is that P is on the way up. I had an 'equivocal' screening years back and I know the whole scene. Yuk.

Your folks came over on Saturday and we had the best time. Carey was down (and is doing well, now). I was worried because my delightful ex-husband – did you meet? – was there, too, spreading terror and confusion. Guess I'm still bitter! But it was OK. Carey gets on well with him and Dougall is pretty much straightened out, still on the hippy trail in New Mexico but working again. He was flirty with your Ma – she got cross as only J can! (I love her, though – she is a stayer.)

The folks tell me you are planning to be a journalist and writing a lot of articles. I think that is just a great idea. It is an exciting time at home and abroad with many maps being redrawn. Any room for poetry? I have not written for years. The Hat and Feather is full of video jukeboxes.

I hope to see you again one of these days.

Go well, Daniel.

Love,

Frankie Schumacher.

PS. Ian Bachelor – large, hairy poet, used to edit *The Ninth Wave?* – has been caught reading it. At his *wedding* to *Tina* – from the leather stall!

May 1 [1990]

Long live the Revolution.

From May 10, you can write Carey Schumacher at 1429 Santa Maria Blvd West #3, Albuquerque, New Mexico 87378, or c/o University of New Mexico, Albuquerque, NM 87131, USA.

Bye. CS.

Real Time

Everything is fine until we touch. In the narrow, bottleneck hallway to my flat, Carey's stick proves an encumbrance and so he proffers his arm. 'Best if you lead,' he says. I wipe my hands on filthy jeans, try not to stare at the insectoid blacks of his sunglasses, and reach for him. He smiles, but his bicep feints, like the bubble in a spirit-level, as my fingers close on it. We jostle three-leggedly to the brink of the two steps into the kitchen, and I change hands, remembering the upstairs-downstairs drill, ready to hold and support along the back, expecting soon the shudder of the legs which is so discon-certing the first time it happens, and which you never afterwards get used to – though I did try.

'OK, Daniel,' Carey laughs, a little embarrassed. 'I can manage a few steps. Just take my hand.'

I am behind him at this point, my chin nuzzling the nape of his neck, my arms around him in a professional embrace. The soapy notes of his skin and shirt collar are sleepily familiar. For a second or two, we both resist. My arms linger because of the sweet smell, to which the body I'm holding somehow doesn't quite belong, and Carey's muscles clench indignantly, mindful of a basic impropriety.

'I can smell trees,' he says, once I've sat him down. 'That

must be the garden – that patch of light.' He waves, accurately enough, at the kitchen door. 'Why don't I sit out there while you have a sleep? You're tired, Dan. You've been up a long time.'

This arouses my curiosity.

'How can you tell?'

'Body odour.'

Carey laughs again, mechanically.

'Sweat has a different signature before sun-up and after,' he explains. 'And you've got two signatures, so I figure . . . you've been out – or in – somewhere, without washing.' His nose dimples. 'Somewhere underground, maybe. I can smell, uh, damp.'

I check my armpits, which have the usual tang of gluey chemicals, and my admittedly filthy shirt.

'Quit that,' he chides. 'Don't get self-conscious on me.'

'Me? Hardly,' I protest, aware that insincerity may have a saccharine pong all of its own. 'You're right, though. I could do with a hose-down. What about you? You're the weary traveller.'

An orthodontic miracle beams back at me. The brilliance of those teeth is a new feature, I suppose, like the thickening of a once etiolated neck into the present raised deck of shoulder muscle. But nothing in Carey's faddish physique is ever beyond recognition – in a way, it's his most distinctive feature – and none of it disturbs me like the constant echo of mockery in his exquisite manners, ready to tax me with resentments unforgotten, things we have both always known about each other but would rather not face. The blindness I knew about.

The man in the thousand-dollar suit strokes his turquoise tie.

'Business class is a wonderful thing,' he purrs. 'You eat and drink, you sleep. You wake up feeling like a million dollars.'

'Bet you earn that anyway,' I call out from the bathroom, pulling off my shirt and wondering if a bit of opportunistic streaking could possibly cause offence. I'm stupidly turned on by the idea, and traipse back into the kitchen with a semi-erection.

'Oh no, no way,' Carey giggles, doffing his glasses to reveal clear, cold green eyes. 'I earn *much* more than that.' He frowns affably and sniffs the air – then points straight at my wilting cock. 'Say, that's too bad. You should get a robe.'

*

In the garden, our tongues loosen and we chat about work. Carey is now Network Systems Director of Development (US) for Vector Corp., your average desk-top runaway success story – 'an out-of-town IT grad start-up that was nowhere for two years until this new age New Mexican futures freak – made his fortune in dry grains – threw us seventy million in research and said, "Get Gates." '

'Microsoft? You're kidding.'

'The same.' Carey shrugs it off. Either that or he has a stiff neck. 'The thing is, it's all hack work – PCs, domestic and business software, profiling, Net access. The technology is so goddamn basic, it's scandalous. The whole deal is manufacture and rights: you can't compete without muscle, de-da, de-da, de-da, which – by the way – I don't deny. Until you offer the market something it didn't know it was missing, like we're doing with Plus. Then all you have to do is sit back and watch them come running.'

He shifts in his canvas director's chair, distracted by the shuffle of a thrush in next door's – Neville's – lilac.

He says, 'You write on an Apple – in QuarkXPress, right?'

'Right.'

Carey draws a white finger across his throat.

'Plus Design will be the industry standard in five years. All the papers. All magazines. Across the board. European launch Wednesday.'

'I'm impressed.'

This is to be polite, though the strain shows in my voice: the problem being that I have worked on practically every program and system in existence over the last three years – Quark, PageMaker, Atex, Xywrite, Adobe, Hermes – and it's hard to believe there isn't one that can't be jinxed by a three-second power cut.

Carey's nostrils widen. He stares inwardly at the pond, reminding me for a moment of the flame-haired thirteen-year-old with his ZX81, so happy to boast capacity, so vague about necessity. Things have changed since then, of course. My whole profession now depends on computers, and I am a 'core user', as the strategists like to say. But that's only made me more suspicious, because the programmers – the human element – have stayed the same: for ever unhappy with what already works.

'You don't sound it,' he says, frowning. 'And know what? I don't blame you, so don't apologize. It's the same old shit.'

While I am thinking of reassurances – at least it's shit with a high salary tag – a grin steals across his face.

'But let me show you something that's not.'

He leans back, reaches into his pocket and pulls out a smooth, flat, metallic lozenge somewhere between a cigarette case and a mobile phone. The sun on its tilted casing turns one edge into a toothpick laser.

'This is *mine*,' Carey says, stroking its polished chrome

shell, leaning forward again, close enough for me to see pinheads of sweat in his eyebrows. 'This is me – what I do.'

He finds my hand and palms me the prized gadget: warm from his touch, even slightly greasy. It's ultracompact, too small surely to support the weight of its own sophistication, and so probably lethal, as if with a flip and a tap it could reduce the house behind me to a pile of smoking rubble.

I ask the obvious question.

'Open it up,' Carey says, a shade impatiently. 'Find out.'

To begin with, I can't see how. The casing is so seamlessly bonded, there's no way to prise it apart. It's like a jigsaw in reverse – one of those puzzles designed to prove the genius of hitherto confirmed idiots.

I give it a lengthways squeeze. The bottom end depresses suddenly, like a ballpoint pen, and two oval eyelids rise out of the clear top surface. The springloaded lids slide sideways – one to the right, one to the left – and subdivide into strips to form arms. The spectacle lenses revealed beneath the lids are mineral black, separated by a pair of much smaller lenses, like dead railway signals – : – on the bridge. The insect whine of micro-hydraulics ends in a series of contented clicks, and a green 'on' dash fades up on the inside of the left hinge.

They're goggles rather than spectacles, curved around the edges to exclude peripheral light. With them on, the outside world – daylight, garden, pear tree, house – disappears. My night vision is of no use. An unearthly shimmer from the 'on' dash registers to one side; otherwise it's like trying to see through lead.

I can feel Carey squirming opposite me, aglow with ingenuity.

'I know what these are,' I say, working up to a wild guess. 'They're virtual screens, aren't they? They're more like Lanier headsets than shades. That's why I can't see anything through them.'

Carey grunts.

'Nice design, though,' I add apologetically. 'Very – neat.'

Slow seconds later, he mutters, 'Thank you,' with enough unintentional emphasis to betray the accuracy of my guess and the depth of his rage, and strips the goggles from my face.

The play of his fingertips is a shock; they feel like tentacles chasing prey, tearing at a shell to get at the flesh underneath. Another is my sense that something more than a pair of glasses has been taken from me. He has my imprint, now, I think with a shiver. Carey knows the shape of my face – its long nose and tilted brow. Fingernails, surprisingly sharp and ragged, have mapped its contours.

The sun returns, and Carey, his back to the pond and trees, develops like an overexposed photograph. For a while he is a mass without feature, the smile gone. Then I see that he has replaced his shades with the goggles, which give him a corporately alien look.

'Yeah,' he says, not moving his head. 'There's a VR component in here. Kind of.' His fingers twitch. 'Half VR, half AI. AOI, in fact.'

'Any old iron?'

Carey freezes.

'Artificial Optical Intelligence.' He clears his throat, settles back. 'You won't have heard of it.'

'Of course not.'

'Practically no one has. I've been co-developing it with the med lab at Albuquerque for two years. At least two years. Since we last met.'

'What is it, then? What does it do?'

Vector Corp.'s IT guru breathes out with calculated

displeasure, happy to explain his supertoy but piqued by the ignorance that necessitates enquiry.

'What does it do?' he repeats, searching for a bearable paraphrase. 'Well . . . let's see.' His head swivels slowly to the right and back. 'Loosely speaking, AOI marries virtual imaging with real-time movement – for those with a severely reduced visual facility.'

'Loosely speaking.'

'Loosely speaking.' Carey permits himself a flicker of a smile and continues. 'The two spots on the bridge?'

'What about them?'

'The top one's a digital camera. It tracks the space through which you move and plays it back in sync with a pre-recorded virtual program of that space – the bottom spot's a kind of projector – to let you know where you are in real time.'

'Clever.'

'You load the "projector" with the virtual layout of, say, the inside of your house – where the furniture is, height, depth, width, and so on – and the camera places you *in* the layout, so you can move around.'

'Very clever.' My voice holds steady.

'That's not the clever part,' Carey drawls. 'That's just the content of the image – what you see. The clever part is how you get a damaged eye to see it. That's AOI. A network of extra-optical receptor cells designed to edit and collate at least some of the information that would usually be processed by the retina – before it gets there.'

'Brilliant.'

'Sure,' Carey agrees, removing the goggles. 'But still primitive. The next step is for us to in-build – make it smaller, put it in the brain.'

'Well, *I'm* impressed,' I say, weakly.

'You said that before,' he snaps.

'OK. But this time I am. Really. Impressed.'

Carey flicks the ends of the goggles together. The whole contraption modestly retracts. His coralline eyes blink vaguely.

'Yeah, well, it's way ahead of the game in digital optics, but that doesn't mean . . .' He pauses. 'I mean, it isn't, like, an actual substitute for the eye or anything, because AOI makes comparisons within such a limited signal field. The variables in the program have to be finite, which is why you can only use it indoors. Outside, it's not much use. There's too much going on that you can't control, or predict.'

'You mean you can't see anything, here? Now?'

'I don't have a scan for your apartment.'

'It's no help if you go for a walk?'

'I told you, the variables have to be pre-set.' Carey's voice goes up a key; a frog responds. 'OK: AOI assists your routine domestic orientation. I suppose if you took the same walk every day, and the elements of that walk remained constant, then maybe . . .' He shrugs.

'But if there were any surprises – if a car came straight at you?'

Carey unclips his shades from his top shirt pocket. 'I don't know about you, Dan, but I've always found it best to stick to the sidewalk.'

He looks down. The frog disappears with a plop.

'What you're saying,' I carry on, as taken with the idea as if I had thought of it, 'is that it measures where you are against the plan in its memory. The glasses – the specs, whatever you call them – are comparing visual records, updating a sort of 3D film.'

'Something like that,' Carey concedes, brightening.

'You see mostly what you've already seen.' I stop. 'You see the past.'

The overall shape of his smile remains, but a facial spasm pushes the lower lip in and lifts the brows.

I wish I hadn't said it quite like that.

*

In the kitchen to make more coffee, I remove my wallet from yesterday's trousers and see the slope's twin legacies thrusting out: one ruined photo of a baby, and the letter from Norman and Liz Spillings. The queasy sense of no longer being able to avoid a subject overtakes me as I return to Carey with full cups and shaking hands.

'You mentioned news, on your message,' I say, sitting down heavily. Hot coffee splashes on to my hand. There's more rustling from the lilac as Neville shuffles out into his yard, shifting a few pots here, adjusting a trellis there. 'I heard–'

'You got the message?' Carey raises an eyebrow.

'The machine cut it off. I was going to ask you about it, because you sounded almost jovial – and I had a letter.'

'You're upset.' Carey smiles. 'I understand. But you gotta remember that whole period doesn't have quite the same associations for me that it has for you.' He clicks his tongue in understatement. 'I guess . . . what some people idealize as growing up is what I'd rather, uh, leave behind. I don't mean that *you* idealize, Dan – I'm not making any accusations. I just mean that I don't. Far as I'm concerned, they could have knocked it down the day we left.'

Knocked down what? Exam-room confusion overtakes me: prickly calves and wadded ears, the sense that I have missed the point. My lips move involuntarily; I could be saying something, or shouting it. As I finish, Carey's last words float back on an airborne swell of coffee and pollen. He has found my hand again, his slippery grip alive with the old fear of desertion.

'Hey,' he says. 'I didn't mean to bring up other stuff. Jeez, of course you miss him. Everyone does. He was – look, I was jealous. I understand my dad now, but Philip was always amazing. It's OK. I know, I know.'

'Knocked down what?' I tug my hand free.

'The school. Lyncombe. What else?' Carey's eyebrows arch and flex; a flush deepens, adding lustre to the roots of his hair. He rubs a red ear. 'The site's been developed – y'know, light industry, infotech. Anyway, it's gone. You got the school's letter.'

'I got a letter, not *that* letter. The school never wrote to me.'

The rustling next door stops.

'So . . . what was in yours?'

He waits.

My mouth drains, like seawater from sand.

I have to remind Carey of a past he's said he'd rather leave behind. But how? What do I say? He hasn't been told – and that's already an insult: you're in the know or you're not, where death is concerned.

*

The moment before you tell someone that someone else has died is a moment of separation like no other. It is a moment to be extended by mental division, half over and half over again, in the hope that Xeno's paradox will prove benign. It is never quite up. You face each other – the informer and the informed – across an infeasible corridor in time.

The garden now becomes that corridor and Carey fades

from view. (The jasmine next door sours medicinally; the pond is a pile of bed linen.) Carey is replaced by a nurse, taking short steps towards a pair of double doors. She is outwardly composed. Her shoes smudge the lime linoleum.

What she knows will change the lives of the mother and son on the other side of those doors for ever. The instant before they see her, the nurse wonders – as parents with children wonder, looking at the world – what she can do to protect them from it. And the answer is: not much. In the end, frankly, nothing. She could choose not to tell them. She could pretend not to know, walk away, leave them complaining about the undrinkable machine coffee. But the point is that *she* would know, and they'd find out anyway. And if you lie about things that simply *are*, or are bound to be, or if you withhold that kind of information, then your original responsibility to share it becomes responsibility for the consequences of deception – which may be worse than the effects of knowing.

The walls of the corridor disappear; its smooth floor yields to size five wellington boots. Small colourful figures are toiling up a broad white incline stuck with matchstick flags and lost woollen gloves.

It is winter – the unremarkable Bath winter of 1981–2. There's been some of that famous 'snow on high ground' overnight, and Carey and I are putting Frankie's old Corsham sled through its paces on a gentle golf slope that planes down towards the Royal Crescent. Carey wants to try a shorter, steeper run which drops from Sion Hill to the bottom of Cavendish Road, but I am unwilling. Once the sled picks up speed, there's no stopping it. On the steep side of the course, you'd have to bail out inside thirty seconds or risk brain damage on the perimeter trees and railings. I am about to say all this, when Carey asks me if I dare him. Well, if he wants to be stupid . . . Fifteen seconds later, the clang of runner against railing brings a well-fed lady in tartan skirts striding from the houses on the other side of the road. She kneels down and puts her hand through the railings. Carey's forehead is bird-egg blue from temple to temple.

Do I feel guilty? Not immediately (the crying starts while I am at the top of the hill, looking down, counting chimney stacks). But that night I overhear my parents talking in bed, saying how easily Carey might have been killed. And I realize that I knew as much all along.

Now, though – as my garden and the tang of Neville's jasmine reasserts itself – knowing something that Carey doesn't seems so counter-intuitive, the thought of it makes me hot and sick.

The corridor may not be as long as it was. Losing Dad may have made things more equal, but there are still gulfs of experience between us. I don't know what Carey went through after Flo's DNA test, and I don't care to remind him of it. Perhaps he'll cry when he hears the latest; perhaps he'll cheer; perhaps he'll try to say the right thing. From the informed person's point of view, the actual moment you're told isn't the problem.

*

'The letter was from Craig's parents. He's dead. Plane crash.'

The words slip out simply enough.

Carey's mouth makes an equals sign. 'What happened?'

'His plane crashed. He crashed it.'

Looked at brutally, I suppose you might say that Carey has reason to be grateful to Craig, who freed him from parental responsibilities he was probably too young to shoulder. As, indeed, was Craig.

'*He* crashed it?' Carey whispers.

'Last week. It was in the news. I didn't know it was him.'

Seconds drift by – ample time for me to reflect on what kind of sub-editor doesn't even skim the second paragraph of a lead story.

Carey, meanwhile, is struggling. 'Craig flew planes?'

'Not very well, it seems.'

We laugh together, and then Carey waves an excited finger, as though recollecting the crucial part of the story.

But 'how awful' is all he says, his face curiously dappled. 'No, really. I mean it. This is terrible.'

'There's a memorial service, on Tuesday.'

'Are you going?'

'I've been invited.'

A distant little-piggy squeal, no more than the whee-whee-whee of temporary tinnitus or the robotic white noise of AOI turning itself on, catches me offguard. Carey rolls his head, as if in search of the sound, until it fades. His throat relaxes.

'Oh, well, you must,' he says. 'If you've been *invited* . . .'

Carey gets up and makes for the kitchen door. I catch him by the arm to offer guidance, but he brushes me aside. After an apparently aimless pause, he walks the four yards to the door with perfect, straight-backed confidence, and disappears inside.

*

A wispy head sprouts on top of the fence.

'I was just saying to my Auntie Betty, that young man knows how to dress of a Sunday. And what a difference it–'

'Not now, Nev. I'm not in the mood.'

Neville, not to be put off, pushes a low-hanging plum branch to one side. He has clearly rallied with the sunny morning, and looks spry in button-down green plaid shirt and khaki shorts, the capillaries in his cheeks flooded with genial outrage.

'Nev?' he chokes. '*Nev*? Do I sound as if I come from Harlow?'

'No.'

'To whom, then, do you refer? Not, surely, the crisp creature recently retired hence.' Neville lowers his voice and points at the kitchen. 'He's gorgeous, Daniel. How did a little streak like you bag that one?'

'He's an old friend. I've just upset him.'

'Bit of a domestic?'

'Not exactly. You know that news I had yesterday?'

'Ah, yes.' Neville drops a pair of secateurs and clasps his head in his hands. 'I'm sorry. I was only joking. Is he all right? Are you?'

'He's fine, just a bit jet-lagged. But we've got to go home tomorrow for a couple of days and sort a few things out. Could you water the plants, top up the pond while I'm gone?'

'I do anyway, dear. How else would anything survive?'

'Thanks.' I turn to go. 'You look nice,' I add, guiltily. 'Going out?'

Neville studies my face without replying. He is expressionless for maybe five seconds, unblinking, remote – before reaching some private decision and blushing deeply. He brings a hand to his cheek.

'Last night,' he explains, with a palpitant gasp.

'Oh yes . . .'

'Someone I met.'

'Really?'

Neville beams. 'Second bass in a shocking Sidney Jones do at the Queen Elizabeth. He's only just left! I'm seeing him later. I thought about Kew, or the V&A. What do you think? Or perhaps just the cinema?'

'You met him last night?'

'That's right.' My neighbour runs his thumbnail, slowly, up the easy grain of the fencepost. 'We met last night.'

'I hope you had a nice time.'

'Thank you. It was deeply satisfying.' Neville inhales the complex perfume of the garden and shuts his eyes. When he opens them again, they are glassier. 'He looked a bit like you.'

'You should ask for a refund.'

I am aghast at my careless betrayal of the truth, but Neville, seraphic with self-deceit, only digs his nail deeper into the wood.

An instant later, he pulls it out. 'Ouch,' he says, and childishly thrusts his thumb over the top of the fence so that I can see the dot of red.

'Bite and suck. It's just a splinter.'

Neville looks distracted. 'The second today,' he complains. 'Is that bad luck? I got the first from that silly box–'

He breaks off, twitching.

'What's the matter?'

'With the box? Oh, nothing,' Neville laughs. 'It pricked me, that's all. I thought it was walnut all the way through, but it's not. The veneer's cracked on the lid.' He steps back from the fence. 'It's a fake.'

*

Blind people in the movies fall into four categories: fumbling dependants, florists/newsagents, soothsayers, and brilliant musicians. For the purposes of most screenwriters, the blind are simply metaphors for the provisional nature of sight. See better, the movies tell us, and you won't die horribly in a serial killer's sexpit. Truth – survival – is seeing properly.

Yeah, right. The real truth, as the rest of the day with Carey demonstrates, is that the blind are for ever making huge mental concessions to the preconceptions of the film-going public. *That* is why they look spaced out. Our pity exhausts them.

Carey spends most of the afternoon on the bed in my front room, skim-reading a manual in Braille and tapping into his laptop. Still I keep getting up, whenever he gets up, ready to take him from chair to door, from door to kitchen to bathroom, and back again. I even find myself apologizing in italics for the awkward topography of the flat (those *two steps* into the kitchen), and the cumbersome intricacies of *doors* with *handles*. In the end, he claps me stiffly on the shoulder and begs me to shut up, says he's got the layout more or less fixed and really doesn't need any more help. With anything. And can he have a bath?

The irony is that, whereas blind men are supposed to have all sorts of ESP which marks them out from the common herd, I really do have an extra visual sense – and all I can make out are similarities.

Once he's worked out the length and breadth of the front room (gauging distance by aural resonance) and felt the height of the light sockets, Carey discards his cane. He flutters a bit in the kitchen with packets of things and cutlery, and he holds *Hello!* up very close to see if it makes any more sense that way; but otherwise it's difficult to tell, from his actions, in what sense he is blind at all. Memory, touch and smell soon take up the slack, and develop their own culture, he says. (This could be a political obstacle for AOI: 'Sign linguists got mad when the docs came up with cochlear implants. Betcha the Braillists do the same.')

The other similarity, or reverse oddity, is that we are alike in the dark. Stumbling to the toilet in the middle of the night is no more of a problem for him than it is for me. He feels; I see.

Asleep on his side, one leg drawn up, he looks at peace. These days, Carey Schumacher is a beautiful man. The scrawniness of adolescence and the fat of depression have reached an adult compromise in long legs and a solid chest (perhaps the shoulders are narrower in repose). His body hair is light brown; he has freckles along the forearm. His fingers curl to form querulous fists, like those of the new born or recently deceased.

I get out the photo in my wallet, and look at it.

Don't Eat the Chrome Yellow

Daniel,

Hard though it may be for you to believe, it was with the best of intentions that we both (repeat, *both*) decided not to tell you earlier. It isn't a question of keeping things secret; there just didn't seem to be any point saying anything while we didn't know for sure. Mr Yea had high hopes we'd got the tumour early, and you would only have worried. (You're *very* like me in that respect, although I know it pains you to think we have anything in common.) What else can I say? The news is not all bad and stage three is not the end of the road, but I know that P is sending a letter too, so will leave him to explain the state of play. And I promise to let you know anything else as soon as I can, only please don't *shout* at me.

I am not silly.

I know how close you are, and how frightening this is. I'm trying not to say 'How do you think I feel?' but frankly that's what I feel (like saying). You do belittle me, Daniel. I appreciate that (for some reason) I make you very angry – my father used to drive me potty, as all parents do! – but I would never have dreamed of swearing at him and carrying on. I *can't* really be as stupid as you make out, or you wouldn't be so clever yourself, would you? (Which you are, as I'm only too pleased to admit!)

Are you registered to vote in Brighton? I can't remember. Anyway, a card has turned up here with your name on it.

Love,

Mum.

P.S. It is always lovely to see you, and you know that you are always welcome with whomsoever you choose to bring down. I wasn't discouraging you at the w/e – I genuinely thought that with London and the Reed course coming up you might have wanted to stay in Brighton to pack, see friends etc. I am *sorry* if I misread the situation.

April 10 [1992]

Dear Dan,

I think it's fantastic news. Major will never last. Six months max, and they'll all be gone in a puff of carcinogens. Then we can vote in a Labour government, pour the military's undeclared billions into the NHS and find a cure for me! Yes!

No – I don't think you should shelve the course and come back home. There's nothing you can do here at the moment, and I am fine. In fact, I feel much better now than I did a few weeks ago because of the painkillers I've been prescribed, which encourage me to do little but smile wanly and nod off. The downside is that I feel a bit rough if I take them too late, or at irregular intervals so that I have a weak patch, say, in the early morning. The headaches are OK, but the pain in my back is pretty debilitating. I used some colourful language last week when Yea asked me to describe it – as if doctors have ever taken any notice of patient diagnosis – to which he had the cheek to reply that a little loss of temper was inevitable, and that we shouldn't worry about it. Jane coughed at this point. Then he suggested chemo, and since there isn't really a choice, that's what I'm getting: the full whack, two cycles, six weeks each. And a wheelchair when – if – moving around gets to be a problem.

Well, moving around *has* got to be a problem, but I'm not completely helpless yet. I'm getting physiotherapy once a week and J has just dug out a pair of her Dad's old crutches: extraordinary brown objects you wedge into your armpits to make you look like a shell-shocked poet. J says I cut a dash. Don't get me wrong – I'm not too proud to be helped, and I suppose I'll use a wheelchair if they give me one. I don't give a toss about dignity. It's just that, in some weird way, *not* giving me one would feel like more of a vote of confidence in my prospects. Apparently, I have progressive bone 'involvement' in my spine and at the base of my skull, whatever that means. Yea says the realistic chances with the chemo are sixty-forty. So.

The drugs are kicking in, Dan, and I must rush to finish this before I fall asleep. Have you sorted out your career development loan thing with Barclays? Remember, banks are evil. You are getting ripped off whatever the bastards tell you. I'd rather you take a wodge from me and pay it back when you can, or not at all. How much do you need? I've got £900 you can have. I don't need it, do I?

Hope the move goes well. Will I see you before?

P.

May 29 [1992]

Daniel,

P is so looking forward to seeing you, but I hope you won't

expect too much. He is bald as an egg and looks a sight. His skin was always pale, but it's like glass now, poor thing. I've got used to it, though it's a bit of a shock first thing in the morning! (P also gets tired, and when he's tired can be a bit of a handful, so no long interviews! I know you will be sensitive to this . . .) There's a break in the treatment for a couple of weeks while he has more tests (including a full CT scan, at *last*) so he should be feeling less queasy by the time you both get here.

What is your friend's name again? It is exciting to be starting out in London. I can hardly believe it – time goes so fast. It doesn't seem a day since Melanie Giggs and I used to buy offcuts from the wholesalers in Brick Lane. (We made all our own clothes back then!) And I am truly pleased you have found somewhere nice to stay in Brixton, which I am sure is nowhere near as fraught as 'the media' make out. (I was born in Highbury, as you know.) Naturally, I'm glad you're staying with people from Sussex; I think that makes it easier to find your feet. Did you meet your new 'friend' through them, or on the course? She will be very welcome, rest assured.

Thank you for being so selfless and understanding about the money. I trust and hope it doesn't come to that, but it would be foolish not to think about these things. I haven't told P, and feel wretched about going behind his back, but I feel sure you will get a job and be all right.

We are still waiting for the Dept of T's decision on the Swainswick and Batheaston roads. The protesters are already planning their tree-top protests! I wish them luck.

Love,
Mum

Dan,

Nice to see you and Ryan. Don't want to sound like a know-all, but I had my suspicions, if that's the right word, and I'm glad you felt able to tell us. What does it matter? Families shouldn't have secrets, though we all do. I know that my father's stepfather was pretty keen on him, or so mother used to hint when she felt like making mischief. Funny – I've been dreaming about them both recently.

Feeling awful today and wish the pain would go away. CT scan plus tests tomorrow and Yea is bluff about it. I'm not, I must say.

J has gone out to Harris's to get some paints and canvases. It pisses me off not being able to stretch my own. I have tried to show J how to do it (she used to do it all the time at Corsham) but she says she isn't strong enough and that I make her nervous. Rubbish.

Don't worry about her. She'll come round, but do be sensible, like she said, won't you? Be yourself, not what other people expect you to be, that's the point. You are my dear son in any case.

P.

Dearest Daniel,

This is just a short note that I am sending with Philip's letter (which I have *not* read) to thank you for your visit.

I much appreciated your straight-forwardness in saying 'I'm gay and this is Brian'. It was very like you to be so adult, open and sensible, and Brian seemed equally level-headed, as I'm sure he is.

I hope you will forgive me if I was a bit upset. I cannot pretend the thought had never occurred to me that you might be 'homosexual', but I had indeed prayed it was not so. I remember finding a Durex in your schoolbag and thinking, well, that's all right then. (Don't ask me what I was doing looking. I certainly didn't make a habit of it.)

Nothing you have said, or could ever say, has any power to affect the way I feel about you. You were such a surprise, just when I had begun to think I might not get pregnant after all, and I was overjoyed.

Things are very different now and I am conscious of not having caught up with all the 'right' ways of thinking. My school reports always said that I was a chatterer and would do better if I listened more attentively. I know there is some truth in that. I, too, had certain 'feelings' about other girls when I was growing up, but it would never have crossed my mind to act upon them in any way. And I must say I'm glad I didn't.

I won't say any more about it. (Don't want to say the wrong thing.)

P is very nonchalant about all this, of course, which is wonderful – but he has his dark side, too. I don't think cancer has done much for his sense of common decency. Our nice new neighbours, Amanda and Simon, called in yesterday with a jug they'd bought from the Amalfi Gallery in Manvers Street, and P told them it was a piece of worthless s–t. (Well it *was* ugly, but they liked it, didn't they? They're in advertising.)

Frankie has agreed to keep watch next w/e so I am planning an escape on my own to Porlock Weir. Do you remember walking to Culbone along the cliff-top path? That harbour was full of sewage, but we all swam in it!

Lots of love,
Mum.

Daniel,

Sorry for the phone melodrama. I am all right, but P is in a bad way. Are you free this w/e? We need to put our heads together. The hospital was sitting on the results. I can't tell you how angry I am. Ring and I'll fetch you from the station. (I'm driving again – after fifteen years.)

J.

Dan,

I'm a bit nervous about putting pen to paper, since I'm now being read by a fucking journalist. Don't want to be misquoted, do I?

Latest hospital stay was awful. Physio is total crap. What's it for? There's nothing they can do – secondaries are all over the shop, frontal lobe and medulla whatsit, so might as well give over. Message received and so on. But can you believe there is no bath on the cancer (*sorry*, 'oncology') ward, just a shower! How many people with brain cancer do you know who can stand up, let alone have a fucking shower? The wheelchair is also *hopeless*. It's a kid's fucking wheelchair and I will have to wait a month for one the right size. J in panic about this and I have no energy to waste on calming her down. She cannot get me up the stairs on her own, so I am moving into your old room next to toilet at street level. Not allowed to drink, have sugar, eat cheese, milk or game. *Game?*

That box of yours is still in here. Am using it to keep paints in.

Steroids making me fat after only two weeks! Big neck developing.

P.

PS. What's this? What's this? I see from second glance at your card that you are going for an interview with advertising magazine. Who is *Media*? Loopy Greek tart wot killed the nippers? Good luck anyway. Our shiny new neighbours, Amanda and someone, are in adverts or something. So boring, and they keep dropping in. Always a smile on.

August 9 [1992]

Dan,

I am re-sending the cheque which J removed from a letter I sent months ago and I want you to bank it. I'm not so enfeebled I can't keep track of statements, you know. That's it on this subject.

September 15 [1992]

Dearest Daniel,

If you can get hold of a copy with bigger type, that would be ideal as P's sight is not wonderful. Apparently in certain lights I look like a big grey blob in a boring Patrick Heron. (Jane the speaking blob.)

We won't do anything very adventurous for his birthday, but we might stretch to a meal out if you can make it down and P is not grumpy. I thought I'd invite Frankie, too, as she has been so supportive of late. We have not always seen eye to eye, she and I, but I cannot fault her loyalty. And anyway, she's always been potty about P, which I don't mind.

Isn't the carnage in Sarajevo shocking? I hope you don't get posted out there as a war correspondent. Is that what subs do? Excuse my ignorance, but what is a sub? I've heard of a sub-machine gun. Submarine of course. (Lemon s–yllab–ub?)

Talking of subversives, the Swainswick conservationists have got everyone up in arms, so to speak. K. Carlisle has said no to the Limpley Stoke road – the council are furious! – but yes to the Swainswick bypass. One of the Dimblebys, I think, and his wife have written to the Chronic. Of course, they're on the side of the protesters (as is yours truly), but there have been angry letters from the villagers in Batheaston who are all in favour of the road because it will take the traffic *away* from them and dump it on the rest of us. I am thinking of writing myself. Those water meadows are just about the last in the West Country. They'll rush it through, that's what I think will happen. It's wicked.

I expect the Dimblebys can afford to move elsewhere.

Enough for now.

Love,

Mum

October 5 [1992]

Dan,

Row with J over paints. She doesn't think the smell is good for me, toxic or something, like it makes a difference, and tells me that I have been shouting 'Don't Eat the Chrome Yellow' in my sleep. This is A Bit Rich, as I have repeatedly asked her for chrome yellow to finish the latest small set of Nolde-ish oils and she is deliberately failing to get it from Harris's where I know they stock it because everyone does for Christ's sake. I mean, everyone. It's ordinary fucking cadmium yellow but with a bit of lemon yellow and yellow ochre in it neither of which I have any more of or I'd be mixing my own wouldn't I?

How am I supposed to make use of time remaining when my own darling wife can't remember a SIMPLE INSTRUCTION. Then it's drug time (been put on tranquillizers) and that's another day gone. Tired now might not send this. And I am not sure J doesn't vet my letters so may write this out or do short version and keep it in the slippery-slope for you to read whenever. You must meet my physio. He is shirt-lifter, too. (Small.)

Odd – feeling best now in the small hours, when everything is clear and I think of all I want to say. 3 a.m. very vivid, but no energy to write then and can't remember it in the morning. Thoughts come in phrases. Only ones I can remember now are 'unconditional dinner money' and 'forgive by forty'. Total gibberish, but at least I know it. Apologies in advance. Can read better than write. Write, write.

P

October 24 [1992]

Dearest Daniel,

It is a beautiful autumn day. P is napping and I have just finished fiddling with the ceanothus. I hope I have not cut it back too early.

The bypass is going ahead, I'm sorry to say, and will be visible from the garden. I try not to look eastwards too much as it puts me in such a lather. Frankie was saying that it is supposed to be part of a European trunk road, but that it will be obsolete as soon as the Channel Tunnel opens and all the freight goes through Kent instead. Your friend Gregory Bray wrote such a good short letter to the Chronic, which I enclose forthwith.

Dear Sir,

The root of the problem regarding traffic in Batheaston and Bathampton is not congestion but cars. More roads make room for more cars. It is that simple. I would like to use public transport more often, but public transport is now privately owned, and costs too much for the people who need it most.

Sincerely,
Mr G. Bray,
Larkhall.

Isn't that good? Succinct and to the point. It goes to show, doesn't it, because he was never what you'd call 'academic'. He lives just down the road, too, though I haven't seen him about. He was in Cornwall a year or two back, I believe. I wonder what he's doing.

When are you down? Next w/e?

Love to you,
Mum

January 3 [1993]

D – letter lovely. When you're here I forget to say or can't what is the word, I have such a lot I still want to say explain, not easy all in a rush big things and no time. Sorry you didn't have brother or sister for example. Not for want of trying? Look through few things, albums, exercise books, but mostly tired. Morphine not as nice as all that. Sick. Be nice to J that is most important. Hard to know, worth it though I found. Have avoided hospice so far. Would like to go on a bit here. Sorry didn't get to more things with you in which you were. Enjoy flat garden. See you. P.

Dear Daniel,

I hope you will forgive the liberty of this letter from two almost total strangers. Amanda and I moved in next door to your parents last year, and we are very happily settled. We have met you once, fleetingly, when you came down on a visit, but didn't get a chance to say hello at Christmas as we had relatives staying and it was manic, as Christmases often are.

We just wanted to say how sorry we are about your father's illness and how incredible we both think you and your mother have been. My own father died of the prolonged after-effects of a stroke last year and I feel for you as a witness to a parent's decline. It is so hard to accept one's final powerlessness and see one's way clear of the vastly complex emotions involved. We were not lucky enough to know your father before he had cancer, but other people in the street have spoken about him and we have just bought two of his wonderful paintings (and a collage). We also bought a small vase for your mother and he was very funny about it!

I do not believe that the vitality of such a mind is wasted, or otherwise extinguished after death. My father, like yours I suspect (forgive me if I am speaking out of turn), did not always suffer fools gladly. He had affairs and hurt my mother terribly, while enriching the lives of his colleagues and pupils (he taught History and French at a school in Sheffield), who adored him. He could not speak after his stroke, but my mother said she could understand some of the sounds he made and, more importantly, *felt* that he was trying to explain things. I am not religious, and nor were my parents. But as Mum said to us (I'm one of three) after he died, any God worthy of the name would be asking Dad what he did with his life, not what he did wrong.

I hope that this letter doesn't presume too much, and that if it does I can make sincere amends the next time we meet.

With very best wishes for a peaceful end.

Simon (and Amanda) Hooper

January 26 [1993]

Announcement on the 15.15 Great Western intercity service from London Paddington to Bath Spa.

'Good evening, ladies and gentlemen. This is your conductor Martin speaking. I'm sorry about the go-slow we're experiencing. The driver has received reports of children placing things on the line in the Box area and he is currently clearing the way ahead. We'll be picking up speed as soon as he gets the OK. Once again, we do apologize for the delay to your journey today and for any inconvenience it may have caused you.'

Death Squad

My father died in the winter of 1993. He was fifty-four. It was a pretty swift exit; after one cycle of chemotherapy the preceding summer, the doctors gave up, and so – not without relief – did he.

Illness failed to ennoble him. In October, the disease turned metaphysical, suckering from brain to mind. Of all transformations this was the worst, if only because while lucid, Dad was too appalled by his periodic fugues to offer any apologies or explanations. It wasn't that bad, in retrospect – he threw his food around a bit, pissed and swore, cried in the night. We had been warned to expect this, but it could be embarrassing in public, and knowing that his wife and son were sometimes embarrassed put an unrealistic pressure on him to be sympathetic the rest of the time – as though we were the patients and he the nurse. The disabled are good at this role reversal. Ugly people, too. Philip Rathbone wasn't.

I shared confidences with him, but we said little. It was as if all conversation strayed from the point, or petered out unless disciplined by practical considerations.

One mild weekend in November, Dad visited my flat and my mother and I sat him in the garden, under the plum tree, where he looked almost healthy. He gave me some stern instructions about ground elder and foxes, and an hour later asked to go home. I wasn't offended; he preferred to order his thoughts as far as he was able on paper, where the dwindling present was less, well, present. The script grew spidery, the thought patterns crudely repetitive. His last letters to me, written two weeks before he died, were short and mad: lines of continuous characterless scrawl converging like twists of raffia. He said that he had something to tell me, which was probably a plea of sorts, and stopped speaking to my mother when he found out that she'd been looking into hospices for him. A week after the funeral, we opened the slope. It contained about six tubes of unused yellow paint, and all my letters; there were also a few barmy copies of his missives to me, together with odd things squirrelled away from other secret places in the house, like my school reports and old exercise books. There was one piece of paper addressed to Jane – a shopping list in angry upper case: '3 MID GREEN, 1 BLACK, 2 CHROME YELLOW FOR CHRIST'S SAKE, PAPER FOR WRITING AND HEAVY CARTRIDGE, STAMPS, MOISTURISER, SAUSAGES, BACON, CHEESE – CAMEMBERT OR ANYTHING REALLY BAD FOR ME, BUTTER, EGGS, CHOCOLATE, BOOZE. *STAMPS.*'

The end was scrappy – I was, and wasn't, there.

Dad had seemed fine at the weekend, but I got a call on Tuesday at work and caught the train that afternoon. It was delayed; there were kids on the line on the far side of Box Tunnel. We crawled through it, creaking and chafing, and I remember thinking 'There's nothing I can do about this,' which, oddly enough, is what Mum said to me at the hospital. Dad had been conscious until four o'clock, when he slipped into a coma. I turned up in Ackerly Ward at six, but he didn't come round, and by the next morning it was all over.

There were no relatives to invite to the cremation. My parents were only children. Mum's widowed father died soon after she married Dad, and Dad's divorced, estranged father had succumbed to heatstroke in the south of France in 1979. Dad's ancient mother was still alive in '93, but in a home and somewhat distressed, which presented us with a dilemma.

'I can't not tell her,' said my mother, tempted. 'Or can I? Not?'

The confusion was pardonable; Caroline Isabella Rathbone was a more than averagely confusing person.

After a traumatic late divorce in the early seventies, she had developed an obsessional mania which involved the serial theft of doorknobs, handles and related items. At the one clan gathering I can recall – I could only have been five or so – Grandma Rathbone had disappeared upstairs for a lie down in the afternoon and gone straight to the bathroom, where I later surprised her in the act of disengaging the toilet flush with a penknife. I walked in on her – an accidental intrusion. I was barely house-trained, she said. But I only walked straight in because the door wasn't locked, and the door was only unlocked because Caroline had already unscrewed the lock and pocketed it.

'If I tell her,' my mother reasoned aloud, 'I'll have to invite her.'

She stroked an eyebrow meditatively. 'You see, I don't know how much to say. She might get upset: she won't really understand, but she might react. And then if she came, well . . .'

'Get the nurse to check her handbag,' I suggested. 'And don't sit her anywhere near the coffin if it's got handles.'

Of course, when we rang the home – in Radstock, a little way off but not quite far enough – Caroline was creepily enthusiastic ('Jane, dear, I'm so looking forward to it . . .'), so we decided on a plain box with no fittings and steered the once imperious matriarch to a safe pew by the window.

An hour before the service, I spent a few minutes with Dad in the Crematorium's thickly carpeted, overpolished chapel of rest. From the adjoining room, with its sale-of-the-century pelmets and hidden furnace, floated familiar voices. Frankie Schumacher pressed random consolations on Jane and old friends from Corsham. Simon and Amanda Hooper, the neighbours, introduced themselves in sympathetic counterpoint. And a West Country accent with transatlantic vowels that I recognized as belonging to Dougall Voss exchanged pleasantries with Carey, who had co-founded a software company and shed thirty pounds in the last four months. They'd flown back together, father and son.

My mother had clear eyes when she came to fetch me at 3 p.m. She was dressed in a deep charcoal suit and white shirt, her brown-grey curls swept back in a resisting bun. She looked at me across the casket.

'That's a nice hair cut, Daniel,' she said, directly. 'Is that the fashion now – you know, to have it so short?'

'It's not that short.'

'No, well . . .' she allowed, 'but it is fairly short, isn't it? I mean, you couldn't have it much shorter, could you, or you wouldn't have any hair left! Still, I'm not saying it's not nice. Although,' she paused and blinked, 'long – longer – hair suits you, too.'

'Thanks.'

'Well, it does! It suits the shape of your face. You've got long features, like me.' She sighed. 'Anyway . . .'

And we went in.

I remember a plain, square room with two shallow alcoves either side of the disguised caterpillar-track on which Dad lay, waiting.

The pews were pale and unaged, with gold-trimmed hassocks. One whole side of the Congregational chapel was made of tinted glass, giving out on to the wintered scrub of Monkton Combe, with its ganglia of blackthorn and bramble. The Reverend L. Deldridge, one of those tactless exquisites ('I have another funeral at five . . .') in whom the Church of England specializes, paid excruciating tribute to Philip Rathbone's 'special skills as an artist', which made him sound retarded. I played 'The Lord's My Shepherd' on a three-and-a-half-octave Casio keyboard; G below middle C stuck at the beginning of the second verse. The coffin trundled into a black hole behind the curtains, and I tried not to think of the kitsch cremation scene from *Diamonds Are Forever*, in which Bond is consigned to the flames by a couple of freelance gay psychopaths. The service dragged on, and Grandma Caroline sang an extra verse of 'Abide With Me' all by herself in some parallel universe where disinhibition, like nudity in the morgue, goes unremarked.

It was a subdued occasion, though not exactly sad. Grieving is not the same thing as being miserable and there's a lot to be said for the mental distraction of having to deal with other people. It stops you thinking about those moments when the coin-op in the launderette jams, or when a much thought-upon lover sounds irked at the other end of the line. Trivial, emptier disappointments.

There was the funeral tea to negotiate, too, at which Dad would be present in a small pewter urn. (A stipulation of the will.)

'Is that all?' I heard my mother say to the funerary clerk on the chapel's back doorstep as he handed her the ashes. She clattered the lid off and on.

He spoke softly, comfortingly, while I waited in the car. She remonstrated, unmoved, and he made a helpless gesture. This went on for a while, until the spade-faced clerk took the urn and disappeared inside the Crem. My mother crunched back across the rain-sharpened gravel to the car, and handed me the extra scoop of God knows who or what with an air of placid vindication.

'That's more like it,' she said.

* * *

A couple of weeks later, I was feeling randy and took myself off to a backroom. I'd not been to one before, but a subtle coercion of sympathies from workmates, friends, ex-lovers and neighbours had made me feel oddly euphoric, as though I deserved a long break from responsibility. Ryan and I were undergoing a trial separation, so . . .

Even on a Wednesday, the Stack, which then clung to the scuppers of Bermondsey, was packed. The flyposters on the inside door advertised a 'uniform and discipline' night, and depicted a City guy on his knees in front of a marine. The whole of the interior was painted black – walls, windows, barstools, ceiling, floor – and from the cornices the proprietors had hung swathes of webbing into which everyone stumbled and fell. Yet for all its murky fetishism, the pub's ambience was one of familiar repose. True, there were a few dolled-up squaddies hanging about looking daggers at each other, and a 'boot-camp' barber offering buzz cuts. Otherwise, the bar

accommodated no more than the usual mixture of local loi-
terers and men on their way home from work.

The boy on the door, straining to stay the right side of
thirty, said goodnight to those already on their way out, and
told them to look after themselves. He turned to me
and bunched his lips.

'Have we seen you before?'

'No.'

'You know what kind of club this is, don't you?'

'Yeah.'

I tried to sound off-hand.

'Bless,' he said, and slapped my fiver in the ancient cash
register. (I had the change, but it was too deep in my pocket
to get at.) 'It's not frightening once you get used to it. Just a
lot of pooves in poor lighting. Come and ask for Pat here if
anyone gives you any lip.'

The huge black guy at the coat check winked once, and
went back to his shattered copy of *Great Expectations*.

I ordered a pint of Guinness at the bar, remembering to
keep my eyes down so that the bar lights – the only ones on in
the building – wouldn't make them glitter too unnaturally, and
edged towards the thin partition wall at the back of the saloon.
To one side, furthest from the bar, was a door in the wall,
slightly ajar, beyond which a minimally illuminated coppice of
limbs swayed to and fro.

The backroom itself was essentially a pen, its bay boarded
up in consideration of the neighbours. It might have been a
dining room in a previous life, but felt, even on a cold night in
February, more like a sauna. (From the outside, you could see
steam pluming through the vents of a defunct fan.) A dullish,
respectable-looking man in his late thirties or early forties,
who'd come in at the same time as me, said 'Christ' under his

breath. I looked back: his spectacles were already white eggs; hands budded and unfurled next to him.

There were about sixty men in that small space in various states of excitement and undress. Many had their eyes closed.

As a sample of their sex they seemed representative, if weighted towards thirty- to forty-year-olds, of whom many were probably – typically – homeowners with safe jobs. Their blind couplings seemed less safe, it must be said, despite the crotch-level provision of free condoms and lubricant in handy dispensers. A body or two to my right, I saw the man in glasses inexpertly stroking a rubber on to his dick with one hand (a ring on his marriage finger) while attempting to hold his trousers up with the other. An obliging boy in front of him bit through a sachet of lube and applied it vigorously to his arse, urging the older man to fuck him, which he did – having discarded the condom in exasperation.

Their rhythm quickly established, the two men became the focus of the room's attention. The fair-haired boy, thicker-waisted from the side view and wearing – just about – a plain shirt saddle-bagged with sweat, scrabbled open the flies of two men caressing in front of him and wolfed down the contents of each, gulping and gagging with every thrust from behind. His lover meanwhile let his suit trousers fall to the ground with an unbuckled clank, and bent his knees, drawing the boy back on to his cock so as to penetrate him at a deeper, steeper angle.

A shrewish specimen, of uncertain age and complexion, insinuated himself into position behind the couple, dropped onto all fours and made a pretence of licking the man's buttocks. But his agile fingers were more interested in the trousers on the floor, from which he lifted a leather wallet and a pager before getting to his feet.

'That's it . . . nice . . .' the thief whispered, retreating.

The man in glasses pounded his way to a long, vocal orgasm, confusedly echoed by his partner's groans. Then, after resting a moment on the boy's back, he pulled out with a sinewy squelch and bared his teeth in distaste at the residue smeared over the end of his dick.

'Shit,' he said, and someone laughed.

He picked up his trousers and searched the pockets for a tissue.

And again whispered it, 'Shit, shit . . .' as the weightless tinkle of small change betrayed his loss. Scared eyes, until recently half-closed and crossed with lust, opened wide. Inches away, the shrew-like thief played with himself in the shadows.

I slipped out and found 'Pat' by the cigarette machine.

'Is it Pat?' I asked.

'It is,' he replied graciously.

'Well . . . there's a pickpocket in the back,' I said. 'He's nicking wallets. It's the skinny geezer in blue – the one with the grey hair and goatee.'

'Mary – she's trouble,' Pat sighed, lighting up.

He gave me the kind of look that can go either way. If the pupils lock on, you're looking at a month in plaster; if the eyes roll up and the lids lower, you're not worth the hassle. On the back of Pat's grey roadie T-shirt, the words 'We All Need' stood out in big white letters. The chest-hugging front read, simply, 'Security'.

A vein moved in the bole of his neck.

'Word of advice, my little geezer,' he said, lids lowered. 'Don't speak common if you're not common.' Pat leaned his massive bulk against the machine and shook a gold ID bracelet.

He indicated a yellowing notice above his head that read

'Beware pickpockets. The managment [sic] accepts no responsibility, etc'.

'I thought you should know,' I mumbled.

Pat laughed. 'Oh, I do,' he said, and swivelled so that a single crease divided the plate of his belly. Stretching over the cigarette machine, he reached back to a panel of switches on the inside wall of the bar.

The lights went on beyond the partition. Cries of disappointment and surprise greeted Pat as he filled the doorway and placed the great pink flats of his hands against its wobbling jambs. I could barely see around him. From the back, the folds in his neck made a five-line stave.

The posh man in glasses got as far as 'I think I've been rob–' before Pat cut him off.

'Listen, girls,' he called out.

Around the pub, men whooped and crowed.

'Save yourselves a trip down the station and *please* put your valuable items in the coat check. That's what it's there for – to give everybody's guilty conscience the evening off.' Pat nodded to a chatterer on his left. 'That's right, darling. You think about it.'

'Actually,' began the respectable man in the measured tones indicative of panic, 'I think I dropped my wallet in the, er – at the, um, bar. Do you know if it's been handed in?'

In the returned light, the poor man seemed crushed by responsibility. People were tittering. He tried to hide his silver cufflinks, kept putting one hand over the other, then thrust both into his pockets and squeezed past Pat without waiting for an answer. The grizzled pickpocket followed.

'Have we met?' Pat said, and barred his way.

' 'k off,' the wan-looking thief replied, dimly scratching at an armpit, where the dark blue of his Fred Perry shirt bore a series of tidemarks.

Pat put an arm comfortingly around the little man's shoulders and in one movement swung him out of the room so that his legs trod the air like a stuntman's in freefall.

'I'm sorry?' Pat said.

The thief wriggled and cursed. Pat pressed him against the partition, knocking a clutch of empty bottles off the makeshift shelf.

'Wallet. Come on. Cough up.'

'I haven't go' a fuckin' wallet. 'k off.'

Hardly moving his arms, Pat folded his prey into a necklock and fished the stolen items out of the pickpocket's combats.

'There, easy wasn't it?' Pat said, shouldering him towards the exit. 'Have a nice trip home–'

''k you.'

' – and if I see you again, I'll put you on a drip.'

''kin' black cunt.'

'Oooh,' Pat exclaimed, kicking open the outer door. 'I don't think we can have that.' And with the bored élan of a cook slinging guts into the bin, threw the little man into the open road.

There was some desultory applause from the saloon as Pat tapped the cuff-linked homeowner on the shoulders and, wordlessly, returned his possessions. Back at the bar, he picked up his copy of Dickens and lit another cigarette.

The lights dimmed, and men began drifting back into the wings of the pen, where they struggled to restage the earlier scene of abandon.

But darkness is a fragile state and cannot bear much inspection. People go to it to have sex for the same reason that they like to pray in it – because they want to feel something without seeing it. Backrooms are plain spaces, like Lutheran churches. Too much visual ornament is a distraction from the divine, or the transcendent. The congregation is there to forget time, a forgetfulness dependent on averting one's eyes; you are communing with the Almighty and the Extremely Big, remember, not listening to Laurence Deldridge in his ratty cassock and surplus, or being fucked by the Asian guy in the dodgy slacks.

The more you see, the less you seem to feel or know.

I felt cut off from all the shoving and groping that night. In any case, it died down after the theft – after the orgiasts had seen more than enough of each other – and so, perversely, I began to relax. I even closed my eyes and reached for the fair-haired boy as he brushed past me on his way out. He felt taller and older to the touch; more willing to embrace and to kiss than have sex, yet again. His tongue tasted of chewing gum and other men. I felt him looking at me.

'You're nice,' he said drunkenly, and hugged me.

This could hardly have been true. I had bags under my eyes and spots the size of radishes nestling in my eyebrows. All attempts to turn a terrible short haircut into a hard 'look' had failed. Instead of squaring off my head, the remaining tufts of hair made me look like a hedge-trimmed bride of Frank-enstein.

I opened my eyes. The boy closed his in reply, and I counted the freckles on his flattish nose. His mouth hung open with post-coital fatigue, enough to hint at a small gap in the front teeth.

We held on to each other for a while, moving our hands around each other's moistened backs, sometimes under the shirt, sometimes over. I counted vertebrae. Then he let go of me and left.

It was the last time I saw Craig Spillings alive.

* * *

I rang my mother last night and told her about the service.

She was horrified, hadn't realized, didn't know the family well, felt that 'that boy' had made a mess of some people's lives, but still – what a shock, and so young. To my surprise, she asked if she could come along; and I said yes. She's good in this kind of situation, with a self-strengthening sympathy for near strangers in their hour of weakness.

I invited Carey, too. At three in the morning, the tremors got to me and I had a waking dream about the statistical improbability of the three hundred boys in my year at Lyncombe all making it to their mid-twenties without a few casualties. My dream guide was an ethereal young man in jeans that hung about his pipe-cleaner legs like Goliath's hand-me-downs. His name came to me as I wiped the sweat from my chest and got up to make some tea: Peter Lillingston, the boy with weak bones.

Anyway, it made me think – but Carey said no, he didn't want to come. Not nastily; he was sorry, really – but he had meetings. (I called in sick.) He'd be down soon enough to see Frankie; it would just be too painful and uncomfortable seeing everyone again. So I left it at that.

*

The twelve-fifteen from Paddington is on time. We've just left Chippenham and will be entering Box Tunnel in a few minutes. The sun is high and the swift shadows of railside

214

objects – chimneys, trees, bridges, signals – flame noiselessly on the table in front of me. I am studying a Xeroxed photograph of a child retrieved from my twenty-fifth birthday present, a Victorian writing slope with a thin walnut veneer.

Light has passed twice across the face of this child and almost erased it. The first wave of light imprinted me standing in a garden beside a plastic paddling pool with one hand on my round stomach and another pointing at the lens. It would have been a good photo, originally. There are two adult figures in the left-hand side of the frame, laughing proudly. The rubble of infancy surrounds me: a castle-shaped bucket and spade (no sand), a doffed rug, hoops, discarded sandals, and a book.

I remember the tan-coloured sandals, and how their buckles bit into the sides of my feet when new. The resulting sores gave me a precocious vocabulary, full of 'blisters', 'verrucas', and hopeful references to Doctor Scholl, who sounded nice, although strangely he was never in the shop. But these are memories by association, no longer visible in the crumpled glare of this photocopy, where the second mechanical wave of light has destroyed most of the detail and defaced me with ink-blot acne. I suppose the hair is distinctive – white-blonde, voluminous, awry.

The child's gesture is also unnerving because he appears to be pointing straight at me across two decades.

Oh, I know – he's not really pointing at me, but at my father, the man holding the camera. Still, the outflung arm does look like an accusation (I'm frowning, too), and innocence often comes across as a rebuke.

Box Tunnel is seconds ahead, at the end of the cutting. The speed of approach has changed over the years; passengers' eardrums no longer stretch and strain; even the tidal roar of entry has been mopped up. And yet, here it comes, with a jolt

– a leap into the dark that spills drinks and stuns the kids . . .
Demons grind and snicker under my feet, newspapers are
lowered, and along the carriage eyes stray towards those
double-edged reflections in the window as they drop their
double-glazed jaws.

The hillside releases us into a molten confluence of valleys.
A disordering love for my birthplace catches me in the throat:
for all its sulky citizens and ransacked architecture, its gothic
follies and raised pavements. This is where I was brought up.
When someone asks me where I come from, I nearly always
say 'South London,' and then apologetically, 'Bath, originally.'
'Lucky you,' they say then, and I know they're right.

Now the carriage ignites, and the Georgian terraces of the
London Road incline to us in brilliant serpent's coils. (The
road is straight, but warped by our orbit.) The houses are too
dazzling to look at. Their gardens grow; they turn slowly.
The birch trees waltz along the riverbank towards the turbid
certainty of Pulteney Weir.

★

'Daniel!'

Christ Church, Julian Road, lies halfway up Lansdown Hill
on the northern slopes of the city. It has been cleaned since I
saw it last, and the mid-Victorian oolite stone is lime-white in
the afternoon. The forecourt seems to preserve the high echo
of chippings flicked against the wall by a succession of three-
point turns, but the cars in it are grave and still.

The sober-suited congregation is already inside, apart from
my mother, who waits on the steps and hails me diffidently
when she sees me across the road. I am sweating unpleasantly
in my suit; my mouth is dry.

Before we go in, I give her the Xeroxed photograph.

'This was in the slope. Someone put it there.'

My mother looks small-framed today. She is wearing a black Chinese jacket from the market and an oddly tight, Quantesque woollen skirt. She must be sweltering, but her face is lowered.

'I had the box cleaned,' she says. 'There wasn't anything in it. I checked.'

'It was Dad, then.' (I'm out of breath after running up the hill.) 'There was a compartment, with a spring catch. I used to keep stuff in it.'

'I don't know anything about that.'

'Who is it?'

'Look at all that hair—'

I interrupt. 'It isn't me, is it?'

'I don't—'

'It's Carey, isn't it?'

My mother freezes for a moment and then folds the sheet of paper. Her lips are set together, pushed out slightly. She has begun to smell of fear, a compound perfume of lipstick and morning coffee – and something else entirely foreign, like a fermentation of weeds.

'Isn't it?' I insist. 'Dad had an affair with Frankie, didn't he?'

This brings my mother's head up. The lines on her forehead are deep for her age; the skin has dried up; the eyes oscillate like spinning plates.

'I guessed anyway.'

She puffs out her lips, and manages a punctured sigh.

We both wait a little while; then she nods, as if in dispute with herself.

'I loved your father very much.'

A sort of congested snort escapes her, and she laughs,

217

fiddles a bit with the hem and smoothes the sides of her jacket; at last puts one arm decisively through mine.

Beyond the rotating doors, I can see the Reverend Deldridge beckoning, coaxing, looking at his watch. I stop her, as she tries to steer me inside.

'What? What were you going to say?'

She lets go of me, and is spun into the nave.

The day behind us is bright; in front, it thickens into flagstone and brass. The air is cool, peculiarly freshened by the papery smell of *Hymns Ancient and Modern*, and of psalters full of amiable ridiculousness. 'He taketh no pleasure in the strength of an horse, neither delighteth he in any man's legs.' I had a few organ lessons here in my teens, and sang in the choir, where the cross-bearer was a robust Jamaican and the lead soprano a blue-lipped Afrikaner who had a heart attack halfway through the Old Hundredth and was not greatly mourned. I sit near the back, not wanting to look around and see the scattered lights of my old friends' eyes, housed in faces that will either be the same, or indelibly changed.

I can see only necks and hats. There are some RAF officers here, and many couples; no one I recognize. In rows, we somewhat resemble a class of schoolchildren, bewildered by a sudden, dizzying superannuation. These are proper clothes we're wearing. We pray as though we mean it, and not because it's a meaningless chore.

That one – there, in the grey suit, balding, with the pregnant wife, third row from the front – that's Bruce Hartt! (We're singing 'To Be A Pilgrim' and he's moving his lips to the music, shifting from foot to foot the way Death Squaddies used to when forced to do something they didn't like.) Next to him, the fleshy young guy in the waistcoat with the curly hair

– who's he? Like a puddled reflection, the features of Tom Burns-Wilson, my erstwhile assailant from King Edwards, take a minute to resolve themselves. Both men look shifty and well off. What would they be, in nineties Bath? Antique dealers? Wine merchants?

By the last verse, the singing has become unbearable, and the pained expression on the sensitive young organist's face says it all. Disharmony he expects; it's our slowness he can't bear – that terrible Anglican undertow that turns every tune into a battle with time and gravity. Bunyan's pilgrim 'knows he at the end/shall life inherit', but at the rate we've been going I wouldn't be so sure. By my side, my mother warbles into her hymn book. Across the way, a large-breasted woman, with an air of the military wife about her, yodels into the gallery. She sings up; my mother sings down. The Reverend Deldridge drifts palely to the lectern.

'Blessed are they that mourn: for they shall be comforted,' he begins.

Of course, this being a memorial service for friends and colleagues, and not the funeral, Deldridge can afford to be relatively upbeat: '. . . and so we come together,' he continues, 'not merely to mourn our loss, but to seek solace for the humanly incomprehensible in the greater mystery of a deity who was made flesh and died upon the cross.'

A few coughs ricochet around the church.

'And to give thanks; to thank God for the life of Craig, beloved son of Norman and Liz, friend to so many of us; to celebrate, in words and music, the wealth of affection and love that he inspired in others. We remember especially Craig's special skills in the . . .'

As the tape unspools, a scattering of snivels disturbs the shafts of sunlit dust around me. Stained blue and red nearer the windows but losing definition by the time they hit the pews, the rays are opaquely animated by grief and allergic reaction.

A young girl in a blue dress, two rows in front, bobs her head impressively. She's trying to keep a sneeze down, and wants someone to admire her self-restraint. She turns, looks at me and puffs her cheeks. The sun comes out from behind a cloud and she is momentarily hidden by the increased veil of light, though I can see her behind it, still looking and wondering. Her face is a complicated blank of puzzlement and recent experience. The sneeze has been forgotten. And then her mother, whose hand she has been holding, gets up and makes her way to the choir steps.

She is familiar, this short, self-contained woman. Her rolling gait and arm-length black hair strikes a chord, louder than the lingering suspensions of hymns and sing-song platitudes.

She stops at the top of the steps.

'This is a very short reading,' the young woman says. 'So I won't keep you.' (A ripple of laughter.) 'Someone read this out on stage at Glastonbury when I was there – with Craig – and there were queues at the tattoo tent all day afterwards. It was the only bit of the Bible Craig ever heard, I think. It's the famous bit from the Song of Solomon.

' "Set me as a seal upon thine heart, as a seal upon thine arm: for love is strong as death; jealousy is cruel as the grave: the coals thereof are coals of fire, which hath a most vehement flame. Many waters cannot quench love, neither can the floods drown it: if a man would give all the substance of his house for love, it would be utterly contemned." '

When she comes back down the aisle, Karen Kale smiles at Norman and Liz Spillings and acknowledges a few other people with tiny gestures: a raising of her eyebrows here, a covert wave there. The atmosphere of the service has changed; as people turn to each other, it is as though they have been given permission to speak freely. I would not formerly have credited Karen – the Karen I knew, blear of eye and caustically perfumed – with such a transforming power, but then she is not that Karen any more, clearly. Her shoulders are relaxed, her once-sour complexion ruddy and colourful. She moves nimbly, compactly. She is liked; you can feel it. She has a comic instinct equal to a sense of propriety.

Karen does a double-take on seeing me, looks nonplussed at first, then sits and swivels so quickly she catches Flo with her arm. Her mouth is wide open with delight and consternation.

I am confounded by her reading, and can't respond as I would like.

I keep mangling the tissues handed to me by Mum, and thinking of Dad, I suppose, who taught all those people for all that time and never had a proper send-off, because he died slowly during the winter.

But there is something about being recognized that takes you out of yourself. Karen waves away my confusion, though she is not so very composed herself, and points me out to Flo. Her lips move excitedly.

'That's Daniel,' I can see her saying. 'Daniel – Daddy's friend.'

*

Flo has gone home with Karen's mother, because Karen says she wants to talk to me. So we walk to the Chequers Inn, a wormeaten freehouse at the end of Julian Road, where you can still buy mild, and where the addled darts players broadcast their arrows like handfuls of seed.

'I told Liz to get in touch,' Karen says. 'I'm glad she did.'

She taps a fag into a dead pint, and folds an arm underneath her chest. She looks content and confident. She runs a temping agency, and does promotions for a local computer publisher – 'keeping my hand in'.

'Craig rated you, you know,' she reveals suddenly. 'He said you were all right. He talked about you.'

My fingers are clamped around my third pint of Guinness. The pub is filling up with brickies from across the road, where the black facades of St James's Square are being sand-blasted; it must be seventy-five degrees outside at least, but I still feel cold.

'We didn't really keep in touch . . .' I begin, and give up.

Karen shuts her eyes and smiles.

'I know,' she says, cautiously.

I look at her. She is offering reassurance as the downpayment on further disclosure – and I am resisting, because I know such offers are usually only requests in kind.

'And for what it's worth,' she shakes her head, 'I know you two had a thing at school.'

She waits to see if I want to add anything.

'Face it,' she almost laughs, 'he had a thing with half of Bath, didn't he? And he never could keep a secret.'

The voice of sympathy slips a key into that of revelation.

'He didn't think full stop, mind, that was his trouble,' Karen continues, momentarily deaf to the world. 'But I didn't care at first – when it all came out – because I thought, like, if you're going to have a child at seventeen, you might as well get the father right.'

'I could never see Craig as a father,' I put in, without thinking. Before the words are out of my mouth I'm stumbling to retrieve them.

This time, Karen's laughter is hollow. She looks away, puts a handful of hair behind her shoulders, settles down. And says nothing for a while, knowing as I do that this silence is the point at which, one way or the other, many things are decided.

'No,' she says, finally. 'Maybe not.'

'You don't have to–'

'I know I don't. But it's nice, Dan.'

She reaches over the table and, in an intimately bungled gesture, slaps the back of my hand with a wet beermat.

'It's nice to – to speak without explaining. Or just, you know, explain whatever.' The fag has died in her hand; a gust of wind blows a plastic pint tumbler in from the street, its rim torn into strips.

Quietly and inexpressively, the water wells up out of Karen Kale's round, brown eyes and runs down her cheeks. It pools surprisingly quickly – actually forms a small puddle – on the table.

'You lose your chance,' she says, after a bit. 'To explain – when something big happens to you. There's no going back.'

She sniffs, and for the first time does something that reminds me of her former self: wipes her nose on her sleeve.

'Carey was gone, like that.' Karen snaps her fingers without making a sound. 'But I worried about him. I did worry. I've heard . . . I see his Mum, down the shops sometimes, though we don't speak. He was like me.' She stops. 'And he was the first to take an interest.'

For some reason, this makes us both smile.

'We were going to open a stall in the market,' she says. 'Health food.'

'Another one,' I say, not meaning to sound unkind.

Karen wags a finger. 'Ah, yes. But not the same.' She rummages for a cigarette, finds one and carries on without lighting it. 'We were going to do it properly, you know, build up a little co-op, sign petitions . . .'

'I'm sorry.'

'Oh, no. There was no way . . .' she says, simply. 'Not at all.'

I wait a bit.

'Because?'

Karen is motionless, which is answer enough. It's a pretty stupid question. Soaking lentils can be like white-water rafting with the right person, until the wrong one comes along.

Eventually, she says: 'I asked Craig to marry me.'

'Why?'

'Why?' Karen raises her voice, and drops it again apologetically. She indicates the rest of the room with her head. 'This is Bath, Daniel. Not London. Poofs and single mothers aren't welcome, not if you live in the ordinary parts. Don't be fooled by the big houses and voices. It's sleepy and small and suspicious, and people don't like people like you or me in places like this.' She gives a last sniff. 'And I asked because I thought he wanted me to: he was the one who came looking for me, remember.'

The mental picture of my last encounter with Craig Spillings fizzles briefly as Karen talks.

'Anyway, he said no. We had a good year together, but he said no.'

'And that was that.'

'Practically, yes.' She pauses significantly. 'I mean, things were fairly dreadful for a time after that . . .'

'I can imagine.'

'Can you?'

Her mouth makes an ugly shape.

'Sorry,' she concedes. 'I know you can.'

'That's OK.'

'No, well, you were right. He just wasn't a father. Flo hardly ever saw him; he was someone Mummy knew. So she knows, but she doesn't really *know*. He paid support and pissed off.'

Karen is only my age and in some respects, without all that black make-up, she looks younger (and healthier) than she did when I saw her last, seven years ago. But her brow is also tauter in a way which suggests the hidden lines of someone who has decided not to see certain things.

'Mind, he could afford it. He was loaded.'

Karen picks at her teeth quickly, watching me digest this one.

'*Craig?* He always made out he was broke.'

She gives a shuddery laugh and leans forward, so that her chest all but rests on the tabletop.

'To think our Hunter should be so blind,' she says. 'The Spillingses were rolling in it. How do you think his parents could afford to send him to King Edward's, then? Did you ever go to his house?'

'Actually, no.'

'It was a bloody mansion out along the Lower Bristol Road.'

'But he lived in Twerton!'

'Twerton, Texas. His dad was way up in the MOD.'

'Craig was the one who took the piss out of me for being posh.'

'Yeah,' Karen reflects sombrely. 'But everyone lies about sex and money, don't they? And influence.'

With renewed scepticism, we both scan the pub, ready to winkle out the lottery millionaire in the corner, drooling over his shove ha'penny. It's true; Craig was always going abroad for his holidays.

'His dad got him the RAF cadetship, which paid for Uni, and made sure he got into Signals and Radar at Malvern. Found him a place on a new technology development programme. All the classy stuff: lab work, occasional test flights. Classy, controlled and safe.'

Karen pauses, forced to admit an irony at which the world might laugh.

'Until it wasn't.'

'What went wrong?'

'I don't know.' She shrugs. 'Instrument failure.'

'I read that.'

'And that's the last you'll read, what with the security blackout.'

'There has to be an inquiry, though.'

'Doesn't mean anything. Norman knows, I reckon, but won't let on. Liz said that it was something to do with a virtual navigation thing for low-attack night raids. They were trying it out and it – well, it didn't work.'

'Trust me,' I say, recalling Carey's politely unanswerable certitudes about Plus and AOI, 'it never does.'

'Thing is, though,' Karen considers, her scepticism less dimly prejudicial, ' "virtual" means what it says in the end, so it's no wonder the plane crashed. He was flying a videogame. Virtual reality is, like, "almost" reality, isn't it?'

'But not quite.'

'Exactly.' Karen breathes out and smiles sadly. 'And you can't have the real thing twice, whatever anyone tells you.'

'You should tell Carey that,' I say. 'He works in IT. He makes–'

The evening sun goes in, and the Chequers' interior is

suddenly close and dark, as though a dusty, gilt-edged cloak has been shaken out over us. We look at each other unwillingly.

Through rather than under her breath, Karen says: 'So there.'

The shadow passes. We finish our drinks, and the first of the serious long-session boozers begins kicking the jukebox, with its weird menus of do-wop, punk, re-mixed Dusty Springfield and Take That.

'Remember me to your mum, Dan,' Karen says, getting up and brushing at the drops of beer that have fallen onto her lilac chemise. 'I always liked her. She still says hello in the street.'

'I will.'

We step outside, and walk back along Julian Road, past the boarded-up windows of what was once a sherbert-rimed confectioner's, and the stained lower reaches of the Balance Street flats, waved through in the 1960s when Grade Two listed terraces didn't cut it with the council.

I wonder briefly if I should tell Karen about Carey – and dismiss the idea. She would have asked, surely. And what would I tell her, anyway?

'I hear Lyncombe's gone,' I say, as we reach her blue Polo, its back window measley with yellow WWF stickers.

'Mmm. Sad, isn't it?' she agrees. 'We went to watch the day the contractors moved in. It was a good school.'

'Mr Dooley always said you couldn't be angry for long in an environment like that. Jesus, it had a park for a playground. All the way to Combe Down Tunnel and back over the cliff. So . . . who's "we"?'

I can't tell if I've caught her out, or if she's genuinely surprised.

'What d'you mean?'

'You said "we" went to watch. You and . . . ?'

Karen is frowning a smile at me, her mouth hanging slightly. Then she shuts it, decides I'm having her on and flourishes the ignition key.

'Gregory. You know.'

'Oh. No.'

'You did know, come on. I told your Mum.'

'As a matter of fact, I didn't. Maybe she forgot.'

'But we've been together *ages*. Three years. Three . . .' – she starts the car – '. . . years already, Christ.'

'I'm sorry.'

Karen doesn't say anything to this, and sits back for a moment, still smiling as though my confusion might lift like the morning mist.

'No, well – *I'm* sorry. I just assumed.'

'He wasn't here today.'

I sound cross. Karen pauses again, treading carefully.

'No – he's away. He's a field officer for the Conservancy Council. He's reforesting bits of Wales this week.'

'Right, right.'

'Daniel?'

'What?'

'You all right, my love?'

She is cheerfully concerned, making light of what was, after all, an innocent oversight on her part.

'Absolutely fine.'

I can smell the plastic of the driver's seat.

'No, I was just thinking the usual – well, no, not the usual – what's that? – just, you know, what a small world.'

'Are you sure?'

'I'm delighted. Of course I am.' My laugh is pubertally stark. 'Sorry, what was the question?'

'Are you sure – I can't take you anywhere?'

'No, no. I'm just up the road, really.'

Karen chuckles roundly and pulls the door to.

'Come and see us soon,' she says, winding down the window. 'We've just moved out to Corsham. Come and have a drink. I was going to invite you anyway – even more reason, now. You still in the book?'

'Still there.'

The blue Polo swerves out into a running thread of traffic, and the air is suddenly sweet with the scent of hot stones and petrol.

'That's it, then,' Karen calls back. 'There's no escape!'

Old Games

Alone – almost – in her new, dark kitchen, Jane Rathbone soothed the single stuck-note of the fridge with a repeated whisper. At the other end of a Formica-topped table, Wicked Thing blinked greenly and would have purred if stroked.

Four years into her marriage, Jane was resourcefully happy. A late miscarriage had knocked her back a bit just before the move to Upper Alpine Gardens on the poorer side of Lansdown, but she had rallied well and was ready with a smile for neighbours and children alike. At St Luke's C. of E. Primary School, a picturesque Victorian cluster of high-ceilinged halls and classrooms in Lansdown proper, she was adored by her pupils, who endorsed the emphasis on slapstick in her art classes and wanted to go home with Miss at the end of the day. Round-bellied Gerard Felton, so shy he had to be walked to and from the school gate, clung to the sleeve of Jane's flowery pink round-collared shirt, yelling at his mother: 'I'm not coming. I don't like you. I want to stay with Miss.' Painful laughter ensued, and Jane didn't know what to think. Mrs Felton was a serious-faced mother of four. 'Don't worry,' she said sarcastically, squeezing Gerard by the wrist so that he squealed, 'he's like this at home, too.'

At home herself, Jane swung with the decade, though

only so far as common sense and a certain physical self-consciousness would permit. The beautiful set from Corsham had headed straight for London after graduation. Several girls were still in touch with Philip, and visited every few months, with secretive smiles and hash breath. Dougall and Frances came by to share in the dinner and argument. Tales of druggy escapades in dim Chelsea basements impressed them both, particularly Frances, whose allergies forced her to inhale vicariously, but left Jane feeling cold and exposed. Whenever St Luke's was mentioned, she noticed, the new Londoners flared their nostrils or asked for ashtrays.

Little things boosted her confidence, like learning to drive (difficult on Bath's hills). Freedom behind the wheel of their second-hand Hillman Imp made up for a pedestrian timidity she would never conquer as long as Evans and Owen tiled its shopfront with mirrors. The juxtaposition of slimline mannequins and repeated square reflections was an unhappy one, and Jane did not accuse herself of vanity for wanting to drive past it. Philip's ignorance was benign; he liked her as she was, and knew – hoped, trusted – that she did too. He took her to concerts and gigs; did, curiously, what she had never seen her father do for Mum – which was always to introduce her in company, straight away, by her first name.

In the kind silence that followed these introductions, Jane thought she could detect surprise. She was, she supposed, the unexpected choice: a girl who still put a cardigan over her shoulders in midsummer.

At smoky tables after 'indo-jazz fusion' upstairs at the Hat and Feather, no one asked her what she thought about the band. They said instead: 'Did you like that?' She always said yes.

And yes was seldom a lie. She *did* like a lot of the new

music, especially 'A Day In The Life' on *Sgt Pepper*, if that qualified. She wasn't informed, of course. And the way-out stuff – 'modern' classical – was too much. Philip had come back from his evening stint at the Academy last week with a composer friend, who said he was 'preparing' a piano. 'Well, I'm preparing vegetables,' Jane joked, and the man left.

Sex, too, Jane enjoyed. The early hindrances of inexperience – on both sides, she was relieved to note – had been dealt with, and the doctor said, about the other thing, that they would have to give it time.

She had a great deal to be thankful for; so much so that when, on those rare occasions, thankfulness deserted her, she was secretly afraid.

They were usually midweek evenings, at dusk.

Philip's last class at Sydney Place was at nine on a Tuesday, and the news until then was full of grim excitements: Ho Chi Minh and midi skirts ('daring to be demure' – did that make sense?), hippies, moonshots.

Dinner was in the oven, and tomorrow's art class prepared. Her day complete, Jane tried for a while to lie down, to spare her back – but the newness of the brown carpet in their bedroom disturbed her, hinted at corrosive luxury. The kitchen, too, when she had nothing to do in it, was a galley of gleaming affronts. There were no ghosts of former forms in its wipe-clean surfaces as there were in wooden fixtures or fittings, no pockmarks in the brass doorhandles.

These were superficial matters of decor, perhaps: the concerns of mood and taste. About the location, at least, there could be no doubt, for the three terraces that made up Alpine Gardens followed the natural contours of Margaret's Hill, and commanded spectacular views of the southern city.

The new house was warm and comfortable, its rooms laid

out in passable imitation of the old rows it had replaced, with a kitchen and dining room pegged into the hill, two rooms at street level and another attic-floor above that. (Philip's family had helped with the deposit.) The first month after her miscarriage Jane had spent at home, unpacking, arranging furniture, sitting upstairs where there would once have been a bay window. Philip bought a black kitten which they called Wicked after it trod dirt into one of his canvases. Wicked – more often, Wicked *Thing* – loved Jane, and sat with her while she looked out over the city, watching the yellow cranes dive and peck.

It was a strange prospect.

Now, from her window seat, Jane followed the river down to Beckford Row, a damp stretch of artisanal housing between Walcot Street and Bridge Street where she and Philip had rented a poky flat for three years. Cranes, diggers and a yellow cloud of dust marked its redevelopment. When the cloud lifted, Jane knew, Beckford Row would be gone.

This foresight lent her present situation a sentinel irony, for she had watched Upper Alpine Gardens rise out of a similar fug of loose plaster and saturated brick eight months ago.

'What have I done?'

The words tumbled out like falling masonry.

It was not her fault, she said to herself, and went back downstairs into the kitchen. Wicked Thing followed her. They sat in the protective gloom, away from difficult views and opinions.

*

Jane worked late the next day and spent a couple of hours in the Old Games Room, adjacent to the hall, where she was painting the scenic backdrops for the Juniors' production of *Jack and the Beanstalk*.

Light hit the yellowing sash windows at a low angle and spread across a worn-out billiard table, on which patches of grey slate showed through the receding baize. A local league of some sort – ex-servicemen, probably – had used this room in the past. Now it stayed locked most of the time. There were empty cue racks on the far wall, just beyond a set of steps that led backstage, and a mounted wooden shield of champions with names that stopped at 1962. By the near door, a delivery man had left some of the small crates that carried the children's morning milk.

The main drop lay on the floor between the table and the racks. Jane painted steadily, soothed by a sense of after-hours sanctuary. The Head had expressed reservations about the turgidity of her first beanstalk, and she was behind schedule with a more modest revision. The bite below her thumb still ached occasionally, making it hard to grip the brush.

At seven, with the light almost gone, Jane began to tidy up. She pondered the luxury of a cigarette and rummaged in her bag.

Frankie Voss burst into the room, yelling 'Caught you!'

Her husband slunk in behind, and shut the door.

Jane put away her lighter, smiling, and cupped an ear with one hand. Outside, the deserted playground rang with the echoes of what sounded like horses' hooves.

'Are those clogs new?' Jane asked, pointing.

'Uh-uh.' Frankie shook her head.

They were, but that wasn't the point. In the strong weave of their friendship, both women acknowledged a catch of self-deception. Frankie sought to offend the dignity she admired, and Jane determined not to offer satisfaction: nothing could visibly surprise her, though much, invisibly, did. (When Frankie married Dougall last year, hadn't she, Jane, cried on the way home? And hadn't a shallower, if no less excitable, nerve raged when the two newlyweds, with all of Colonel Schumacher's money behind them, took over a squat in Larkhall?)

Dougall tried to stabilize the pile of crates which his heavily shod wife had knocked sideways.

'How did you know I was here?' Jane said.

'Oh, you know . . .' Frankie leaned against the billiard table, her fingers twisting an amulet. She had news, but wanted Jane to be curious first.

'We called in at yours,' Dougall revealed. 'Philip was back, told us you'd be here most like. Anyway, thing is, Frankie's–'

'Oh, Ja-ane . . .' Frankie cut him off at a tangent. 'Ja-ane, we never see you these days. You don't drop by, you're always working.'

She stopped, wondering herself what this might lead to.

'I *know.* You're busy. It's OK, I understand. You're *embarrassed* by us.'

She went back to winding the amulet's leather strap around her finger.

The cleverness of forcing someone actually to deny the thing it would be a relief to admit was not lost on Jane. A polite deflection sprang to her lips – and found, unusually, no breath to inspire it. Instead:

'You're right,' Jane said, simmering. 'I have been busy, I'm sorry.' She felt Frankie's eyes on her. 'Could one of you give me a hand with this?'

She indicated the long backdrop on the floor.

'It needs to go up the steps, backstage. We can't roll it – it's still wet.'

Even in the gloaming of the Old Games Room, the blush on Frankie's cheeks was visible. The flipside of Jane's impassivity was supposed to be her quickness to reassure – that brisk, kindly 'don't be so silly' that put everything in its proper perspective. Its omission seemed ominous.

The drop filled almost the whole of the back part of the room. One vertical edge was already lying at Jane's feet near the steps, the other was over by the window. Dougall walked straight there from the door, skirting the billiard table in the middle. On the wrong side of the table but anxious now to be of use, Frankie turned and clopped the quickest way to the window – right across the glistening trunk of the beanstalk. The heavy material on the floor took the edge off her clogs' painful click-*clack*.

She saw her husband already in place, with his hands rigid on the paint-stiffened tarpaulin, eyes shut. He looked handsome, she thought, with the light behind him, his hair edged with fire, the beard and moustache darker in front, strong wrists marbled with sinew . . .

Frankie came to herself and looked down. A trail of fat green and brown clog prints marked her unthinking passage across the painted sky. She was still two and a half yards from the window and in the middle of Jane's epic storybook illustration. The white cheesecloth shirt she had on felt suddenly damp and shapeless.

'Oh,' she said. And 'ohhh . . .' a sad second later.

No one moved.

Then Jane said: 'Stay there, Frances.'

Her voice sounded neutral. She put down the drop at her end.

'But I've – I'm–' Frankie whimpered, a child in quicksand.

'Are you deaf? I said, *stay* where you are.'

Jane's anger was touched with exultation.

'Now,' she said, 'ease your feet out and stand on the tops of the–'

'I can't,' Frankie pleaded. 'I'm stuck, unless I–'

'You can. Stand on the tops of the clogs and jump to the floor. That way you won't get paint on the parquet.'

'I can't. I can't get my f–'

'Do it.'

'No.'

'Just do it.'

'No.'

'Get on with it, for Christ's sake' – Dougall spoke for the first time.

'NO!' Frankie exploded. 'STOP telling me what to do. Everyone's *always* trying to tell me what to do. Like I'm a *little girl*. Well, SCREW you. It's only a goddamn kids' painting . . . if I can just–'

Frankie moved towards Dougall, waving her arms, and skidded on a cloud. Her right foot slid forwards, her left slewed back; she fell and got up, her shirt, dress and purple suede waistcoat smeared with paint.

'Nnnooo! Nnnooo!'

The two yelps echoed back and forth.

Eventually, Frankie made it out of the picture and on to the floor.

She slipped once more, at Dougall's feet, and without lifting her head raised an arm. Her attitude, dignified by sunset, was allegorical: shoulders bowed, fine clothes besmirched, one hand thrust out in an ecstasy of need.

Dougall did not take it straight away. He stood looking instead at Jane, until his wife called his name for the second time, her anger dulled with pleading. As he helped her up, unhurt, she spluttered the words, 'I had to *ask*, of course . . .' and, as quickly, gulped to recall them.

Too late. Frankie shook off her shoes.

When she at last lifted her face, the room and all in it – her husband, the woman he really loved – seemed sharp and distant as a garden glimpsed from the wrong side of a keyhole.

Jane knew then that Frankie had asked, possibly begged, Dougall to marry her, and that she had done it – waged the whole ludicrous post-graduation campaign of flattery and seduction – out of spite.

It was a bitter comfort to Jane to realize that quiet, practical Dougall would never have offered himself, and in her throat she tasted the gorge of pride: a sick relief that she had not done as Frankie did when she had the chance – when, who knows, it might have made her happy.

The scar on Jane's hand pulsed. Six years ago, Dougall Voss had wrapped a clean tea towel around it in the deserted cottage at Norbin's End, and had bowed quickly to kiss it better, just once, while Philip was outside with the sleds. Frances Schumacher had seen the kiss, and Jane remembered her clock-like face, marking more than time in the pantry doorway.

She felt again the cat's claws, saw shapes shift in a multiple mirror.

'I'm going home.'

Frankie's bark ended the reverie. The round and cunning face moved in different directions. It was planning something.

'Let's all go,' Jane said. 'Come on, I'll take you.'

The streaked figure laughed.

'I'm going *home*,' Frankie repeated, 'next month. There's a lease come up on a house back in Pound Ridge, and Dad wants us to help him fix it. I've got some teaching lined up in

Stamford. That's what I – we – came to tell you.' She paused. 'Sorry about – all this.'

In the shallow yellow of dusk, Frankie's clog prints on the backdrop had already lost their shine. Jane's mouth slackened. The smile she summoned to her lips went into spasm.

'Well, that's something, isn't it?' she said, in a shocked vibrato.

Nausea forced her to sit on the steps leading backstage.

She hated being this weak – and yet, as her legs buckled, she sensed the weakness itself giving way to some other waking instinct or desire, which whipped and whickered like thrown rope.

'Yeah,' said Frankie, cruelly. 'I thought it would be a surprise.'

Dougall winced, and Jane wondered at his forbearance.

'We're going in November,' he managed at last.

His wife swung his hand.

'One other thing,' she said.

'Not now, Fran,' Dougall advised softly. 'It can wait.'

'It cannot. It's the best bit!'

Frankie's eyes were wet grapes.

'I'm going to have – ' she whispered, patting her stomach – 'a *baby*!'

'You are?'

'I am!' Her fat face beamed. 'Me – a baby. How about that?'

The room spun, and Jane's consciousness divided evenly in two. One half offered garbled congratulations; the other screamed behind a wall of soundproofed glass. *Oh! She must be delighted. When did they find out? How long? Was it safe to fly? Were they sure?*

The rope of instinct went taut.

239

Oh, and was she all right? She must try not to fall over . . .

Frankie softened at once, and apologized again for the drop, secure in the knowledge – or suspicion – that the pregnant can always expect a full pardon. Only Dougall, watching, noticed Jane ball her fists.

'Have you told Philip?' she asked, still smiling.

'Oh no,' Frankie giggled. 'I had to tell you first. I just had to come and find you. I knew you'd be thrilled. I so wanted *you* to know straight away!'

Dougall turned to look out of the window.

'I think . . .' he began, and Jane picked up the thread.

'*I* think,' she said lightly, 'that you, Frankie, should go and tell Philip now, while I finish clearing up here, and I'll join you in half an hour.'

'That's OK, we can wait.'

'Honestly, I'll get it done much quicker on my own.'

'Uh-huh. Whatever you say,' Frankie sighed, piqued that the offer of a lift home had been forgotten. She dragged Dougall to the door, and was through it herself when Jane called out.

'Oh, Dougall, sorry – I still need to get this thing up the steps – do you mind? It won't take a minute.' Jane bit her lips. 'Go on ahead, Frankie, he'll be with you by the time you get to the gate.'

And so, because Jane had told her to go, Frankie went, clopping blithely at first across the grey playground, but reaching the entrance fifty paces later in shapeless distress, as though sensing that she had been separated from Dougall – whom she rarely let out of her sight – for a purpose.

She waited there ten minutes, feeling tricked and apprehensive, bereft of excuses for going back, while her husband moved the drop and followed Jane into the wings.

Frankie was cross by the time he emerged from the hall corridor and jogged, grinning, towards her. He put an arm out to the flagpole in the middle of the yard, and slapped it in passing. The wood buzzed. What a carry-on, Dougall laughed. First Jane wanted the tarpaulin dumped behind a couple of flats, then it didn't fit and she wanted it rolled up after all (it would have to be done again anyway . . .), then she didn't see why it couldn't stay where it was. Bit precious, wasn't she?

Dougall's frightened wife sighed, inexpressibly reassured by this hint of criticism which was to her roses and truth and an unlocked door. They walked off together, and the children on the St Luke's Green swings stopped calling out to Frankie now that she was with a man.

Back in the Old Games Room, Jane rearranged her clothes and cleared up slowly, rinsing the brushes with turps, dabbing at swipes of paint on the block floor. Her walk home, over the Green and down the beech-clad Beacon Steps, was tranced, with a buoyancy of detail that seemed to keep the sun from sinking. Her eye drew down the falling leaves; the ratio of nuts to cases on the kerb was apt. The trees gripped, split, inclined. Her mood made her associate, and for a while it seemed as though the hippies were on to something – vectors of fate directed her fancy: this Volkswagen Beetle, that patch of sky, are like eggshells, she thought. She'd blown three eggs as a child, three perfect shells which pastry-fingered Melanie Giggs, trailing a yard of plaits, had crushed with squawks of disbelief.

A stream runs beside Mt Beacon Steps and down to Camden Road. It has been culverted for many years; the source is one of Bath's less celebrated springs. Jane heard it as she stepped out of the wood into the numbed evening, and gasped at the deliberacy of things.

'What have I done?'

It must go underground, she decided. No one need know.

* * *

I expected evasion and pride, and have been confronted instead with the desire to be loved and understood – a desire that irks the self-possessed because it recalls a time when we were all too honest to be proud.

The kitchen is much as I have always known it, except that Mum has taken down the photographs and cards that used to overlap each other, like a game of Patience, on the cork wall. Dad's porcelain bottles and bowls are still on the dresser; inside the lower cupboard, spice packets consort with gravy and treacle in the granular dark.

She talks, is angry and disconsolate, presses on. Not in her words so much as in Dad's removal, and in the brooding but purposeful continuity of my mother's single life – the passage has been repainted, she has a tin of Johnston's undercoat by the back door – I sense the returning seepage of pre-history, of a whole existence before him and without me, to which I am none the less imaginatively obliged.

*

'Who knew?'

'No one.'

'Did you see him again?'

'I said goodbye to them both, the day before they flew back. Dougall dropped in, I think, once or twice, but we never – we didn't even talk about it. I didn't.'

'You didn't want to.'

'No. Because I'd made up my mind. I'd – made up my

mind. I think it was harder for him, going off – you know, severing all ties. He was a garage mechanic's son from Chippenham, after all: even Bath was strange to him. What he must have thought . . .'

'But you loved – I'm sorry–'

'No. I'm sorry.'

'It's the way you talk – you, you must have missed him.'

'I think I did. I – I'd been a bit off colour for a while. Nothing too bad: the move and – and all that. I wasn't up to much – well, people would call it depression now, but we didn't have a word for it then. I certainly had a few heaves when I thought of them – of him – all those miles away.'

'You let him go.'

'It wasn't all up to me.'

'It could have been, though. If he'd stayed – if–'

'Oh, no. I was married. He knew. I'd made up my mind.'

'You didn't want him back, ever? You didn't miss–'

'I missed his smell.'

'His smell?'

'It was a scent. It was – oh – it was that clean skin smell some people have. The smell of no smell. It's with you as soon as they look at you. It can – it can come at you across a room, from the other side of the street. One minute you're breathing normally, walking along, and then it's in your nostrils and you need to slow down and touch something solid. I missed that. I did miss that.'

'Did he miss you?'

'I think so.'

'He must have written.'

'Yes. He did.'

'What happened?'

'I–'

'I'm sorry.'

'No, no, it's all right. I'm all right. You carry on.'

'You were saying.'

'What?'

'He wrote.'

'Oh yes. Well, of course, I – I threw them away.'

'All of them?'

' – one.'

'You kept one?'

' – one, with the housekeeping. Philip never touched that. That was my money – he was very good – and then–'

'Then?'

'I lost it – it was just a short letter. It was with the housekeeping in the drawer. I dropped it at a counter some-where, probably. The money was a muddle then. Ten-bob notes and fifty-pence pieces. It was all a muddle. I was – then I found I was two months gone, just after Christmas.'

'What if Dad saw the letter? What if he guessed?'

'When you came, I just stared at you. You were with us, in the top bedroom, for a long while. Sometimes you'd wake in the night and just stare back. Staring, moving a bit. Wicked was jealous; I had to keep her away from you. And she wasn't well, she sort of dwindled.'

'What if Dad knew? All the time.'

'I don't know.'

'You *didn't* know? Or you don't know *if* he knew?'

'I don't. I don't know.'

'You don't know that he didn't find the letter – or you don't think he realized you'd been having an affair?'

'I don't know. I–'

'You keep saying "I don't know". What don't you know?'

'I don't *know*.'

'OK, OK. Calm down.'

'It wasn't an affair. I *loved* Philip, Daniel. What do you want me to say? What am I supposed to do? To have done? I *stayed*. It wasn't easy. He wasn't an easy man all the time. He wasn't whiter than white.'

'You just said he was good.'

'Well, he *was*. And we were so lucky. We had you.'

'OK.'

'Let's not be angry.'

'I'm not – I'm not angry. I just feel – tired–'

'Well, it's – it's emotional, isn't it? I don't know – I'm not good at–'

'I don't like parading emotion.'

'I know – I mean I *know* what you mean. But it's true, Daniel, we were lucky. You do – feel that.'

'I suppose so.'

'He cried. He never cried – I never saw Philip cry. Except when I had you and he waited outside. He was so relieved.'

'He told you that?'

'Yes.'

'I can't see it. I mean, you're right, he never got upset.'

'Until later.'

'That was different.'

'But before that, he was always very – he lived intensely. Privately.'

'I miss him.'

'I know. I – now that I'm on my own, I miss–'

'Do you miss him?'

'Oh, Daniel. What have I *just* said?'

'I know.'

'Well, then.'

'But I have to ask – but – I don't want to rake it all up–'

'It's all right. Oh, look at this . . .'

'Here.'

'I'm a mess. Can I have another–'

'Here.'

'Thank you.'

'OK?'

'Yes. Go on.'

'He was my dad, wasn't he?'

'Daniel.'

'He was my dad.'

'Of course he was your dad. Oh, *Daniel*.'

'You have to say it.'

'Say what?'

'*You* have to.'

'What?'

'Say it.'

'Dan – put that away–'

'You see, you can't.'

'Daniel, it's just a picture.'

'Here.'

'What?'

'Here it is. This is it.'

'I know, I can see. You showed me.'

'Dad put it in the slope for me. Why did he do that?'

'I don't know. He did a lot of odd things at the end.'

'Why did he put a copy of a photo of *Carey* in our – in *our*, mine and his – secret hiding place? I know why.'

'I don't.'

'You do, only you won't say. I know.'

'Know what?'

'You know.'

'I know you take after him, that's for sure.'

'Come on.'

'You get the bit between your teeth and you – you just go *on*. I don't like it when you do that. It isn't nice–'

'You won't say it.'

'I don't like it. I'm your mother.'

'You're a bit of a coward.'

'I – I – why are you doing this?'

'I'm not doing anything.'

'You saw your father doing it, that's why.'

'Did I? I don't remember.'

'Always belittling me.'

'Don't *change* the *subject*.'

'Yes. You do. You belittle me. Silly little me who only looked after you both for twenty, thirty years. How *silly* I must have been.'

'Belittle you? *You* said, only just now, that he was very good.'

'I've told you; he was. Now stop it.'

'You started it. One minute he's a loving husband, the next he's some kind of robot who never appreciated you. Which is it?'

'Stop it, Daniel. It wasn't my fault.'

'I didn't say it was.'

'What are you implying?'

'I don't think he had any affairs at all. You had the affair and you've felt guilty ever since.'

'Your trouble is you think you know everything.'

'I'm just trying to find out.'

'The things I could tell you.'

'What do you mean "it wasn't your fault"?'

'I think we should stop.'

'If that's what you want.'

'I just think . . . I never really knew if he–'

'If he what?'

'He never said – oh, wait–'

'I can wait.'

'Wait a bit.'

'Here.'

'He was a good man.'

'But?'

'And he loved you anyway, you see. But he never really loved me. That's what this – this is–'

'How can you say that?'

'It's true.'

'It is *not* true. You know he did. I've got letters . . .'

'He never said – said it to me.'

'And you did to him? Did you?'

'Say what?'

'Say that you loved him?'

'I – no, well–'

'You see?'

'Oh, who does *say* that kind of thing?'

'I don't know. I never have, but then I take after him, apparently. Or is it you? Why wasn't it your fault? *What* wasn't?'

*

We have been talking since I got back from the pub. It is very late now, about four in the morning; the night wanes and an early swift arcs over Lower Alpine Gardens. We have not touched the food we made: pork chops and rice, red cabbage with raisins.

'This,' says my mother after a long pause, shrinking down and sideways into her chair. 'All of this.'

248

Her voice gurgles to a halt. When she speaks again, it is with that automatic clarity of which only the exhausted are capable.

'If it had been wrong,' she says, 'if I'd done something so bad, I wouldn't have been allowed to keep you. I would have lost you.'

She hangs her head and goes blank for a moment.

'Mum?'

I'm on yellow alert. When you've been with terminally ill people for any amount of time, it is the moments of unresponsive blankness, the neural cut-outs, that you learn to dread. Mostly, they're having a rest, but you're never absolutely sure until they start up again.

'And then,' she lifts her head with a shudder, 'everything else – Philip's going – would be my fault, too.'

She brings her knife and fork together.

'Anyway, you're right about the boy in the picture,' my mother says, almost to herself. 'Dougall took it when they visited in '74. He and Frankie separated soon after.'

She takes a deep breath – 'So . . .' – and starts to clear the table, scrapes our congealed chops into a plastic container, runs the hot water. I am spent, too, by this point, with my head on my arms.

'Carey is your half-brother and Dougall is your father. Philip wasn't very fertile. There was something wrong.'

My mother adds a dash of cold.

'Daniel?'

The fridge clicks off.

'I don't know if you knew that.'

Quietus

Vernon Melchior was the NASA scientist turned civil engineer who built the lifts in Evans and Owen, a self-consciously superior Bath department store of the 1960s and 1970s. Melchior's contraptions bullied the laws of physics: your brain hit haberdashery before your bowels had left kitchenware, and when you came back down, parents looked like their grandchildren.

The last two months have been a bit like that.

After the night of the long sighs, my mother and I went to pieces for a day or so; then we cheered up and got on with things. One minute we were mired in the imponderables of devotion and duty, the next we were arguing about the perished flashing on the roof. (The lead needs stripping out and replacing with a pre-formed zinc valley – I've had it done in Brixton – but Mum won't listen. It was only put in ten years ago; she has to find the money for her TEFL teacher's course first; if need be, she can do it herself, etc. The fact is, she'd rather live in a colander than pay over the odds.) Neville has since offered me some sage advice; he says that most people forgive their parents by the age of forty and that I should be grateful for the opportunity to do it sooner. He's right. Not that I've actually said anything, you understand. The big decisions in my family have always been silent ones – internal accommodations.

And anyway, what is there for me to forgive? Jane Rathbone nursed a troubled affection which she kept to herself. Why? Because other people, as she saw it, were more important. At the same time, she kept other people *out*. Good for her. There is altogether too much letting in.

I'm glad no one let on, either. Perhaps I should feel the burden of such privileged information, but all I really feel is a natural concern, being freed from suspicion, that I don't abuse that freedom myself.

For what it's worth, my interpretation of events is this: Dad – Philip – may have known about Dougall, or he may have read a love letter; later on, he probably doubted his paternity, and that may have become a private obsession when he was ill. The Xerox in the slope was his way of saying that he suspected something; that all was not as it seemed. And others – Dougall, Carey, though not, I think, Frankie – may have suspected something, too. These are the ties that bind.

The fact is that he's gone, and it can't be helped. Biology be damned, a little bit of you goes with them if you loved them, whoever they were.

I saw Carey when I got back in the middle of the week, and told him nothing – quite civilly – on the flawed principle that what he doesn't know can't harm me. He is my brother, of course, but consanguinity is a fickle thing. In any case, I think he knows. I met his – my – father once, long ago, when he arrived in Bath to take Carey on holiday, and there was the same suppressed horror in his smile; the same thinly masked disappointment in his own, most recent guise – a car dealer – as though the world turned principally to others' advantage.

Dougall shook my hand, at Dad's cremation; his fingers were white and eager.

Carey flew home after a lightning visit to Frankie, and I haven't heard from him since. He left behind his AOI goggles, which appeared to have been stepped on, or dropped. They looked helpless, on my desk, like an old box of tin soldiers. The micro-hydraulics had jammed with the two eyelids stuck halfway across the chrome casing, so I tried to unjam them, without success. I sent them back with a note.

His other bequest has had wider repercussions. The launch ('pan-European roll-out') of Plus Design at the Olympia Systems Fair went horribly well; so well, in fact, that my employers at *Media Weekly* (part of Conqueror Business Press) bought it and announced the whole company's immediate reconfiguration to accommodate the new IT package: amazing ISDN and Web uplinks, superfine digital imaging, short-term contracts (for editorial, not advertising) and the itemization of all phone calls. It's the 'benchmark integrated desktop publishing solution'! Plus has completed trials in Mexico (on *MásTV!* and *TeleFiesta*), and Vector Corp. anticipates a phenomenal 'take-up' in the coming year. There are a few glitches – the letter 'e' doesn't print in Times Roman – but it's nothing the formatting guys can't solve. They're working on it now.

My contract stipulated three months' notice, so it was chastening to be escorted off the premises the morning I resigned. For an awful moment, I thought maybe I'd made a mistake: all I could think of was the legend on fat Pat's T-shirt ('We all need security'). And then I saw Will, one of our more highly strung junior subs – hair unwashed, cracked glasses awry – glaring at me from the coffee-shop window and mouthing a string of obscenities. I put my head round the door to say goodbye.

'Piss off,' he said brokenly. 'You lucky shit.'

'Right you are,' I said.

★

'What's that?' the young girl asks, standing on tiptoe to reach a more promising clump of fruit. 'What does that mean?'

Her fingers are stained purple with juice, and she is concentrating so hard on coaxing the blackberries towards her – the best ones are always behind leaves – that she doesn't notice the scratches on her arm, which have begun to put forth redcurrants of their own.

We are discussing what I used to do for a living.

'Well,' I reply, 'a sub-editor is someone who rewrites the stories in newspapers before they're printed, so that they make sense. He, or she, checks the spelling and writes a headline.'

'The big words.'

'The big words. And then the editor – that's the person in charge – comes along and changes everything.'

'Why?'

'No one knows.'

The girl is quiet a moment, her white arm lost inside the bramble's stringy maw. She shakes her head. Florence Kelly Kale is not yet ten, but she has already acquired that nice vocabulary of disdain with which youth signals the utter fatuity of adultkind.

'That is sad,' she says in a low voice. 'You are *sad*.'

My citadel of grief receives no visitors for the next few minutes, until Flo steps back from the bush and holds out her Tupperware box of fruit, which is two-thirds empty.

'Look how many I've got,' she says. Her face is serious

beneath a basin haircut deliberately at odds with fashion – Karen's doing, I imagine. The carrier bag at my feet has about two pounds of fruit in it; Flo looks at it and again at her tub. She waits until I have moved a little way along the hedge, and then carefully tips her blackberries into the bag. The box is now empty, but the bag – our bag – is full.

'I'm going back,' she announces, suddenly. 'Are you coming?'

'In a minute. Do you want to take the bag – can you manage?'

Flo withers me up with a glance.

'*Course.*'

The fruit is heavier than she expected. Weighed down on one side, Flo totters back along the cornfield ditch as though walking a tightrope. She stops to untie the gate and eat a blackberry or two. It is six o'clock, and a peppery fuss of insects chivvies the hawthorns, maples and oaks. There may be a storm brewing.

Gorged horseflies pursue me into the shady cleft of the road that leads down to the cottage at Norcot End, where I am spending the weekend with Karen. (Greg is in Somerset until this evening.) They do not seem to bother the two old ladies rootling for rosehips where the road bears left towards the quarry. One of them starts at my approach. I call out 'Hello,' and she looks round, though not at me, not directly. She smiles; I see her lips move. But whatever she says is lost in the drone of tiny wings.

*

Norcot End is the sole remaining edifice in the lee of Cat's Hill, an anomalous mound that looks as if it might once have been a Stone Age settlement. The cottage is a mile from the Rudwick Arms and two from Corsham proper. There were two quarrymen's cottages on the site originally, but the other one disappeared in the mid-1960s.

Being a conservationist, Greg has made a feature of the gardens: roses, berberis and crocosmia in the front; ancient apple trees, herbs and dazzling banks of cornflowers to the rear. A couple of erratic boulders from the quarry sit in the middle of the back garden like sleeping lions.

The inside of the house is Karen's domain, and a mess. Horribly done up in the 1970s with plasterboard and wood-chip, very little has been added to it since. The galley kitchen has an ice-blue ceiling with two long fluorescent strips, its job-lot beige units and pasta-clogged sink arranged in a kind of hairpin bend. Rind of indeterminate origin and nuggets of translucently hard cheese litter the floor. In the sitting room, things are more orderly, although the green-plush sofa and brown pile are an uncomfortable reminder of soft-centred Christmas chocolates.

Karen happily admits that she doesn't know why she and Greg bought the place: 'Except that it was falling down, and all we could afford.'

Flo licks her knife and Karen, without looking, takes it from her.

'Bath is crazy now. The prices! You can't buy anything. Besides, we fancied living out a bit.' She gathers the plates. 'It'd help if we were tidier, mind, but there doesn't seem to be the time, what with getting muggins to school, going to work, picking her up, doing the shops.'

Flo heaves a sigh, and mutters something about a video. Karen shoos her into the lounge and fills the sink.

'I thought Greg was a stickler for clean living,' I say. 'Remember when he worked in Wilson's sports shop? He was always immaculate.'

'Christ, *yes*,' Karen exclaims, as though she'd forgotten. 'He came to the hospital in ironed jeans. I thought that was a bit, like, odd.'

'Not too odd, though.'

She giggles.

'No. Not too odd. Anyway, he puts up with me and my ways.' Karen looks round sheepishly. 'Says I'm like that Helen Burns.'

'Who?'

'You know, Helen Burns – *Jane Eyre*. O level. Wore a sign round her neck at school saying "Slattern". That's me, Greg reckons.'

'But Helen Burns was a model of patience and virtue.'

Karen throws me a tea towel.

'Yeah, well it's always the quiet ones.'

She smiles to herself and, unbidden, I see them together – Karen and Greg – in the morning. She has jogging bottoms on, and a voluminous T-shirt; her hair is tangled, hiding sleepy eyes. He is getting heavier, growing sideburns, making tea in her kimono and pinching the leaves of a lemon tree that needs a bigger pot. He has a runner's legs, of course. Supple feet, slender calves. There is a direct mail catalogue yellowing on the window sill; the furred kettle reminds Greg that he must get some descaler for the loft tank. They are probably trying for a kid.

'What about you, Dan, then – your man, what's his name?'

'Ryan.'

'Ryan, that's it. You don't talk about him much, do you?'

'No.'

'I see,' Karen says, flatly. 'Superstitious, like.'

*

After the Saturday night video – *Terminator 2* – there is a brief altercation between Karen and her daughter, who wants to stay up because Greg is on his way back from Bridgewater. From the front door, you can see the lights of cars and lorries passing over the brow of Rudwick towards Corsham. They are not numerous, and Flo insists that each one is the one that will slow down at the top of the rise and bend its lights towards her.

In the end, I leave them to it and climb the stairs. I'll see my old schoolfriend in the morning.

But on the way to my room, along a short, narrow pass-ageway whose boards creak and slope to one side, my resolve weakens. Should I go down again and wait with them? Or wait up here, until I hear the car pull in? It is false pride, surely, to let the moment pass.

The rain begins. The room is dark; the wind wrestles the latch.

On the window-dresser is a three-panelled mirror, incon-gruously well preserved. Its two outer panels face inwards and offer a multiple receding diptych of the room and of its dith-ering occupant. Logic says that my bony frame must be infinitely reflected, far beyond the point at which even I can see myself in the concertinaed curve of images.

Rain falls steadily. Out of the window, in the rising blue of Cat's Hill, I can see creatures among the roots of thorn and ash and elder. I am sure of some of these animals and less certain of others, though their dimensions are clear enough. So I try, now, to observe my eyes' searching; to see how the scattering of shade acquires new meaning in the light of memory and experience. With each sweep, more is revealed – more of all that there is to be revealed. Two hares at the end of the orchard; an owl away towards the quarry and chalk pit; by an outflow, rats.

And something else, in front of me, as the rain clouds unexpectedly disperse: so close, upon the nearest hunched boulder, so black and evident, I cannot believe I missed it. It springs from the rock and lands silently on the grass beneath me, looking up. One eye shines bright and green; the other glows dully, like a spirit lamp.

Flo calls me. She has seen the car turning.